I0653946

THE BRUTAL TIME

BOOK SIX OF THE ANGELBOUND ORIGINS SERIES

CHRISTINA BAUER

COPYRIGHT

Monster House Books
Brighton, MA 02135
ISBN 9781945723858
First Edition

DEDICATION

For All Those Who Kick Ass, Take Names
and Read Books

CONTENTS

THE BRUTAL TIME

EPILOGUE

BONUS STORY - BARBIE DOLL DEATH MATCH

ALSO BY CHRISTINA BAUER

APPENDIX

THE BRUTAL TIME

MYLA

*T*ime to kick some *old lady butt*.

And no, I'm not kidding.

Right now, I pace inside a hallway of the Sunset Retirement Community for Quasi-Demonic Women. Like most of Purgatory, this place is all chipped walls and threadbare carpet. A sign at the corridor's end reads:

Quilting Contest with the Great Scala
Activities Room, 10:30 AM

It's true that I'm the Great Scala—meaning the only person who can move souls to Heaven or Hell with my igni —but saying this event is hosted by the Sunset Retirement Community?

Not exactly.

Truth is, this building houses a powerful coven of quasi-demonic witches called the Bloody Knights of the

Round Table. These ladies can see the future, which they think involves *yours truly* ending the world in a great demonpocalypse. So I volunteered to judge this contest … and will instead uncover the coven's plans.

A lady tips her head out into the hall. "Are you the Great Scala?"

I want to reply, *how many chicks have red hair, a dragon-scale tail, and wear white Scala robes?* But I need to keep a low profile. For the purpose of today, I am a bubbleheaded demi-goddess.

Blinking hard, I imagine my body's filled with sunshine, moonbeams, and large air pockets. "Why, yes. I'm the Great Scala."

For the record, I'm also the Queen of the Thrax, wife to Lincoln, mother to Maxon, daughter of Purgatory's President, and recent winner of the annual *Quasi Enquirer* award for the *sexiest demon alive*.

But I digress.

"We're ready for you." This woman is on the shorter side with shiny brown eyes and a wrinkly smile. Her white hair wraps about her head, cotton-candy style.

"Perfect." I flash her a grin that hopefully says, *don't worry about me. I'm totally not here to snoop.*

Entering the activity room proper, I find a boxy chamber with cinderblock walls and—surprise, surprise— more frayed carpet. A dozen ladies sit at a circular table that's covered with fabric, scissors, and spools of thread. Each woman holds a little quilt that's about three feet square.

So far, so good. Then I notice a surprising *lack of snacks.* As in, there aren't any at all. Good thing I sent my latest assistant, Alli-something, off for cookies already. With any luck, she'll arrive with chocolaty stuff and soon.

"Thank you for coming here today, Great Scala." The speaker is Rose, the same woman who greeted me before. Up close, I can see how she—and everyone else here—sports a great little invention called *the name tag.* It's a life saver considering how 1) I'm terrible with names and 2) these women all kinda-sorta look alike. In related news, I'm also craving cotton candy.

I slap on another smile. "Happy to be invited."

"Each of us created a mini-quilt," explains Rose. "Today you'll review them and declare a winner."

I shoot her a thumbs up. "Ready."

Rose turns to the woman beside her. "How about starting us off, Lucy?"

"Here's my entry." Lucy holds up a mini-quilt that's sewn from bits of red cloth. "My muse was Colossus."

"Colossus, eh?" I scan the quilt, careful to force my face into a blank of confusion. "Do you mean the King of the Archdemons?"

"That's the one." Lucy pats my hand like I'm a toddler who just shoved peas up my nose. "You know how your father is one of the nine archangels?"

Blink, blink, blink. "Sure!"

Lucy holds up craggy fingers as she counts off the archangels in question. "There are seven archangels to battle each deadly sin, then an eighth to fight a combination of *lust and wrath* … that's your father. Finally, the ninth archangel is their king, Lucifer. Or it *was* Lucifer. The King of the Angels is now imprisoned. Ring any bells?"

My honest reply? *Hells yeah, that rings a whole chorus of bells.* Best to keep playing dumb, though. Looks like these women might spill their secrets via quilting. Sweet.

I puff out my lower lip. "No bells," I lie.

"There are also nine archdemons," continues Lucy. "Only they got unruly, even for demons. Colossus was their leader. Ages ago, a human king named Arthur locked them into magical dungeons. Didn't anyone tell you?"

"King Arthur? Doesn't sound familiar, either." *Which is another lie. Everyone knows the Arthurian legends. Sword in the stone. Merlin in the house. Lancelot in Guinevere.* "So why is your quilt all red?"

"Colossus has no physical form," answers Lucy. "He must possess others, usually his archdemons, when he wishes to kill or cast spells. Yet Colossus can also take over humans. At those times, the archdemon king explodes them from the inside-out in a shower of blood." She twiddles her fingers to show said blood-rain in action. "That's why my quilt has little red triangles."

Okay. Eew.

"Ah, I get it." And by this I mean, I *get* how these women would surely love a demonpocalypse-style bloodbath. And with Colossus running the show, all the after-realms could be wiped out in nasty and painful ways. I shiver at the thought.

"Here's mine." A woman named Edith hands me a mini-quilt that shows a hooded figure. "This is the Crimson Scourge. Soon this mage will help free Colossus."

"Wow." I stare at the square carefully. "You totally stitched the image of, uh, some mage in a red cloak riding a white horse. Go you."

Note to self: track down the Crimson Scourge. Clearly, the coven has an outside accomplice. Looks like it's this mysterious mage.

Another woman—her name tag reads Florence—slides her mini-quilt over. "This is my creation. Can you guess what it is?"

"Um, a mountain?" I ask.

"Not just any mountain," corrects Florence. "Lucifer's laboratory is hidden in here." She taps some runes at the bottom. "I added the exact coordinates on Earth. Inside this lab lies a signet ring that the Crimson Scourge will use to free Colossus. It's called the Band of Epochs, and it empowers the wearer to travel through time."

"Interesting." I scan the table. The remaining entries are more of what I'd call, *Gruesome Colossus Kill Porn.* "Did anyone *not get* inspired by Colossus?"

"Oh, me!" cries Rose. "Mine's a fading angel."

I do a double-take. "Did you say a fading angel?"

"Yes, dear." Rose slips me her mini-quilt. Sure enough, it shows a frowning dude with droopy wings and a ghostly body.

That's a fading angel, all right.

And they're my biggest worry these days. Why? Fading angels are spirits who enter Heaven even though they're only *mostly* pure of heart. Sure, they don't deserve Hell. But sending these souls past the Pearly Gates isn't a great idea, either. Once in Heaven, fading angels go all mopey until they disappear. And by *disappear*, I mean *die*. Permanently.

"What do you think?" asks Rose. "That's what a fading angel looks like, right?"

"Oh yeah," I say. "Nailed it."

And with that, the *snooping around* portion of the morning is over. I've seen all the quilts. These creations are more of a *request to team up* than an actual contest. It's time for some honesty.

"Let's talk," I state. "This isn't a real contest."

Rose blinks innocently. "It isn't?"

Let the record show that I use the same blinking-routine ... and I'm much better at it.

"Absolutely *not*," I repeat. "You ladies are the Bloody Knights of the Round Table coven. I knew you had visions of the future that involved me and a demonpocalypse, but after what I saw today? You've also roped in Lucifer's lab, Colossus, the Crimson Scourge, and the fading angels. And you want my help. Now am I right or am I right?"

Everyone starts fiddling with their sewing stuff and avoiding eye contact.

"So that's a *yes*," I say. "Spill."

Quasi-demons all carry an animal-tail-slash-power from one of the seven deadly sins. Mine's a badass dragon-scale number with an arrowhead-shaped end. After my last statement, the ladies' tails all curl over their respective shoulders to reveal their animal origin. *Rattlesnake.* A creepy noise fills the air as a dozen rattlesnake tails do their thing.

The ladies' irises blaze with demonic red energy. No question what that means; they're accessing their wrath power. The air takes on an electric charge. *Magic.* Quilts and sewing things fly off the table to whirl around the chamber.

"You must go to Lucifer's lab." The women speak in a unified monotone. Not gonna lie; it's more than a little creepy. "There you will find a ring called the Band of Epochs. Use it to visit King Arthur in the past; he will help you build your own *knights of the round table* in the present day. Do as we command and you shall save the fading angels. It is the only way."

I frown. Is this combination of magical display and *otherworldy to do list* supposed to entice me to join them? Nuh-uh.

"Wow," I state. "What total B-S."

At these words, the magical show of spinning sewing supplies comes to a screeching halt. Scraps of fabric, quilts, and other stuff all tumble onto the table. The ladies' eyes return to normal as they stare at me in disbelief.

Rose is first to speak, and I'm happy to report the icky monotone-thing is toast. "What?" she asks.

"Here's my take," I state. "This has zero to do with helping the fading angels." I gesture across the tabletop. "You've got blood-n-guts images on your quilts. Clearly, this coven wants to bring about a real-life *slaughter fiesta.*"

"Only a little," mumbles Rose.

"King Arthur locked up all the archdemons. If I grab that time-travel ring from Lucifer's lab? There's a chance the Crimson Scourge will snag it, journey to the past, and free Colossus. By using me—and the Crimson Scourge—to change history, you'll get a carnage party *today*. Am I right or am I right?"

At this question, all the ladies start fiddling with the gunk on the table again.

I roll my eyes. "And that's another *yes*."

Rose shakes her head. "Ignore our visions at your peril. We brought you here under false pretenses, it is true. But we only did so to share our wisdom. You must gain your own knights of the round table."

I rub my neck. "Let's step back here. Why do you think I need my own knights?"

"You only work alone," explains Rose. "That's why you're a failure when it comes to helping these unpure souls. Fading angels are too big of a problem for any one person to solve."

"Hey, I get help."

"Every time you have trouble as the Great Scala, you rely on your friends and family. Yet they have other things —as in whole realms—to worry about. Such assistance is simply not the same as your own knights."

Ouch. I've taken *gut punches* that hurt less than what Rose just said. Sure, I have leadership issues with folks I'm not related-slash-married-to, and I'm working on it. I'm just not making any progress, that's all.

I sigh. "You have a point."

"So you'll aid us in our scheme?" asks Rose.

"Uh, no. It's like this. Lucifer has a long history of creating junk that causes mega-trouble. If you have his lab's coordinates, someone else probably knows them too. Which is why I'll go explode the place ASAP." To emphasize my point, I grab the map-slash-quilt in question. "Later, I'll create my own *knights of the round table situation* without leaving the present day. Bing, bang, boom, done."

Plus, it'll be hella fun to detonate Lucifer's lab and shred all his magical crap.

Rose rises. "If you take that map and leave now, we shall not stop you. But know that you are dooming the fading angels to death. One way or another, magic will not allow that to happen."

"So your magic will *force me* to help you?" I make little quotation marks with my fingers when I say the words, *force me*. "Good luck with that."

The ladies all share knowing looks. It's as if they have the inside skinny on how to enchant my ass to do, well, anything. Meh. Better covens have tried and failed. Enhanced magical immunity is one perk of being the Great Scala.

The door swings open. *Yay, a distraction!* My assistant Alli-something slowly shuffles in while holding a large tray. She's got big eyes, a small frame, and a snail's tail. Why I thought it was a good idea to have an assistant with *sloth* as her mortal sin, I don't know.

I take it back; I absolutely know. I go through assistants like a hot knife through brownies. Finding replacements isn't easy. Honestly? I'm lucky to have *sloth girl*. It's more than a little depressing.

Years ago, I was an invincible Arena warrior. Best of the best. I never met a demon—or an evil soul—that I couldn't take down. Now, I'm the Great Scala. It's a much bigger job, yet I'm bottom-feeding with assistants. How did it come to this?

My shoulders slump as I realize the truth. For the first time in my life, I've run smack-dab into something I really want to do—meaning create what Rose called *my own knights*—and yet I seriously suck at it.

An unfinished scrap of quilt catches my gaze—it shows me in my Scala robes. My heart sinks. That's my life, right there. I'm more a fragment than a leader. Forever disconnected. Nothing larger ever gets created or healed, especially the fading angels.

My assistant taps my shoulder, snapping me out of my thoughts. *Huh.* I must have been off for a while there. It's not like sloth folks move quickly.

"Do you need me, Great Scala?" she asks. At last, her full name pops into my mind. Allimari.

"Yes," I reply. "Please deliver this map-quilt to King Lincoln STAT. Tell him to meet me at Lucifer's lab as soon as possible."

"What?" Allimari pales. "The ghouls always gave us checklists. Don't you have one for this task?"

Sheesh. My assistant is being a total wiener. Ghouls used to rule Purgatory and they had rules and checklists for everything. Not my bag.

"You don't need any checklist." I jam the mini-quilt onto her hands. "This is easy peasy."

In my experience, the most important part of assistant management is this: *walking away before they can corner you and ask a million questions.* All of which is why I speed-march toward the door.

With every step, a heavy sense of dread seeps into my bones. A magnetic pull rises from my soul; its force draws me back to Allimari. A calm female voice whispers in my mind.

Return to Allimari. Talk to her.

My igni chatter in my mind like frantic children. This new speaker is older, calmer, and like nothing I've heard before. Is some fresh entity rolling around my soul? What the ever loving Hell?

In the end, I do what any sane person would in this situation. *Ignore the fuck* out of the weird voice in my head, wave everyone goodbye, and head for Lucifer's lab.

Blowing things up. That's a much better way to spend my morning. And I already have an idea how to derail this wrath coven's demonpocalypse train.

Maybe.

Possibly.

Okay, I really have no idea.

But I'll still go blow shit up.

MYLA

*A*fter leaving the wrath coven, I use a transport charm to reach Lucifer's lab on Earth. The good news is that I land almost-not-quite on the exact coordinates in the map-quilt. The bad news is that it's cold as Hell out here.

Even so, I'm grinning my face off. Somewhere inside this mountain hides a place I can't wait to explore. And by *explore*, I mean, *send it sky high*.

Eat death, Lucifer's lab!

In other news, that eerily calm voice has stopped chattering in my head. Total sanity bonus.

I shuffle-walk across a thin rock ledge. The mountain's peak soars above, its pinnacle wrapped in heavy clouds. Below me, layers of freezing mist stretch *really really reeeeeeally* far down.

Don't look don't look don't look.

Oops, I looked.

Jolts of fear twist up my spine as I consider the pointy rocks lurking in that lower haze. With my luck, I'll tumble off this ledge and land smack-dab on a super-pokey boulder.

I lift my chin. *No, I won't. The lab entrance isn't far.*

Gusts of wind scream in my ears. Little ice daggers—I refuse to call them snowflakes—sting my eyes. Sadly, my dragonscale fighting suit is doing zero to keep me warm. I'd ask to borrow a hat, but these are the Himal-something mountains on Earth. No one's around for miles.

My tail jabs my shoulder as if to say, *can we leave yet?*

And yeah, I could magic my ass out of here. I don't want to, though.

Here's the deal. Lucifer's lab is close. Sadly, there's a magical null zone around it. In other words, my *transport home charm* won't work unless I shimmy my chilly butt in the opposite direction. Not a fan of that concept. I'm here and I'm finding the lab, end of story.

With careful movements, I angle my face toward the right. Bad idea. A fresh tsunami of ice-daggers slams into me. A new voice echoes through the arctic wind.

"Greetings, daughter of General Xavier."

Blinking hard, I spot an angel hovering nearby. This one's a youngish guy with a baby face and ears that stick out from the side of his head. Random angelic visits aren't as weird as they once were. It all goes with being the Great Scala.

"You got a scarf with you or anything?" I ask.

"I do not feel cold, oh daughter of General Xavier."

I open my mouth, ready to point out that I wasn't worried about *him* feeling chilly, then I decide to drop it. Angels live in another headspace—one where physical needs don't exist. Explaining things like *cold* to them? Total time-suck.

"What's up?" I ask.

"You requested that I keep you appraised of Drusus."

Drusus is my fading angel buddy. He's an older guy with an artistic flair and a sweet giggle. I'm trying to understand why he's slowly vanishing. After all, if I can't save one fading angel, how will I help the millions more out there?

"Refresh my memory," I say. "What did I ask you again?"

"This was on your last visit to Heaven," prompts the angel. "You said, *someone please let me know if his case gets worse*. And I said, *yes*. Whereupon you said, *thanks, Buddy*."

"Oh, I remember now. Your name is really Buddy."

"Out of all the angels, I couldn't believe you knew me so personally."

Now I don't want to burst Buddy's bubble, but I did *not* know his name. Still, there's no way I'm sharing how I call a lot of random angels *buddy*. Plus, it's cold as fuck out here. No time for long chats.

"What's up with Drusus?" I ask.

"I can no longer see him."

I cling to the rock wall more tightly. "What?"

"Drusus is close to death."

My breath catches. "How much longer does he have?"

"A few weeks, nothing more." Buddy pumps his wings and takes off to the skies.

Guess that conversation is over.

A weight of worry settles into my soul. Once I'm done at Lucifer's lab, I'll figure out how to visit Drusus again. Heaven doesn't make it easy to visit fading angels, but that's never stopped me before.

Simply put, there must be some way to save Drusus.

LINCOLN

A nearby sign reads: *Welcome To The Incaenda Docks, Antrum.*

It might as well read: *Welcome to six hours of your life that you'll never have back.*

I stand inside a massive underground cavern. Before me there stretches a long stone pier flanked by hundreds of Viking-style long ships … as well as a river made from molten lava. Today marks a sacred ceremony called The Annual Blessing Of Thrax Vessels.

Shoot me now.

This particular ritual requires I wear my full kit as king, including leather pants, high boots, a velvet tunic and my silver crown. So far, I've blessed fifty-one boats. Two hundred and thirteen remain. Ah, the glamorous life of a royal.

I step to the next vessel in line. *The Demon Smasher.* Captain Wilheard leads this ship and her crew of three.

Wilheard is a young thrax with long black hair and a wiry frame. Like everyone today, he's in his formal best with a long coat and plumed hat.

"Apologies, your Majesty," stammers Wilheard. "The vessel is rather a mess." Captains always explain how their ships are filthy. It's an unofficial part of the ceremony.

I scan the longboat as if cataloging every inch. I'm sure this crew spent weeks getting *The Demon Smasher* into shape. "She appears perfect."

Wilheard beams. "Thank you."

My assistant for the day is Erik, who drags along a small cart that's stacked high with Angelflower wine. Erik has taken a break from his Alchemist duties in the hopes of scoring some free imbibables. And Erik's not alone, either. All the captains eye the liquid cargo greedily. Angelflower wine costs a mint.

Erik hands me a fresh bottle, which I raise high while speaking the sacred words. "I, Lincoln Vidar Osric Aquilus, King of the Thrax, Consort to the Great Scala, do hereby wish this boat another year of success." I make a point to look each crew member in the eye in turn. "May this vessel, christened *The Demon Smasher*, navigate another twelve months in profit and safety."

In the past, my parents would smash the bottle against the hull. Here's one place I've made changes. Instead of ruining an expensive treat, I hand Wilheard the wine instead.

Sure enough, the captain grins. "Thank you, your Majesty."

"You are most welcome."

A new figure races toward me. It's Hollywell, one of my messengers. "Your Majesty," she says with a bow. "Terrible news from Purgatory."

My stance stiffens. There are five after-realms, namely Heaven, Hell, the Dark Lands, Purgatory, and Antrum. Though I now stand in the thrax homeland of Antrum, my wife Myla and young son Maxon currently wait in an entirely different place. *Purgatory.* Pairing the words *terrible news* with that realm's name is nothing less than alarming.

"Go on," I command.

"We've had word," states Hollywell. "The Great Scala and Queen of the Thrax, Myla Lewis, is attempting to free Colossus."

There are two items of note in that statement.

First, my people often read out Myla's entire list of titles, although I'm completely aware of them.

Second, there's no way Myla's trying to un-imprison the King of the Archdemons.

"And who told you this?" I ask.

"The ladies at the Sunset Retirement Community," Hollywell replies. "Queen Myla will work with a mage called the Crimson Scourge in order to set Colossus free!"

The docks fall silent. All eyes become glued on me and Hollywell. By my calculations, it will take about five-point-two seconds for this news to get across Antrum. Less to reach Mother.

"Not to worry, Hollywell." I gesture toward her hand. "What's that's you're holding?"

"A map to Lucifer's lab," Hollywell replies. "This place holds the very magic needed to free Colossus."

I stretch out my arm, palm upturned. "So?"

"Oh, right," says Honeywell. "I'm supposed to give it to you."

Which she does. *At last.* "Thank you."

Turning over the small quilt, I find a rather detailed map of an Earth mountain sewn into its surface. The runes at the top read, *Lucifer's laboratory.* More writing at the bottom provides the exact coordinates. My spies had turned up some intel on this, but I haven't yet seen their final report with the precise location. Evidently, Myla beat them to it. No doubt, my wife expects me to meet her there.

Can't wait.

I raise my arms, which is kingly body language for, *something important to say here.*

"I, King Lincoln Vidar Osric Aquilus, do hereby declare a Royal Exemption in this ritual. I shall appoint a deputy to complete it for me."

By the way, I love the Royal Exemption policy. It's my *get out of jail free* card.

I turn to Erik. "I trust you can finish the ceremony?"

Erik pales. "I'm no monarch."

A chorus of gasps sound nearby as a new figure steps onto the docks. Mother. As always, Octavia looks petite and lethal in her black velvet gown. Every strand of her gray hair is pulled back into a neat bun at the base of her neck.

"Greetings, my son."

I tip my head. "Mother."

Octavia scans the scene. "Clearly, you've all heard the news about Colossus." Mother turns to Hollywell. "You were promoted too early, child. We do not go around announcing potentially frightening news with outsiders present."

Hollywell's brows pull together. "But the queen's assistant said to share everything as soon as possible. The risk here is great considering how Queen Myla is ... you know ..."

"Queen Myla is *what*?" I ask, my voice low.

"A demon," replies Hollywell.

Rage heats my blood. Myla takes her duties as thrax queen to heart, yet some of my people will never see beyond her demonic side. I point at the messenger insignia on Hollywell's tunic.

"You were awarded this duty because my queen, *the demon*, extended this office to lesser houses. Show some respect." On reflex, my fingers rest on my baculum, a pair of silver rods that can be ignited into any form of weapon made from angelfire.

Mother steps between us. Clearly, she's trying to diffuse the situation. *Smart move.*

"You may take the rest of the day off, child." Mother pats Hollywell on the shoulder. "Report tomorrow to my reception room for sensitivity lessons. You need to learn the difference between quasis and demons."

"Sensitivity lessons? Must I?" asks Hollywell.

I stifle a gasp. *Did this messenger just question the Queen Emeritus?* Hollywell must have a death wish.

"Oh, yes," says Mother slowly. "You most assuredly must."

At this point, my anger toward Hollywell melts away. Mother's lessons are notorious in their thoroughness and ability to make even the toughest thrax cry. And after questioning if she must attend? Hollywell will need a pile of handkerchiefs.

I gesture toward the exit-side of the docks. "Best if you leave now, Hollywell." *Before you do something else.*

Nodding, Hollywell takes off at a slow pace. Meanwhile, Mother turns to address the nearby thrax. Octavia never speaks in more than a menacing whisper, yet I've no doubt everyone hears each syllable. "I have closed down transfers out of Antrum for the duration."

"What duration?" asks Erik.

It's an effort not to roll my eyes. How did this become *Talk Back to Octavia Day?* I round on him. "Whatever duration the Queen Emeritus determines."

"Quite right," says Mother. "I can't have you running off to other realms and spreading more needless worries about Myla and Colossus. No, you'll all stay here and follow along in silence as I finish the rest of this ceremony." She snaps her fingers and points to the wagon of wine. "Erik, please set one bottle before each vessel while I speak with my son."

"Yes, your Queen Emeritus-ness," says Erik.

Mother pulls me aside. Over the years, we've become

experts at chatting in low tones so no one can overhear us. "Your Queen Emeritus-ness?" she asks. "What's gotten into Erik?"

"You frighten him," I state.

"Oh, that." Mother waves her hand dismissively. "He'll recover. Now what's this Colossus blabber about? Shouldn't Polly know better than to frighten our messengers?"

I frown. "Polly?"

"Myla's assistant."

"Oh, that was four assistants ago. Now it's Allimari."

"The girl who's part sloth demon?"

How Mother knows Allimari's demonic heritage, I can't imagine. Over the years, I've learned it's best not to ask.

"That's the one," I reply. "We tell her things, but it takes a while to stick, if that makes sense."

Mother sighs. "Myla tries to make her people do new tasks, that's the trouble. She should follow the old Scala's example."

"Which involved sleeping and allowing others to order him about. Myla wants to do what's right, not what's easy."

Mother nods. "Of course." She pats my cheek gently. "Go have fun at Lucifer's laboratory. I'll keep the realm under control while you're gone."

"Thank you, Mother."

As I step away from a ritual that defines the word *tedious*, a sense of pure joy bubbles through my veins.

Myla-la, here I come.

MYLA

*A*nother gust of arctic wind slams into me. Little needles of cold wheedle their way through every hole and seam in my dragonscale fighting suit. Meanwhile, more icy bits glom onto my eyelashes and nose hair. That stings like a mutha. Yet another burst of frost slams into my face and then ...

Success!

Up ahead, I spot an opening in the rock wall. It's definitely a cave, complete with a flat-floored entrance and shelter from the wind. My tail curls its arrowhead-shaped end into a fist-shape and punches the air.

Ha! I knew this wasn't a crap idea.

Shuffle-walking at double-speed, I quickly reach the entrance. It's beyond awesome to have protection from the ice and snow. A long tunnel opens to my left. Howling winds whip past to my right. And before me, there stands a lone figure. My pulse speeds. Even that massive coat can't hide the identity of my visitor.

Lincoln is here.

My guy wears a black parka and an unreadable look on his face. Is it weird to notice how cute he is with his chiseled features all framed by fake fur? Maybe it is, but it don't care. Even with the mega-coat on, there's no missing Lincoln's broad shoulders, strong cheekbones, and loose brown hair.

"Hey, L-l-l-l-lincoln." *Did I mention I'm cold? I am.*

My guy raises his hand, showing that he brought an extra parka for me. "Greetings." He sashays to my side and wraps me in the most cozy jacket ever. Even my toes start to thaw, which means the garment has been spelled to keep me warm.

Enchanted parka. I should have thought of that.

"How'd you get here first?" Not that I'm a competitive little shit. Actually, I'm more of a competitive *big* shit.

"Oh, that?" A smile dances in my guy's eyes. He knows I hate to lose at anything, even a pretend race to Lucifer's lab that I just made up. "I took the opportunity to engage in some climbing fun." He points upward. "I repelled down."

"Wow. I really hate you sometimes." Only Lincoln would have hidden mountaineering skills.

My guy straightens the collar of my parka. "Not entirely, surely."

"Never." I grin.

Lincoln gives me a sly look. "Allimari told everyone you went off to scheme with the Crimson Scourge."

I make a gaspy-face. "She did *not*. I specifically told her just to give you the map." I wince. "Or something." *What did I say again?*

"The message got a tad garbled." Lincoln's trying hard not to laugh at this point. "Mayhem ensued."

I pop my hands over my mouth. "Oh, damn. You were supposed to run some big ceremony this morning. *The hurrah for floaty things parade.*"

"The Annual Blessing Of Thrax Vessels."

"Right, that."

"Sadly, the news included more than the Crimson Scourge. My messenger also informed me that you planned to free Colossus."

"That is *not* what I told Allibaby."

"Allimari."

"Right again. So is Antrum freaking out or what?"

"Mother has it under control. And the map-quilt made your true intensions clear. So I grabbed a few enchanted parkas and came along to join you."

"My frozen ass thanks you, big time." I throw my arms around Lincoln's neck and kiss him all over his face because honestly? He totally has that coming and more.

Note to self: seduce husband later.

"It's Saturday," says Lincoln. "Evening approaches. I'm done blessing ships. Your quilting contest is over. And Maxon is safely in the care of Xavier."

I bob my brows. "Xavier, eh? In all the excitement, I'd forgotten he signed up for babysitting duty."

Lincoln lowers his voice to a conspiratorial tone. "Do

you have plans to convince your father of something, Myla?"

"As a matter of fact, I do. Drusus has gone invisible."

Lincoln's mismatched eyes fill with sympathy. "I'm sorry to hear that. It won't be easy to acquire magic to see Drusus once he's vanished. Heaven is rather particular about those things."

"Hence why I need to manipulate my father. For good, though."

"Always." Lincoln scans the passage ahead while his forehead crinkles into one of his *thinking looks*. "I can't shake the feeling that all this is connected. The fading angels … Colossus … the Crimson Scourge."

"About that." It takes a few minutes, but I review everything I learned during this morning's adventure at the Sunset Retirement Community.

"Let me get this straight," Lincoln says afterwards. "These ladies wish you to create your own knights of the round table to address the fading angels problem."

"And I agree with that part."

"Yet according to these same women, you must also acquire a certain Band of Epochs which—if you use it—could save the fading angels. At the same time, it might also empower the Crimson Scourge, free Colossus, and cause the end of the world."

"And *that part* is crap on a cracker. I can find my own knights of the round table here, in the present, without risking a demonpocalypse, thank you very much."

"You always have Walker and my help, should you require it."

"And I totally love that about you." I sigh. "It's just that I'm the Great Scala. It's a huge job. I could corral you and all my friends and family into pitching in, but it still wouldn't be enough. And honestly?" I take care to meet his gaze when I say this next part. "Doing this by myself is a *thing* with me. A challenge. And you know how I am about stuff like that."

"I do." Leaning in, he brushes a gentle kiss across my lips. "You have my full support, whatever you decide."

Warmth and love spread through me. "Thank you."

"Now." Lincoln bobs his brows. "Let's go blow shit up."

I smile my face off. "Oooooh, I love it when you swear."

"That's why I save it for special occasions."

And so, hand in hand, Lincoln and I step off into the tunnel. As we move into the darkness, I come to an important conclusion.

This could be the best date night, ever.

5

LINCOLN

*M*yla and I move deeper inside the mountain. After a few twists in the passage, the stone hallway opens to a large round chamber. The moment we step inside the room, lanterns flicker to life above us. They're the boxy kind where light peeps out through punch-holes in metal.

"Odd," I say. "Those were enchanted to simply turn on when we entered."

"Right?" asks Myla. "There wasn't even a door, let alone a lock." My girl narrows her eyes. "This is all too easy."

"Perhaps Lucifer just became overconfident in his hiding spot," I offer. *Which is possible.* The ex-King of the Angels is nothing if not supremely secure in his own amaz-ingness.

"Even so, we shouldn't touch anything. You don't know what around here is booby-trapped."

"Agreed."

With that, Myla and I step further into the space. The floor is lined with a patchwork of wooden tables covered in white sheets. That's rather standard for a laboratory.

What's breathtaking are the walls.

Lucifer's lab is a round and towering chamber that's lined with shelves. Hammers, chisels, and other tools lie closest to the floor. Above that come shelf after shelf of books, all of them covered in leather. Next follows a section filled with ingredient jars in all shapes and sizes. Above it all, a network of glass pipes and tubes wind toward the ceiling. At the peak of the lab, a strange suit of armor hangs suspended from chains.

"One thing I'll say for Lucifer," I announce. "The man was organized."

Myla nods. "All he had to do was fly around to get whatever he wanted."

All of a sudden, the hairs on the back on my neck stand on end. Energy churns through my muscles. No question about it. My hunter's sense is going berserk, and for one reason.

We aren't alone.

"Oh, do you see that?" Myla points to a stretch of far wall where an alcove's been carved into the stone. Even with all the dust, there's no missing the bright colors from that spot.

"I do." My hunter's sense goes even further on edge. Every cell in body stays frozen in place as my senses reach out. *Who's in here?*

Myla gestures to the alcove. "Let's check it out."

I shake my head.

"What is it?" asks Myla.

"Someone's close." Tilting my head, I further focus my senses. A gentle scratching sounds nearby. I turn toward Myla. "Did you hear that?"

"Nuh-uh."

Scanning the floor, I find the barest lines cutting through the cobwebs. Something has been flying around this place, leaving trails as the ends of its wings brush the dusty ground. *Interesting.* With silent steps, I follow the path to a tall object covered in a white fabric. The linen rustles, yet there is no breeze.

That settles it. Whatever's in here, it hides under that sheet.

I crouch low for a better look. The linen stops moving. A charged aura fills the air. I've hunted enough to know when a stranger is close. Little by little, I reach toward the dusty sheet.

All of a sudden, something flies out from under the fabric and heads straight for my face. Trouble is, the thing moves too quickly for me to get a good look. That means one thing.

Danger.

6

MYLA

a white blob of fur flies right at my husband's nose. *What the WHAT?*

The thing misses Lincoln's head to land on the floor before me. Turns out, it's a mouse-sized creature whose white furry body is paired with matching wings. In other words, it's a snow imp, a variety of demon that's relatively harmless.

And to be honest, it's also pretty damned cute.

I kneel down. "Hello, there. Did we frighten you?"

The snow imp grins, a movement that shows off its pointy snout and tiny teeth. "Fluffbottom, Fluffbottom," it says in a squeaky voice.

"Is that your name?" I ask.

"Captain, Captain," adds the imp.

"So your name is Captain Fluffbottom?" I clarify.

"Yes, yes. Captain Fluffbottom."

"That's a big name for a little guy." Kneeling, I reach toward the imp. "Come here, Fluff. I won't hurt you."

In reply, the snow imp extends its wings. Swooping up, it lands on my shoulder. I don't feel a thing, though. That's not a surprise. Most tiny demons exude enchantments to avoid detection.

Lincoln eyes my new friend. "Snow imps often take up residence in caves." He steps closer. "How long have you been here?"

Instead of replying, the imp rounds on Lincoln and hisses. Which—considering how Fluff is hanging out right by my ear—is a totally sucky experience. I pat his tummy with my pinky. "Calm down, Fluff. Just because Lincoln isn't super-cool and demonic like you and me, that's no reason to hiss at him."

Fluff hisses again anyway.

Lincoln pauses and holds up his arms, palms forward. It's the universal sign for, *I'm not coming any closer.* "You're safe, little friend." My guy scans the lab. "You've lived here for a while. What's the best thing to see?"

"Oh," I say. "Good question."

Fluff bounces on my shoulder while pointing to a far wall. "There! There!" he cries.

I scope out the spot that Fluff indicated. Sure enough, it's the same alcove that I gestured to before. "Nice pick, Fluff."

Lincoln nods. "Let's check it out."

At this point, my tail swoops around until the arrowhead end points right at Fluff. A long moment passes. *What will my tail do?* It's not like I had pets or anything growing up. My tail normally gets all the attention. Yet now I have a furry Captain Fluffbottom taking up residence on my shoulder. The arrowhead-end arches toward Fluff. I suck in a worried breath. It's really uncool if my tail skewers the snow imp.

"Uh oh," I announce. "Tail alert."

Lincoln pauses beside me. "This ought to be interesting."

Little by little, the arrowhead end closes in on Fluff. Soon the pointy part is *almost but not quite* touching the snow imp's tummy. *Crud.* That's my tail's move when it's about to attack.

If Fluff is intimidated by my tail, the snow imp doesn't show it. Instead, Fluff launches into a long stream of high-pitched chatter. I can't understand much of what the snow imp says, but the words *pretty tail* and *mighty warrior* are clear.

That confirms it. Fluff is brilliant. My tail loves being sucked-up to.

Next Fluff reaches out to pet my tail's end. And with that, it's settled. My tail now has a new bestie. The arrow-head end touches Fluff on the head before going back to its regular hang-out spot by my ankles.

"We're good," I announce.

"Clever Fluff," says Lincoln.

We then cross the room to check out the place Fluff pointed out before. And damn, what a spot it is. Up close, it's clear that the alcove was hand-carved into the rock wall. Shelves of small statues fill the space from top to bottom. I move in for a better look.

What I see is a shocker.

The nook is filled with little dolls related to the King of the Archdemons.

"Whoa," I say in a low voice. "This is like one of those serial killer shrines."

"The top is all Colossus," adds Lincoln.

Sure enough, the entire top shelf is covered with statues of the archdemon king. In the first figure, Colossus stands tall, showing off his muscular torso, four arms, and backwards-style animal legs. Colossus also has a goat-like head complete with wide cheekbones, small yellow eyes, and curly horns. Plus, his entire body is red. So there's that.

Did I mention Colossus is also made from what looks like sand? He is. It's the whole *I'll possess you* power he has going on. If you try to punch him, your fist goes right through his sandy face. Makes fighting him extra-tricky.

I move to the next sculptures in line. Here Lucifer has created a series of figures that show Colossus going down on all six limbs to crawl around like a spider. Not something I needed to see.

Lincoln frowns. "I never would have pegged Lucifer as being a fan of Colossus."

"Same here." I bob my head and consider things. "Still, Lucifer wanted to wipe out all humans. Maybe he saw Colossus as a role model."

"Or a tool," adds Lincoln.

An odd tickle crawls up my arms. "You mean with something like that?" I point to the ceiling.

Lincoln and I both look up and hot damn, that's not a great sight. When we first walked in, I noticed a set of suspended armor. Looking at it now, there's no missing how the metal is forged to hold four arms, two backwards-style legs and one massive goat head.

Lincoln takes in a slow breath. "We are so destroying this place."

"Sign me up." Kneeling, I scan the lower shelves. "There are more statues down here."

Lincoln crouches by my side. "Looks like they're the Seven." These are the seven archdemons—the ones who focus on one deadly sin each. Colossus can possess any of the Seven. The eighth figure, the Archdemon of Lust and Wrath, is a dragoness and does her own thing. She's my fave, obviously.

"Yup." I point to a pair of statues that look like armored knights. "There's Null and Rage."

Deadly sins tend to run in pairs, so Null and Rage are the Archdemons of Sloth and Wrath respectively. Null's armor is all rusty while Rage is all black and badass.

Lincoln nods. "And next to them, it's Plain and Vain." Those are the Archdemons for Envy and Pride. They appear as figures in metallic cloaks with the hoods drawn low.

I point to the next statues. "Skyn and Bone." In this case, Skyn and Bone are the Archdemons of Gluttony and Greed. You'd think this pair would be all chubby, but the driving force for those two sins is emptiness. As a result, they're both skeletons.

Lincoln points to a figure who's dressed in a bard's outfit. "And that's Lester."

"What a loser." As part lust demon, I find it offensive that the Archdemon of Lust is a greasy guy in a pouffy hat who carries a lute.

At this point, Fluff jumps off my shoulder to gesture at a small golden casket on the bottom shelf. "Gems! Gems!" he calls. Unlike everything else in the laboratory, this container isn't covered in dust. It was opened and recently.

Leaning in, I scan the runes inside the small casket. "It says, *Gemstones for the Staff of Avalon.* There's nothing inside, though." I purse my lips. "What's a Staff of Avalon?"

"Not sure." Lincoln inspects the nearby floor. "There are more wing trails here." He looks to Fluff. "Did you do this?"

"No, no," comes Fluff's squeaky response. "Another flew in here, stole the gems, and winged away. Stepping on the floor is bad."

I wink. "Now he tells us." I rub my temples and think things though. Some puzzle pieces fall into place. Others stay stuck between the metaphorical couch cushions.

"You have something for me?" asks Lincoln.

"The Crimson Scourge needs the band of Epochs to travel through time, right?"

"Yes."

"Well, maybe this evil mage needs more than just that

signet ring." I gesture to the empty container. "Do you think these gems could be part of the plan?"

"It's possible." Lincoln taps his cheek. "Staff of Avalon. That must concern King Arthur."

All of a sudden, Fluff bobs on my shoulder. "Danger, danger," he says in his squeaky mouse voice.

Lincoln stills. I know that look on my guy. It's another one of his hunter-stances. In my experience, we now have a fifty-fifty chance of something big happening.

And by *big*, I mean *lethal*.

7

LINCOLN

*O*nce again, my hunter's sense goes into overdrive. Energy pulses through my veins. I scan the laboratory closely. Shelf after shelf lines the towering walls. Cobwebs cover everything. Nothing has changed. That's when I hear it.

Whirrrr. The barest mechanical sound fills the air.

"What's wrong?" asks Myla.

"Not sure." I focus on Fluff. "Do you know what made that sound?"

Fluff buries himself deeper into the hair that cascades over Myla's shoulder. "Yes, yes."

Myla pats Fluff's back. "It's okay. You can show us."

Fluff swoops out to a tall object covered in a sheet. It's the same place where the snow imp hid before. After grasping the fabric in his tiny claws, Fluff pumps his wings and flies upward. He's certainly a strong little fellow. Once the sheet is gone, I find nothing less than the most amazing clock I've ever seen.

The device stands six feet high and is made in a classic grandfather clock design that's tall and rectangular. However, the round clock-face holds no numbers (or arms) to indicate the time. That isn't the most impressive aspect, though. The device is completely made from tiny golden crystals the size of matchsticks.

Myla gasps. "I've never seen apex crystals before."

"Same here. And this clock must contain thousands of them."

Gemstones store magic, some more than others. Apex crystals are the most valuable, considering how they're small in size and yet hold more power than stones that are as big as Mack trucks.

"Fluff," says Myla. "What's the crystal clock for?"

"Boobytrap, boobytrap. Clock makes everything explode."

All the blood seems to drain from my body. With this much apex crystal power, this entire mountaintop could be leveled. "How long do we have before this detonates?"

"Hours and hours," says Fluff.

Myla and I share a long gaze. Fluff is many things, but an expert in time doesn't seem like one of them.

"Let's give it five minutes," says Myla.

"Agreed."

"That's why Fluff only flies in here," says the snow imp. "Step on the floor and the clock starts up. Afterwards, hours and hours go by before *tick-tick-ding*."

"Tick-tick-ding?" repeats Myla.

"Oh." Fluff rubs his little hands over his pointed face. "Tick-tick-ding-boom."

"Understood," I say. "The clock is some kind of bomb. And tick-tick-ding … that's all the warning we'll get before the proverbial *boom*?"

"Yes, yes," replies Fluff. "First hours and hours, then tick-tick-ding-boom."

I'm not happy that we've started a ticking bomb, but I'm not displeased either. It looks like we've plenty of time before the explosion itself, and the boobytrap does save us the hassle of wiring the place. There was no way we'd leave this lab without some kind of detonation.

Fluff swoops over to a nearby shelf of books. A heavy leather tome lays open there. "This, this," says Fluff. "Tell you everything."

"On our way," I state.

Unlike Fluff, Myla and I must step around the tables in order to reach the same spot. I point to the opened book. "Is this the one?"

"Yes, yes," says Fluff.

"And it's okay to touch?" asks Myla.

"Fine, fine."

Myla turns the pages. The volume is large and covered by detailed illustrations all signed by Lucifer. "Whoa," she says. "I thought the wrath coven made some *Colossus Kill Porn*, but this is even worse."

"Indeed." I tap the first image, which shows Colossus himself slicing off a human's head. "Here Lucifer has drawn the archdemon king in the same red armor that hangs above. And Colossus appears to be wielding a sword."

Myla frowns. "But Colossus can't wield anything himself. He's the possession guy. That's it."

"I fear Lucifer has other ideas." I point to the ceiling. "Hence the suspended armor. It's the exact thing he's wearing in these images."

Myla gasps. "Let me get this straight. Colossus is a red mist baddie who can only possess people. But Lucifer says, *I'll make armor so he doesn't have to go through that pesky possession stage. That way, Colossus can get right to the magic-casting and killing-stuff fun.*"

"You got it." I refocus on the book. "Check out the margins here. Lucifer added numerous handwritten calculations to cover magical containment and power." I gesture upward. "That armor is nothing less than a Colossus *kill suit.*"

"Ick." Myla turns another page.

And there it is.

A thick golden band.

Above it is written in loopy letters, *Band of Epochs.*

"Oh, Hell," whispers Myla. "That signet ring is here."

Once again, smaller text fills the sheet's margins. Leaning in, I begin to read the tiny runes aloud. "Hear ye, hear ye! This ring bequeaths the power to journey through time. There you may discover the path to save the fading angels. Lift the ring from the page if you dare."

Myla sniffs. "I tell you what I'm *not* doing, and that's

touching that freaking ring. From what I learned at the wrath coven, once I take the Band of Epochs from this lab, the ring will somehow end up in the possession of the Crimson Scourge. That evil mage frees Colossus and—WHAMMO—the world is trashed."

"I couldn't agree more. We must allow that ring to be destroyed along with everything else."

Myla frowns. "Um, Lincoln?"

"Yes."

"What happened to the Band of Epochs?"

I look at the book once more and sure enough, the signet ring is gone. "I didn't touch it."

Myla worries her bottom lip with her teeth. "The wrath coven said that if I didn't do what they wanted, their magic would make it happen anyway."

Little by little, Myla raises her palms. I exhale. She wears no new rings on her fingers. *Whew.*

Suddenly, a burst of purple light flares at Myla's left hand. A thin tendril of mist wraps around her thumb. The light grows brighter. Then it disappears. When the mist vanishes, I can't believe what I see.

Myla now wears the Band of Epochs.

"Hells bells." Myla yanks on the signet ring, but it won't budge. "Stupid magic."

That's when we hear it.

Tick-tick-ding.

"Uh-oh," says Fluff. And he flies off down the exit passage. *Clever imp.*

"We need to run," says Myla.

"There may be faster options." Reaching into my pocket, I pull out a transfer charm. It appears as a purple ticket, the kind humans use for raffles. The moment the colored item hits the air, something awful takes place.

My transfer charm disintegrates.

"How unfortunate," I quip.

"That happened to me on the way in." Myla sniffs. "Unlike *some people,* I didn't do any mountaineering. When I tried to transport right into the lab, a magical null zone stopped me. Ruined all my charms, too."

I nod slowly. *So charms are useless in here.* I pat my pockets. I've other charms remaining, and they still feel intact. None are transfer magic, but I'm not pulling them out only to have them get dusted. I zip up my parka. "Which means this is the part where—"

Myla finishes my thought. "We haul ass?"

"Quite."

With that, Myla and I turn toward the exit and race for our lives.

8

MYLA

Unholy Hell.

Sure, I wanted me some kaboom, but not while I was still inside the freaking mountain.

Lincoln and I race through the lab. Our goal? Reach the same access passageway that we used to enter the laboratory—AKA the one Fluff just flew his furry butt into—and vamoose.

Running around the tables is too much of a time-suck, so Lincoln and I take to leaping over them, Olympic style. As we rush toward the exit, the floor starts to tremble. Long cracks form in the stone walls.

Not long now.

As I speed forward, my mind snaps into a little thing I call *battle mode*. Everything in the room comes into hyper focus. Time seems to slow. Plans form and shift. I catalog our situation. We have no transport charms, not that they'd work anyway. Lincoln has some other magical goodies from Striga, but those won't function until we pass the null zone.

Images pop into my mind. The short ledge. A long fall onto pointy rocks. The soon-to-come explosion. *How the Hell do we stay alive?*

An idea hits me.

There's a low shelf by the exit. And it's packed with odd tools. I spy a pickaxe and some other goodies. *Perfect.*

Now, it's no secret that I suck at long-term planning. Like, you know, grabbing a coat when I'm off to sub-zero temperatures. That said, give me a crisis and I'm at my best. And my current plan is super awesome, if I do say so myself. Looking to Lincoln, I point to the shelf in question.

"I'll grab the pickaxe."

My guy leaps over a table, his forehead furrowed in thought as he figures out my scheme. A second later, he nods. "I'll take the chain." It's the one the armor's hauled up on, but can easily be unhooked.

Perfect again.

Satisfaction and love warm my veins. *Lincoln's the best.* All I need to do is point and say four words: *I'll grab the pickaxe.* After that, my guy is right with me.

Ear-piercing cracks sound as more fissures open along the walls. Books tumble. Vials shatter. My pulse speeds. The armor lurches at an odd angle.

Only seconds remain.

I grab the pickaxe from its spot along the wall. Lincoln unhooks the chain, then loops it over his shoulder. The opened passage looms before us. We race into the darkened hallway. Right behind us, great chunks of rock break free from the ceiling and tumble down.

Boom! Boom!

The ground shimmies as each boulder slams into the tables below.

There isn't time to contemplate how the lab is literally falling apart. Lincoln and I race down the shadowy passage. From outside, the barest tendrils of light criss-cross the rock floor. Sweat beads on my temples. Behind us, fresh rumbles erupt from the lab.

Then everything falls silent.

Somehow, the quiet is the more unnerving than anything that came before.

Light bursts through the tunnel. Heat sears at my back as a wall of fire erupts from the lab. Lincoln and I race toward the outside. There's no time. Only yards separate us from the end of the tunnel. And from there? Inches divide the tunnel's mouth and a long-ass fall. Fire licks at my heels and burns the back of my coat. Thankfully, my tail is on the job. It takes charge of putting out the flames.

We close in on the cave's edge.

Five yards.

Four yards.

Three.

I've carried the pickaxe all this way. Now I summon my demonic strength, focusing the energy into my grip on the tool. My eyes flare red with magic and power. Letting out a great yell, I slam the axe into the rock floor by the passage's edge.

Crack!

The axe's metal head bites into the stone. Was I able to get the pick deep enough to support my plan? I can only hope.

Without needing a word, Lincoln winds his chain around the end of the axe. "Hold on to me!" he calls.

I move so Lincoln and I stand face to face. Then I wrap my legs around his torso. "All set!"

Looping the chain around his arms, Lincoln waits at the rock's edge. Red light dances across my guy's face, a reflection of the fire as it churns through the tunnel behind us. Blue power flares in my guy's eyes. Before, I tapped into my demonic energy. Now Lincoln's doing the same with his angelic side. His gaze locks with mine as he calls off a single word.

"Now!"

Lincoln kicks off the side of the mountain. The chain loops around the pick-axe above, using the tool as a kind of fulcrum. One side of the metal chain winds around Lincoln's left arm; the other end curls around his right. More chain dangles below us.

Now, I'm no expert at repelling, so it's a bit of a mystery to me how Lincoln manages to loosen the chain and allow us to repel down into the icy clouds below the mountain. I'm just glad he can do it.

We're only a few yards away from the passage's mouth when it happens.

KABOOM!

The entire top of the mountain explodes in fire and

light. Bits of rock tumble around us. My tail takes charge of batting away the smaller bits, but Lincoln must leap from side to side so we don't get flattened by the larger chunks. I can't help but notice how boulders pass us by, followed by a distant smash as the massive rocks burst onto the pointy stuff below.

If those lower rocks can destroy boulders, what will they do to us?

Lincoln repels us down further until we're almost out of chain. The mountain quiets. Moments pass.

Is it over? Are we safe?

At last, I exhale. Lincoln and I share a smile. *We did it.*

"Good thing Lucifer kept a chain around, eh?" I ask.

"Far sturdier than a rope," counters Lincoln.

As if in reply, the chain starts to whine. My blood freezes as I watch the links stretch and crack.

"Oh, no." I guess even chains get brittle after hanging out in a mountain for *who know how long.*

"Quick," says Lincoln. "My breast pocket. Purple quarter. It's a Striga charm."

"Right." With any luck, we're now outside the null zone for spells. Whatever this purple charm does, I can only hope it involves keeping us from becoming royal pincushions.

Reaching into Lincoln's front pocket, I pull out the small round spell and break it in two. For a long moment, nothing happens. Then a puff of violet smoke rises from the jagged halves of the magical coin.

That's the good news.

The *bad* news is that the chain has decided that *now's a good time to die.* The links snap in multiple places at once. The metal cord turns limp around Lincoln's arms.

My guy and I tumble through empty space.

Leaning in, I kiss Lincoln because if I'm about to kick the bucket, I want one last smooch.

With a thud, we land on something hard and round. Looking down, I see a purple platform now juts out from the mountainside. It's the kind thrax deploy on demon patrol when they need to create an observation perch. I've seen these used in trees, but on a mountain? That's new.

Not that I'm complaining. I'm just glad it worked. Lucifer's enough of a dick to make sure his null zone is pretty large.

Lincoln cups my face. His palms feel warm and firm against my skin. "Are you all right?"

"Fine." My tail pops over my shoulder to wave at Lincoln. "And my tail is great also."

A sly look enters my guy's eyes. He pats the tail's arrow-head-end. "Glad you're both okay."

"Hope Fluff made it out all right."

"Me, too." Lincoln scans the skies. "No sign of him, though."

Voices echo in from down below. *Humans.* "We've got visitors."

Lincoln checks his pockets. "Humans must have seen that explosion. We'll need a thrax containment team in here STAT."

I nod. "I wouldn't put it past Lucifer to have more booby traps left over, too."

"Agreed." Lincoln pulls out a small slip of paper. With quick movements, he folds it into an origami bird. Since it's actually a charm from Striga, this folded sheet is not just any creation. The paper bird comes alive, takes to the skies, and vanishes into the clouds. No doubt, it's somehow summoning a demon patrol at this very moment.

"How long before the thrax arrive?" I ask.

Lincoln tilts his head, thinking. "Two, three minutes tops. The platform will hold out for hours, if that's what you're concerned about."

"Actually, I was wondering if the patrol could look through the ruins for more magical items." I sigh. "Maybe there will be something left over that could help the fading angels."

Lincoln pulls me against him. "If they find anything, they're trained to turn it right in."

Those words—along with Lincoln's embrace—should be comforting. And it is, for all of three seconds. Then that odd voice returns. In a super-serene tone, she speaks in my mind once more.

Take the risk. Travel to the past. Save the fading angels. You can't do this on your own.

This is exactly the kind of namby-pamby, sweetie-pie, hearts-n-roses stuff that my inner wrath demon usually hates. Strangely enough, that part of me is completely silent. No coiled fury. Not even a huff of frustration.

Did I get hit with a possession spell? If so, who'd possess me to have happy talk going in my head? I stare at the Band of Epochs on my thumb. Whatever's going on, I bet it has to do with this damned signet ring.

Trouble is, I still have no idea how to keep the wrath coven's vision from coming true.

9

MYLA

$\mathcal{W}$ ithin minutes, demon patrol warriors are every-freaking-where, all of them sporting their special white body armor.

Soon scaffolding and platforms rise up around what was once the mountaintop. Dozens of thrax check out the ruined lab, looking for magical leftovers.

Spoiler: they don't find anything. This is both good (because Lucifer is Lucifer) and bad (considering how I hoped there might be other stuff for the fading angels).

Another thrax team enchants human satellites, recordings and memories, erasing any sign of the massive explosion. You'd think technology would make it harder for magical cover-ups. The reverse is true. Humans are so confident in their computers and whatnot, they won't believe that magic changes things, even when it happens before their very eyes. Then again, humans can't tell when a sloth demon is gnawing on their ass, either. Best to keep expectations low overall.

Long story short, it's hours before Lincoln and I can leave the mountain and head home. We recently bought a new house in Purgatory—living with our parents was *too much togetherness*—so that's where we go.

It's precisely 11:03 PM when my guy and I walk through our front door. Mom's away at her Ghoul Reconciliation Convention, trying to ease tensions between quasis and our previous overlords. It's one of her big *President of Purgatory* things. When we get home, Dad's holding down the fort and Maxon should be asleep.

Notice my use of the word *should.*

Sure enough, the moment we step into the living room, Lincoln and I find a pie-eyed Maxon. In terms of looks, my kid reminds me of a big cherub ... if said cherub had a shit-eating grin and a dragonscale tail. When it comes to age, Maxon's only two. That said, he has the logic and speech of someone much older. And his energy levels? That's uncharted territory.

Case in point: Right now, Maxon's turned the living room into an imaginary lava river. My kid is jumping from table to couch to chair, all to avoid getting *pretend burned to death.* Considering there's a real magma river in Antrum, this is a pretty useful game.

Maxon doesn't look up as we enter to room, mostly because he's preparing for a big jump from the fireplace mantle to the couch.

Yes, I said the words *fireplace mantle* and *couch.*

Maxon does stuff like this all the time. We keep a box of healing charms in the linen closet.

Dad waves as we walk in. Tonight my father wears loose ninja pants and a black T-shirt. As the General of the Angels, my father's fit and lean with cocoa skin and pronounced bone structure. Based on the crinkles by his eyes, he's also tired but happy.

My father rises from his favorite rocking chair. "Someone's been waiting for you to get home."

At these words, Maxon nails his leap onto the couch, which then releases a serious of ominous twangs. Lincoln and I share a dry look. There's no need to say it out loud, we both know the drill here. *We'll need a new couch again. Soon.*

Maxon then focuses on me for a millisecond before yelling at Lincoln. "Arthuuuuuuuuuur!"

No question what our little one wants here. King Arthur is Maxon's favorite book these days. In our son's opinion, Lincoln is the *parent of choice* for bedtime storytelling. I'm picked when it comes to snack time, by the way. So I totally win out on that one.

"Arthuuuuuuuuuur!" Maxon now accents the word by jumping on the couch, a motion that's accompanied by ever louder twangs from the sorry springs inside our rapidly-deteriorating furniture.

Dad pinches the bridge of his nose. "I've read him the story seven times."

Maxon leaps off the couch, speeds across the room, and

grabs Lincoln's hand. "Daddy read! Daddy read! Daddy read!"

When my boy is tired, he tends to repeat short phrases over and over. And this much repetition? My kid's exhausted.

Lincoln guy ruffles Maxon's hair. "Sure thing, bud."

"Yay!" Maxon grins, and it's one of those smiles that radiate pure joy. Once Lincoln and Maxon are safely off, my father turns to me.

"So, you blew up the lab."

There's no question here which *lab* Dad refers to. "Technically, Lucifer set a booby trap on the place. So the King of the Angels blew up his own lab."

"But you found it."

"Yup. I got some help from a wrath coven."

"Let me guess. Was it the Bloody Knights of the Round Table operating out of the Sunset Retirement Community for Quasi-Demonic Women?"

I let out a low whistle. "Damn, you're good."

"Verus has been keeping me apprised." Dad sighs. "Perhaps we should sit down." He retakes his favorite rocker.

At the mention of the name Verus, my worry-radar starts to ping *and how*. Verus replaced Lucifer as the ruler of the angels. Her claim to fame is that she's a super-accurate oracle. And the fact that Verus has been focusing on my life? Not good.

Careful to avoid the couch, I plunk onto one of the love seats. "You should know something before we begin," I state. "Verus has been calling me and I haven't quite gotten back to her yet."

Translation: I'm totally ignoring Verus. Why? The oracle angel is an over-worrier. Last month, she said that if I ate a new deep-fried cheeseburger from McPurgatory, then it would end the after-realms. I ate that burger like a boss. Nothing happened.

"I'm aware you two haven't connected," says Dad. "That's why Verus got in contact with me. She's worried about you and the fading angels." He leans forward, resting his elbows on his knees. "Verus says that if you aid those angels, you could end the world with a demonpocalypse."

"She's exaggerating." Lifting my hand, I show off the Band on Epochs on my thumb. "If I use this ring to travel through time, then yes, I could cause serious trouble. But I'm not dumb as a rock, so I won't do that."

"Yet you still have the ring."

"It's kind of stuck on my thumb." In an act of oddness, the signet ring tumbles off my hand to land on the carpet. "Or rather, it *was* stuck before."

This situation just keeps getting odder and odder. I scoop up the ring and grip it in my fist. At this point, I wouldn't be surprised if it sprouted frog's legs and hopped away.

Dad shakes his head. "You do realize that no Great Scala before you has ever attempted to help those angels. Your predecessors all ran across the same prophecy you have, one way or another. The vision states that you can *possibly* help the fading angels, but it will risk the world."

An odd chill runs through my veins. "So what are we talking about here?"

"Verus asked me to get that ring from you, no matter what."

I narrow my eyes. "And what would you do with the ring?"

"Place it in Heavenly storage, same as with the other magical items from Lucifer."

"But Verus wants to go full Frodo on this, doesn't she?"

"Frodo?"

"It's from this human book, *The Lord of the Rings*. The main character, Frodo, chucks a ring into a lava pit where it melts down to zero. Or rather, his frenemy chucks himself and the ring into the lava. It's complicated. Long story short, Verus wants to destroy the Band of Epochs, yes?"

"She does," confirms Dad. "But I don't. When Luce made this ring, he was still my friend and our leader. He wouldn't have created such a powerful item unless he saw a positive use for it one day."

I scrunch my mouth to one side of my face and think. There's a big decision to be made here. Namely, do I share with Dad the fact that his ex-bestie was already setting up serial killer shrines and drawing death porn of Colossus?

In my mind, the answer appears in big neon letters: *Hell, no.*

"I totally agree, Dad. It must have a good use."

"Well, before we get too ahead of ourselves, I should take a look at that ring. It might be a decoy, you know." My father holds out his hand to me. The request is unspoken but clear.

Give it to me.

On reflex, I clutch the ring against my chest. Dad just confessed how Verus has been begging him to stop me. Still, if Dad were going to nab the ring, he would have done it already. So I hand the thing over.

Father turns over the item on his fingers. "The real Band of Epochs empowers you to travel to the past or future. It can only support a limited number of journeys." Dad presses the hefty signet ring between his palms and whispers an incantation.

"Time and flight
Morn and night
Truth and flame
Reveal the same."

When my father pulls his hands apart, there are five thin rings on his palms. All have a familiar angel feather pattern, only slimmer.

"This is the true Band of Epochs," declares Dad. "Only five journeys through time remain." My father presses his hands together again, saying another, shorter spell.

"Sleep now."

When my father opens his hands once more, the ring has returned to being a hefty signet band. Dad reaches his hand toward me. The ring sits on his outstretched palm.

I wave my father off. "You can take it to magical storage or whatever … if that would make Verus chill out."

"It most definitely would," says Dad. "It's not easy for Verus, you know. We only *hear* the awful prophecies. She's the one who has to get the visions of the world actually ending."

"Out of curiosity, how does the time travel part work?" I don't plan to use the ring, but that doesn't mean I don't want full deets while I have an expert nearby.

"When you wish to journey through time, you hold the band between your palms and speak another incantation."

"World and care
Take me there."

My brows lift. "That's all?"

"The ring chooses the best time and place for you to visit."

I smack my lips. "Hey, now. You know a lot about this thing. Did you help design it?"

"Guilty as charged." Dad chuckles. "Oh, there's something else I wanted to share with you. This may aid your personal mission to find knights of the roundtable."

I frown. "How did you hear about that?"

Dad squirms. "Verus again, only…"

"Only?" I prompt.

"Your mother and I have been talking about it for a

while. We even used the same phrase, *Myla's knights of the round table.*"

I slump into my chair. On the one hand, maybe I should get *Myla Sucks At Her Job* T-shirts made. Looks like there may be some demand. An image pops into my mind—the fragment of the Scala quilt that I saw before. I'm still that unfinished piece, alone. That said, pretending I'm perfect doesn't help save the fading angels. So I straighten my spine and ask the obvious question.

"What are you and Mom thinking?" *Because I know they talked about something.*

"That you need more information," says Dad. "With Cryptan gone, there's a new keeper of the thrax ancient archives—his niece Remy. Word is, she's rediscovering all sorts of important things. As the new archivist, she may have something useful for you."

"Okay, Dad. I'll definitely visit her. And ..." I scrunch up my mouth, trying to think of the right words. "Thanks for worrying about me."

Did that last bit come out strangely? Maybe, but Dad still seems to get it. My father and I share a warm smile. It's a nice moment, so I let it hang there before moving onto more tricky topics. "One more thing while you're here. I want to visit Drusus again."

"Your fading angel." Dad's mouth thins. "Sorry to say, the part of Heaven where Drusus exists has serious limitations. Those who are almost fully faded can not be forced to materialize. It would require a particular spell."

"And since you're a super-powerful archangel, I'm

guessing you might know what magic could help?" Dad gives me a dramatic sigh, which means I'm half way to convincing him.

Dad rises. "I'll consider it."

"Well, I plan on leaving here at 10 AM tomorrow for my visit to Drusus, in case you want to join me." I go up on tiptoe and kiss his cheek. "And thank you for watching Maxon."

"Are you kidding? I love it." Dad wraps me in a big hug. "And I love you too, Myla-la."

Dad doesn't say it, but I can tell by his fierce hug that he's super worried about me. And he's right. Out of all my nutso adventures, something tells me that this quest for the fading angels might be the riskiest of all.

10

LINCOLN

*a*t this hour, putting Maxon to sleep requires a full repeat of the classic bedtime routine. In this case, that means a bath, fresh pajamas, and a half-hearted attempt at toothbrushing. All of this is immediately followed Maxon taking a big leap onto his new favorite place.

The big boy bed.

As in, no more cribs.

This is a thing.

Which brings us up to the present moment. Maxon already body-slammed the bed. Now he bobs on his mattress. "Arthuuuuuuuuur!"

"I'll get the book." Turning, I pull the worn leather volume from its place of honor on the top shelf.

"Arthuuuuuuuuur!"

"Hey now, we aren't doing anything unless you've got a quiet body and a quiet voice." We use this phrase a lot while raising Maxon. My son immediately stops bouncing and folds his hands neatly over the coverlet.

"Ready, Daddy."

"All right, then." I sit beside him on the mattress. Maxon snuggles up against me as I set the volume before us.

"*The Tale of King Arthur*," I read.

"By Dalston Rusus the Bard."

"That's right." I kiss the top of his head. "Good reading, bud."

At this point, Myla slips into the room. She loves watching me read to Maxon. Our boy is a natural hunter, but he doesn't yet sense when Myla sneaks around. My wife's gotten rather stealthy.

After winking at Myla, I turn the page. "Once upon a time, there were eight archdemons who were led by the evil Colossus."

Now, Maxon says I'm the best at reading. In my opinion, I think it's because I ask lots of questions. My son likes being challenged. Which is why I gesture across the page. "Which one is Colossus?"

Maxon points to a misty figure standing alone on a hilltop. "That one. He could possess whole armies."

"That's right." I pause, trying to think up a fresh question. "And which one is your least favorite archdemon?"

"Lester," answers Maxon without hesitation.

Now Lester is the Archdemon of Lust, so it could be a bit of a family issue that Maxon ranks him lowest. This is especially true while Myla—who is part lust demon—stands behind us.

"Why Lester?" I ask.

"Mommy's a lust demon. She's cool. This guy is a loser." Maxon points to the picture of Lester as evidence. The archdemon in question wears puffy shorts and a plumed hat that looks more like a fat pizza than anything else.

"You have a point, my son." Lester is known for wearing the latest dance fashion and trying to seduce humans. For the Archdemon of Lust, his success rate is rather pathetic.

Behind us, I hear Myla's muffled giggle. Leave it to Maxon to find the perfect answer.

I return to reading. "In those days, the thrax didn't have a name. Instead, our people believed they were all regular humans who were cursed with the power to see dragons, demons and mages." I pause. "And why did that happen, do you think?"

"Because humans who aren't thrax can't see anything from the after-realms."

"That's right. Most humans don't see things like dragons. If one flies overhead, they'll think it's just a cloud or something. Unless…"

Maxon catches right on. "Unless it's an archangel or an archdemon that's casting a spell or hurting people. Those types are so powerful, even humans can see them in action. But that's not okay, right?"

"Correct," I reply. "Even Pop-Pops can't use his angelic powers on Earth without getting in trouble." I return to reading. "Back then, not a single thrax knew about our powers, or that their true heritage was part angel. And if a thrax *did* know they had abilities, then they didn't realize how to harness their magic. That's why it was called *the brutal time*."

"Now Arthur," says Maxon.

I turn another page. "Then came King Arthur. He was the first to name the thrax and organize our people. His knights of the round table became the first demon patrols."

"Humans don't know any of this, do they?"

"I'm afraid not."

"So what do they think King Arthur did?"

I purse my lips and consider. "They know he became king by pulling a sword out of a stone. Arthur also gets credit for not using his power to hurt those weaker than him. *Might for right* versus *might makes right*. Oh, and they know King Arthur went after the Holy Grail."

"Humans know nothing about the real King Arthur." Maxon turns the page for me. "Let's get the part where Arthur locks up all the archdemons."

"Sure thing." I return to reading. "But Arthur did more than create the thrax. He locked up all the archdemons in the dungeons under his father's castle." I lean I closer. "Can you point to the castle?""

"There." Maxon points out a square structure with a blocky roof. "Pendragon castle."

"Right again." I go on. "After that, King Arthur did something even better. He decided to up Colossus separately. Arthur was supposed to get help from Merlin, but the wizard disappeared with a water nymph named Nimue."

"That wasn't very nice of Merlin and Nimue."

"It wasn't." I tap the page. "But see here? Arthur was strong in magic. He trapped Colossus under his own castle of Camelot. And the world was safe again. The End."

Maxon frowns. "Why didn't Arthur just send all the archdemons to Hell?"

"The archdemons were so evil, even Hell didn't want them."

"Wow." Maxon yawns. "When I grow up, I want to be King Arthur, and you can be the Pendragon."

My heart warms. "I'd like that, too."

Maxon curls up under the covers. "I'm ready to sleep now, Daddy."

Sliding the book under my arm, I tuck Maxon into his big-boy bed. As I step away, Maxon whispers after me.

"I was just waiting for you and Mommy. I can't sleep if I don't sees you." I don't bother to fix his grammar error, *sees you*. He'll figure it out on his own too quickly.

"It's the same for us, Maxon."

And so, Myla and I share a smile as I turn out the light.

MYLA

*W*atching Lincoln read to Maxon is one of the cutest things in the history of ever. Normally, I can't stop smiling my face off.

Not this time, though.

Instead of focusing on the sweet scene before me, all I can think about are those fading angels. What would King Arthur do in my place? I mean, the guy created the freaking thrax. He organized everyone into demon patrols and knights. He came up with new shapes for table designs.

Arthur even singlehandedly locked up a ton of archdemons, including their leader Colossus. And he did all this with a virtual dagger between his shoulder blades from where Merlin ran off ... all so the wizard could hang out with some random water nymph.

Did I mention that Arthur didn't have any special powers like my igni? He didn't.

Much as I hate to admit it, the wrath coven might be right. Maybe I could learn a thing or two from King Arthur.

Lincoln finishes resetting Maxon's favorite book on the shelf. Together we tiptoe out into the hallway. The moment Maxon's bedroom door is closed behind us, Lincoln pulls me into a deep embrace. I must admit, my guy is a really good hugger. His voice sounds all low and sweet in my ear.

"What's wrong?"

"The fading angels," I reply. "King Arthur would have fixed this by now ... and without risking a demon-pocalypse."

Lincoln brushes a sweet kiss across my lips, then takes my hand. "No one knows *how* King Arthur did anything, you know. And this has been a huge day. We're both rather tired."

"Hey, I'm not sleepy." I force my eyes to open extra wide, which only makes me realize how I had them half-closed before. "Okay, I'm totally exhausted."

"Let's get some rest." Lincoln leads me to our bedroom, where he gently removes my fighting suit and tucks me into bed. Every movement is filled with gentle adoration.

I think back to my *seduction vow* from earlier today. Some alone-time my husband is beyond overdue. Sure, I'm tired, but I'm part lust demon. Seducing is part of my DNA.

Once Lincoln slips into bed, I launch my plan into action. Namely, I press my body against his and kiss his face off. I'm able to keep that up for about fifteen seconds before I roll over and fall asleep.

Some lust demon. Bleugh.

12

MYLA

*I*n my dreams, I hang out on a cloud in Heaven. Drusus sits beside me. He's an old guy with a shock of white hair, piercing blue eyes and a turned-up nose. He's also got those apple-style cheeks that make it seem like he's perma-smiling. Beyond that, he's a standard-looking angel with his white robes, wings and sandals.

Leaning back, I kick my legs out. Heavenly clouds automatically take whatever shape you want to be comfy. I'm picking a lounge chair. A lopsided pouf of white passes by. Drusus points to it.

"That one reminds me of a pear," says Drusus. This dream is taking place back when I first met Drusus, so he's almost completely solid. It's only if you check around the edges of his body that he looks a tad transparent.

I point out another cloud. "Oh, and that one looks like a pot-bellied pig."

"Ah, yes." Drusus laughs, and the sound is a cross between a snicker and a giggle.

"And why's that funny?"

"When I was alive, I had a pot-bellied pig. Followed me about like I was Mary with my little piggy lamb." I've heard about people's eyes twinkling. Drusus' actually do that.

"So what were you when you were alive? A farmer?"

A shadow falls across Drusus' face. "We're not talking about my mortal life. We agreed. Now it's your turn."

A row of tallish clouds gyrate before us. "These are easy. That's a boy band." Since this is a dream, the shapes are super detailed, too. Someone strums a guitar and everything.

"Truly," agrees Drusus. "The drummer is rocking out."

I lift my brows. "So you know what a boy band is?"

Drusus nods. "I've been watching one of my extended daughters play drums. She lives in the new world, a place called California."

"Really? That sounds so badass. Can you show her to me?"

Drusus pauses. We do have a rule that we're not supposed to talk about anything personal, including Drusus' extended family. But I need to understand this stuff if I'll ever help him or the other fading angels. So I press on.

"How old is she?" I ask.

"Eight years, three months."

"Then her soul can't be in any trouble yet," I state. "Her

guardian angel must just hang around all day long saying, *oh how adorable.*"

Drusus pretends to be fascinated by another cloud. "That one resembles a dragon."

"Don't change the subject. You know you want to share. What's her name?"

"Annabelle." Drusus sighs. "Fine, I'll show you." He waves his arm. Threads of blue light and power wind off his fingertips. Even though Drusus isn't strong enough to be something senior—like a guardian angel—he can still cast basic spells. The azure cords fly out to wrap about the dragon-cloud.

Then the magic kicks in.

The dragon-cloud morphs into a sphere, the center of which becomes clear, like we're looking through a window. Through that pane, I see a snug room with an orange couch and lots of photos on the walls. A girl with pigtails and a missing front tooth bangs away on a drum set. We can't hear anything; that's how it works when you're not a guardian angel.

I lean forward. "She's so freaking perfect, I can't stand it."

"That she is." Drusus' smile fades. "Others aren't so lucky."

"What do you mean?"

"My extended sons and daughters, as well as other people. They remain influenced by my, uh, life's work. It isn't going well for them."

Now, I'm dying to ask what kind of work Drusus did while alive, but I keep my yap shut. This is more sharing than Drusus has ever done before, and I've been stopping by his cloud for weeks.

"And it's my fault," continues Drusus. "What I did while alive, it's a poison that goes on through generations. Year after year, I watch people replay my same mistakes. It's…" He shakes his head.

"It's what?"

"I don't want to say. You're the latest Great Scala. You weren't the one who put me in Heaven, but I know how your kind thinks. You believe you're being generous by placing spirits like me here. But it's … painful."

I can't believe this. "Would you rather Hell?"

"Souls burn out there eventually, don't they?"

"It depends on who's running Hell. At the moment, it's Armageddon. He doesn't let souls die."

"But others do."

"Yes, that's right."

Before my eyes, Drusus becomes more transparent.

Suddenly, a magnetic pull yanks me through the cloud. I hurtle toward the ground. This dream ends and something else begins.

The next thing I know, I stand in a charcoal colored desert in Purgatory. The place is deserted. Dark clouds hang low in the sky. Kneeling, I brush my hands against the sand. The warm granules tickle my skin. Things are now absolutely lifelike.

I'm in a dreamscape, which how those who wield mega magic communicate with others in their sleep. And only one person uses dreamscapes to bug with me while I'm zonked out.

Verus is on her way. *Crud.*

Sure enough, a small point of white appears in the grey sky. The tiny figure grows larger as it draws in closer. Soon I see an angel soaring toward me. She's the full deal: white robes, matching wings, and open-toed sandals. But that's standard angel stuff. Verus also has long black hair and almond-shaped eyes.

Yup. It's her all right.

Without so much as disturbing a grain of sand, Verus lands before me. "If you'd accepted my summons, I wouldn't have to do this."

"And hello to you, too."

Recap: In my waking life, I've totally been avoiding Verus. She's all blah-blah-blah-*you're-gonna-die*-blah-blah-blah. My days are packed with reviewing and moving souls. In between, there are tons of worshippers to deal with. Don't get me wrong. Verus is on my list. She's just somewhere between *voluntary surgery* and *lunch with Armageddon.*

Verus lifts her chin. "I must speak to you about the fading angels. It is pointless for you to try and help them. All you'll accomplish is our doom."

Now, my father can lecture me. Mostly because he's rather subtle about the whole thing. But Verus always makes me feel like I'm a toddler who just drew on my face with a Sharpie. Long story short, she kicks up my sass factor.

"Doom." I smack my lips. "Got it."

"This is no joke," counters Verus. Her eyes even flash with blue light, just to emphasize her point. "Do you even know what a demonpocalypse is? It's all of history and time being erased. No more humans, angels, and after-realms. Only demons."

"And you're certain this will happen if I help the fading angels?"

"Absolutely."

I tap my chin. How you ask Verus questions is a bit of an art form. If she can give a true but misleading answer, she will.

"Let me put this another way," I state. "If I help the fading angels, then you're certain this demonpocalypse will happen and be irreversible?"

"I am the oracle angel. My words and predictions are sacred."

"Which isn't really a *yes* or *no*."

Here we go. When Verus is flustered, she starts repeating her resume for no reason. Let the record show that I'm already completely aware that she's an oracle and never wrong.

Key example: before Lincoln and I met, Verus encouraged a mutual friend, Walker, to stick his nose into our love lives. Specifically, Verus urged Walker to make Lincoln act like Sir Douchebag, saying that if my guy and I fell in love, then I'd have to fight Armageddon. Talk about your lying liars. Verus *wanted* me to fall in love with Lincoln *and* fight Armageddon. Walker only helped make it happen. You see, I wasn't exactly boy crazy at the time. If Lincoln came on all strong and lovey-dovey, then Verus' predictions showed me running the other way.

All in all, I take the *visions du Verus* with a grain of salt.

Verus sighs. "You don't believe me."

There's no point lying to an oracle. "Not really."

"Don't take my word for it," continues Verus. "Consider all the Great Scalas before you, going back to the dawn of time. Each and every one has decided not to help the fading angels. Even Lucifer didn't try to change this, and he thought angels were the highest form of life."

I lace my fingers behind my neck and think this through. Sadly, Verus makes sense. Why should I be the only one who does something about fading angels? A mental image appears. Drusus vanishing. And there are millions more like him. I drop my hands.

"Let me get this straight," I say. "You're asking me to look away while millions of afterlives are erased."

Verus' eyes glow blue once more. "Yes."

"Come on. You know that's not me. You must have seen that when you totally manipulated me into this job."

"I did." Verus straightens the folks of her white robes. "I thought things would break differently based on your … experience."

"In other words, you thought I'd suck at being the Great Scala."

"You wish to do things, but that doesn't mean you have

the ability. To repair the fate of the fading angels, the Great Scala must work with others. Like ..." She snaps her fingers, trying to think of a description.

Here we go.

"Like King Arthur and his knights of the round table?"

"Precisely." Verus lowers her voice to a tone I like to call, *gentle but deadly.* "Let's be honest. Is that you?"

Now it's my turn to raise my chin. "It isn't me to give up."

A full minute of silence follows before Verus speaks again. "You care about this fading angel, Drusus."

"I do."

"Tell me why."

"Drusus wants to help the living. Back when I first visited him, he'd follow the guardian angels when they watched over their humans. That's the *big show* in Heaven, of course."

Verus nods. "Only the purest souls can become guardian angels."

"After each trip, Drusus returned sadder and a little more faded. Simply put, Drusus didn't know how to help humans. That desire to make a difference without knowing how, I guess it pushes buttons with me. It's what's draining Drusus, yet I don't know how to fix it."

"And you feel responsible."

At this point, one thing is clear. Getting interrogated by Verus on this stuff ... it's like that dream where you show up to class without any clothes on. At the same time, Verus understands how Heaven works. Maybe she'll have an idea or two. I keep going.

"Are you kidding?" I ask. "I'm absolutely responsible. When the ghouls ran Purgatory, they were harsh on souls. If you weren't perfect, you went to Hell. After we got rid of the ghouls, I changed things. If you were *mostly good,* you went to Heaven. I thought I was sparing these souls an eternity of torture."

"Weren't you?"

I hug my elbows. "Drusus weeps." My eyes prickle with held-in tears, remembering all the times I sat beside him on a cloud, unable to give him any comfort as he cried. "I send these souls—millions of them—to what I think is an afterlife of peace. But many spend eternity watching their extended children make the same mistakes they did without being able to do anything. That's it's own kind of torture." I tap my chest. "And I'm causing it."

"Mortals must live with the consequences of their own lives," declares Verus.

"No offense, but that's easier to say when you're not the one choosing their eternity." Pressing my palms against my eyes, I heave in a shaky breath. "I couldn't live with myself if I didn't keep trying to help them."

Verus nods slowly. "I understand. You're very strong, Myla. More than you know. That is why *she* awakens."

A jolt of awareness moves inside me. "She? What she? Who do you mean?"

Yet even as I say the words, I know who Verus is talking

about. It's that serene voice that sounds in my head, telling me to spend more girl-time with Allimari.

"That—" says Verus "—is for you alone to discover."

Without another word, Verus takes off. And I return to an uneasy night of sleep.

13

LINCOLN

"*D*aaaaaaddy!" yells Maxon. "Paaaaaaancakes!"

My wake-up call has arrived early this morning. And by *wake up call*, I mean my son Maxon now jumps on the bed while demanding pancakes. Not that I'm complaining. Normally, our son wants a breakfast of demon bars from Mommy ... and he doesn't give up easily. Thus ensues a lot of explaining about the benefits of vegetables.

It's about as much fun as it sounds.

Then I happened upon a new idea: pancakes. Considering how this dish includes high-grade maple syrup, the meal is only marginally better than demon bars. That said, it allows a somewhat more equal morning routine. That's especially handy today, when Myla remains completely zonked. She isn't even waking up from Maxon's jump-and-demand performance.

Best to let the sleeping Mommy sleep.

I pull on some pajama bottoms, scoop Maxon into my arms, and head off for the kitchen.

Now, I was never much of a cook growing up. In fact, I snuck into the royal kitchens all of twice in my entire life. And I've certainly been invited to attend various committees related to royal meal preparation. There's the Hen Happiness League, Silver Platter Server's Contingent, and —my personal favorite—the Ancient Order of Melon Rind Repurposers.

Long story short, it would have required navigating about a dozen committees and a hundred thrax traditions to empower me to boil an egg. As a result, I'm thrilled with my self-serve options in Purgatory. Myla and I split our time evenly between realms—six months in Purgatory and six months in Antrum—and I must admit that my time here is rapidly becoming my favorite.

Who would have thought that?

All of which brings me to the current moment, where I make what is now the only meal I can create solo, *pancakes.* While I putter around the all-steel kitchen, Maxon sits at the table on his booster seat, watching my every move with rapt attention. A single question overloads his mind.

"Is it done yet? Is it done yet? Is it done yet?"

As I finish mixing up the batter, an idea hits me. "Not yet. How about you sing your new song?"

Maxon frowns, a motion which involves scrunching up his face in the extreme. It's what he does when thinking something through. "Which one?"

In my opinion, there's only one tune Maxon should

sing for all eternity, namely *The Itsy Bitsy Human*. The words are supposed to go like this:

> *The itsy bitsy human met demons in his town*
> *Out came the thrax and tracked that evil down*
> *None saw the thrax as they make the demons fall*
> *So the itsy bitsy human knows nothing here at all*

Even better, there are hand motions that go along with everything. For the *itsy bitsy* part, you put your thumb and forefinger almost together. That's not the bit kids love, though. More popular is brandishing a pretend sword for *out came the thrax*. That's followed up by vigorous stabbing motions with *make the demons fall*. It's beyond charming.

"How about *The Itsy Bitsy Human*?" I suggest.

"Yeah, yeah, yeah!" Maxon takes in a deep breath, which is how he always prepares to sing. Although Maxon sometimes speaks like an older child, his singing voice is all toddler. So it's no surprise that my son's version of this tune deviates from the standard.

> *"Dee izzy bizzy human met dedons in da town*
> *Out comma thrax and track-a evil down*
> *None saw-a thrax when they make-a dedon fall*
> *So dee izzy bizzy human know nothin' here at all."*

He's perfected the song, in my opinion.

"Brilliant," I say as I pile my son's plate with the first round of pancakes.

Pro tip: I make them all bite sized. Saves on cutting and overall mess.

As Maxon dives in, Myla rushes into kitchen. She's wearing a blue bathrobe and a shocked look.

"You let me sleep in," she gasps.

I kiss her cheek. "You seemed to need the rest."

"Right. Rest." Myla blinks hard. My girl is still waking up. "Has my father gotten here yet?"

"Not that I've seen."

"Okay, good." She pauses. "Ugh, I forgot to tell you. I'm visiting the fading angels today. Or rather one fading angel. Drusus."

"Mind if I join you? Octavia is having a blast running Antrum."

"I'd love it, but who will watch Maxon?"

"I think that will sort itself out. I have a sense that Octavia's taking an interest in our morning."

Myla frowns. "How do you know that?"

"Years of scar tissue." I hand Myla a mug of coffee from the counter. As her husband, I've found it's best to keep java handy in the morning.

Myla's face lights up. "Coffee." She gulps down half the mug and sighs. "Thank you so much."

"You're most welcome."

Myla finishes the rest of her drink and pours a refresher before turning to Maxon. "Good morning, baby. What do you want to do today? Go to the zoo?"

Maxon stuffs his mouth with another massive bite of pancake. "No zoo. Horses."

Myla sits down beside him. "What do you mean, honey?"

I raise my pointer finger, ready to share my theory.

Ding!

The front doorbell rings, interrupting me.

Myla starts to rise from the table. "I'll answer it."

"No," I counter. "Allow me."

I march over to the front door and pull it open. Sure enough, my theory is correct. Two figures stand on the threshold. First, there's Xavier. Myla's father is here to help us check on Drusus.

Second, there's my mother.

Now I don't know how she got in touch with Maxon and informed my child that she'd be taking him to visit horses today, but that's part of the charm of having Octavia as your mother. She keeps you on your toes.

"Good morning, Xavier." I shoot Octavia a sideways glance. "Mother."

Xavier tilts his head. "You don't seem surprised that Octavia is along this morning."

Mother grins. "He's my son. That makes him almost as clever as I am. And to answer your next question, Connor is running Antrum today."

Since the Earl of Acca died, my father has become an excellent ruler ... when you can get him out of retirement. I'd wonder how Mother bribed him to help out, but again, it's probably best not to know.

"That's great news." I step back and allow them to enter. "Everyone's in the kitchen."

Octavia speeds past me. "Did Maxon tell you how I'm taking him to see horses today?"

"Something like that," I reply.

Xavier works to suppress a smile, but honestly? He doesn't work too hard at it. "And did Myla mention the visit to Drusus?"

"She did." I open the front hall closet. Purgatory has quickly-changing weather. Both Mother and Xavier are wrapped-up in coats. I take their garments and hang them up.

Xavier rubs his palms together. "I have a magic spell for today's visit which will blow your minds."

"Excellent." This time, I'm the one trying not to smile—and doing a terrible job at it. Because when Xavier rubs his palms together? He reminds me very much of Myla.

The General of the Angels is working a wacky scheme this morning, and I can't wait to discover what it is.

14

MYLA

*W*hile Lincoln goes off to answer the door, I watch my son eat pancakes. Although *eat* isn't really the right word.

Bathe might be better.

One second, Maxon is neatly setting mini-pancakes into his mouth. A moment later, Lincoln answers the door and—*Boom!*—Maxon has pancake in his hair, down his pajamas, and all over the table. Did he some get in his ear, too? I lean in for a better look.

Why, yes. Yes, he did.

Octavia strides into the kitchen. She's wearing non-royal clothes—namely dark jeans and a button-down—but still looks every inch the queen. Maxon stands up on his booster chair. "Gamma! Gamma!" He reaches for her with sticky hands. I'm about to warn Octavia to wait until I de-pancake my boy, but she simply scoops him up. Maxon plants a big maple-syrup kiss on her cheek while wiping off his hands on her shirt.

"Good morning, my sweet Maxon," she croons.

"Gamma! Gamma!" Maxon wraps his little arms around her neck.

Octavia looks to me. "Hello, Myla."

"Hey there." I lean back in my chair and think this through. Octavia never does anything without about five ulterior motives. "We weren't expecting you today."

"Maxon was," counters Octavia. "I promised to take him to the stables at the Ryder mansion."

"Horses! Horses!" Maxon hugs Octavia with extra energy.

I drum my fingers on the tabletop. "We'd planned on Dad watching Maxon today."

"Your father didn't want to tell you," says Octavia. "But there's been trouble at the Ghoul Reconciliation Convention."

My eyes widen. This is Mom's big event to get quasis and ghouls to set aside their differences. "What happened?"

"A few ghouls thought *reconciliation* meant they were being invited to take over Purgatory once more." Octavia rolls her eyes. "Camilla is handling it."

I nod. "Mom can deal with anything. That said, Dad is a pro at flashing his archangel wings and glaring at the opposition. It's really helpful politically."

"Precisely. Which is why he's joining her today."

Now that I know at least one of Octavia's ulterior

motives, it's time to move onto other topics. "Sorry about your clothes."

"Not a problem. I have plenty of extra things stored in Maxon's room."

Hearing his name, Maxon decides it's been too long since he's shouted the same word repeatedly. "Horses! Horses! Horses!"

"Let's get you cleaned up first, my perfect grandson."

I'd roll my eyes at the *perfect grandson* line—it's especially odd considering my kid is wearing about four pancakes—but *meh*. Octavia can go over the top, but her heart is always in the right place.

As Octavia carries Maxon off to his bath, Xavier and Lincoln step into the kitchen. I hop up to give Dad a kiss on the cheek. "Sorry to hear about the Reconciliation Convention. Guess the trip to Heaven is off."

Sure, Lincoln and I can hit the Pearly Gates ourselves, but it's a lot of hassle. The angels don't like *the living* roaming around their realm, no matter who their parents are. And everyone is especially protective of the fading angels. Long story short, it's easier to have Dad along.

"As a matter of fact, plans have changed," says Dad. "Drusus has decided to follow some guardian angels to Earth. They're working on one of his extended sons." In angel speak, *extended* means there are a bunch of great-great-great-grands that go before the word *son*. Angels live forever, so they don't get caught up in the number of generations. You're an extended *fill in the blank* and that's all.

"How many guardian angels?" asks Lincoln.

"A triad," answers Dad.

I hiss in a breath. "A triad?" That's bad news. Normally, humans only get one guardian angel. They send teams when a truly awful soul is about to do something super-wrong. As in, *welcome to Hell* bad.

"I'm afraid so," says Dad.

"Is it this a *crux* for the human?" Cruxes are the big decisions in a human's life that determine their afterlife.

"It is," confirms Dad. "Do you still wish to see Drusus today?"

"Absolutely." I look to my guy. "What do you think? Still want to join me?"

"Same here," states Lincoln.

Dad smiles. "In that case, I've a charm that allows you to see fading angels."

I shoot Dad a thumbs-up. "I'm in."

"Same here," adds Lincoln again.

Dad closes his eyes and murmurs a silent incantation. A golden haze forms behind my father's back before golden wings appear. Reaching behind, he plucks out a pair of feathers.

I look to Lincoln and frown. The question is there if unspoken: *Do you know what Dad's up to?*

Lincoln shakes his head. *No idea.*

Dad then places the feathers between his palms and whispers another spell. This time, I strain to hear the words. Archangel incantations are their own kind of magic. I'd love more details, but asking now might throw Dad off his shtick and ruin the spell.

The two feathers glow between my father's palms. When the brightness dies down, the spell is complete. The feathers transform into a pair of golden butterflies.

That's pretty nifty, right there.

"Hold out your right palms," says Dad. Lincoln and I do as requested.

The moment my hand is outstretched, the first butterfly flits over to land on my palm. The magical creature then melts against my skin. One moment, a magical insect is on my hand. The next, I'm sporting a new golden butterfly tattoo on the same spot. Beside me, the same thing happens to Lincoln.

Dad gestures towards us both in a motion that says *ta-daaa!* "Now, you can see Drusus."

I inspect my new ink. "I've never had a tattoo before. Is this permanent?"

Dad shrugs. "Do you want it to be?"

"I'll get back to you on that." There's no way I'm keeping or chucking anything until I find out what this butterfly thingy really does. "Thanks, Dad."

"Happy to help." My father steps toward the exit and pauses. "One last thing. You'll find Drusus at the offices of Thornberry And Cross, Public Relations, Chicago."

Lincoln nods. "I know the area. There's a Pulpitum transfer station not too far away."

"Best of luck." Dad slips on his conference sash. It's a

yellow number that goes from his shoulder to his hip and reads, *Ghoul Reconciliation Convention*.

Aaaaaaaand Dad puts it on upside down.

Not that I'll tell him.

Clearly, my father is anxious to be at Mom's side. Besides, if I start chatting about my parents' convention, I won't be able to resist asking why they're being so tight-lipped about it. No television coverage. No papers. No whispers when I'm around.

It's downright odd.

Sadly, there isn't time to focus on my parents and their strange ghoul-related behavior. Once Dad's gone, Lincoln and I prep for our own mission. With any luck, we may discover something that can actually help the fading angels.

Oh, yeah. And *not* end the world.

15

LINCOLN

*a*n hour later, Myla and I stand outside a tall glass building in downtown Chicago. Crisp fall breezes whip bits of paper around our ankles. Large letters above the entrance read, *Thornberry And Cross, Public Relations.* Humans come and go through the revolving front door, some toting pride or greed demons on their shoulders.

Not that these mortals are aware of their Hell-born parasites, mind you.

Both Myla and I wear human-style suits today. All the better to blend in. Reaching into my pocket, I pull out two thin wrist cuffs. The glint of purple shines deep within the metal. *Magic.*

I turn to Myla. "These will make us invisible. We still need to keep our voices down, though."

"Sure." She half-slips the cuff on her wrist and then stops. "And we just put them on in front of everybody?"

I shoot her a sly look. "When the *everybody* in question are humans, sure."

Myla chuckles. "I take it back. Humans are pretty oblivious when it comes to magic."

We both set the magical cuffs on our wrists. For a moment, our bodies seem to shimmer with a thin layer of glittering purple mist. After that, we vanish to human sight. I can still see Myla, though. Only now, she appears as semi- transparent.

"Drusus is interested in a mortal named Charles Bishop," says Myla. "This is a huge building. Do you think we can find him?"

"I'm thrax," I reply. "We've a charm for that."

Reaching into my jacket pocket, I pull a small pad of paper. At first, the top sheet is blank. Then purple writing appears across the surface. *Magic.* This notepad has been enchanted to show Charles' location. I read the words aloud. "Sixth floor, main conference room."

Myla's tail arcs over her shoulder. The arrowhead end flattens toward me in a clear call for a *high five.* Which I grant, obviously. Never leave Myla's tail hanging; it's what I live by.

Together, Myla and I slip inside the building and take the elevator to the sixth floor. The conference room in question takes more hunting to discover. Turns out, there are a ton of meeting rooms on this floor. Any one of them could arguably be the *main* one. Eventually, we find a glass-walled space that's deserted save for one young man with a turned-up nose and loose black hair. He sits at the far end of a long table, talking into the round speaker phone before him.

Could that be Charles Bishop?

Myla grasps my upper arm. "That's him. He looks like a young version of Drusus."

I've never met Drusus, but Charles looks like he fell out of a men's fashion magazine. The man sports an athletic build that's well accented by his tailored blue suit. Charles also has intelligent blue eyes, rosy cheeks, perfectly tousled hair, and a trimmed goatee. If I needed to add a photo of *PR Human* to the thrax archives, a picture of this fellow would be perfect.

While still invisible, Myla and I tiptoe into the conference room. If Charles were paying attention, he'd notice how the glass door swings open and shut, seemingly on its own. Yet Charles notices nothing. The human is simply too enthralled by his phone call.

A tinny female voice echoes in from the speaker. "Any word on our project?"

Charles stands over the phone, his arms braced on the table. "We've gotten the confirmation," he replies.

On my palm, the tattoo of the butterfly pulses. Images fly through my mind. These aren't my memories. Instead, I know they're something related to the call.

What did Xavier load into this butterfly spell, anyway? I'd be surprised, but this is Myla's father, after all. The man has forgotten more esoteric magic than I'll see in my lifetime.

I glance over to Myla. She's staring at her palm as well.

"You, too?" I whisper.

Myla nods. "It's something to do with the call."

Now that I know I'm not alone in this vision, I close my eyes and allow the pictures to wash through my mind. I see a researcher in her lab. The name Penny Brice hangs from a tag on her white coat.

Penny Brice. I've heard about her. The angels are excited since she's found a new drug treatment for multiple kinds of brain injury. Brice wants to make the formula public and have the drug produced as a generic. Less money gets made but more lives are saved.

Back with Charles, a voice echoes in from the speaker. "Penny Brice is a thief and a liar," says the woman on the phone. "You were supposed to find a paper trail to prove that she stole drug research from Xax Pharmaceutical. We must have the patent on any of her drugs. No one is giving our market away."

"I understand the project, ma'am," says Charles.

The nasal voice echoes in from the phone again. "So when will we see some headlines on how Brice stole our research? That's what we pay you for."

Beads of sweat form on Charles' forehead. "It's taking a little longer than we thought."

My stomach twists. As king, I've done my share of interrogations. You get a sense for when someone is doing something they know is wrong. Like Charles. In this case, I've no doubt that Charles is being paid to set up Penny Brice and steal her research. No doubt, Xax Pharmaceutical would like the original patent for this drug treatment.

They could then enjoy years of higher prices before any generics are allowed.

But at the cost of how many lives? A weight of sorrow settles onto my shoulders. This is wrong. Charles knows it.

All of a sudden, three beams of light appear across the conference room. I glance to Charles. The human remains oblivious. Which means this is more magic.

Once the enchanted beams fade, a trio of guardian angels stand behind Charles. If the three see me and Myla, then they make no sign of it. Instead, all their focus is centered on their human.

"Don't do this," says one angel.

"You can't imagine the pain it will cause," adds another. Their voices are like sweet music. It reminds me of how Myla describes the sound of her light igni, the power that pulls souls to Heaven.

The third angel sets his hand above the cell phone that's propped on the table. A beam of blue magic cascades from his palm, settling onto the small device. The image on the device changes. Where there was once the picture of an email message, there now appears photos of Charles and his family. The third angel is trying to make a point and encourage a connection.

You love your family, yet you're hurting the loved ones of others.

In the world of guardian angels, this is called creating a serendipity. It's their main way to influence humans.

A new shaft of light crosses the conference room. This one is more sickly and thin than the others. When the brightness fades, another angel is here. Unfortunately, his body is barely visible, more like a conglomeration of dust motes than anything else. Even so, I can see this figure is indeed a more grizzled version of Charles.

It's Drusus.

Myla rushes to his side. "Drusus, it's me. Myla."

"You can see me?" asks Drusus. "I thought I'd faded from everyone's view."

"Yes, I can see you." She gestures toward me. "So can my husband, Lincoln."

Drusus grabs Myla's arm like she's a lifeline. "You must help me," says Drusus. "Talk to Charles. You can become visible. Make him understand. He doesn't want to end up like me."

Myla pales. "We discussed this. It's not about Charles following a list of rules just to avoid punishment."

"It isn't fair." Drusus frowns. "Everyone does things like this. How can it be wrong?"

It's a good thing there are no breezes in here because if one hit me now? I'd tumble over in a heartbeat. How can it be wrong to deny people life-saving drugs? What did Drusus do in his mortal life—kick kittens for fun and profit? No wonder he's not fitting in at Heaven.

Back at the conference room table, Charles stares at his cell phone for a long moment. "Something's come up," he says. "I'll call you back in five."

The line goes dead. Charles slumps into his chair.

All of us stare at the mortal. Tension spikes in the room.

This is it. The crux. Will Charles decide to do the right thing? He certainly seems to be considering it.

The door swings open. A young man with white-blond hair and a predatory smile saunters into the room. "How did it go with Xax?"

Charles doesn't look the newcomer in the eyes. "Not clear yet, Mister Radovan."

"This is a big client for us. Time was, you were the kind of guy who made things happen." Radovan stalks closer to Charles. "You know who's an up and comer? Blake. Real team player. Wants a partnership, you know." He points to the phone. "Do this."

Radovan leaves. Charles pauses, then picks up the phone.

Oh, no.

There's a lot of pleading from the angels and Drusus, but this time, nothing breaks through to Charles. In fact, the human seems to sense another force in the room, yet chooses to ignore it. Charles rises and turns his back toward the angels.

Sure enough, once Charles turns, I see part of his problem. A greed demon is attached to his spine. It's a long lizard-like creature with a pointed head and six eyes. Ringing sounds from the speakerphone before the line picks up.

"Xax Pharma," says the woman. It's the same voice from before.

"The story will run tomorrow," says Charles. "It's air tight."

"That's what I pay you for. Which pubs will take it?"

As the conversation continues, the greed demon hisses at the guardian angels. The trio leave in columns of white light. Drusus also vanishes in his own pale beam.

Myla hugs her elbows. I step to her side and wrap my arm about her shoulders. Sometimes, there's nothing you can say that can top an embrace.

"Drusus didn't understand," says Myla, her voice rough. "What Charles is doing is *wrong*. How do I change that? How can you teach someone to have a good heart?"

I rub her back in long strokes. "Drusus faced his own cruxes when he was alive. It's the definition of a crux that the human can either turn toward good or bad. Who knows? Maybe if Drusus' guardian angel had tried another serendipity, it could have worked out differently. Maybe he would have grown."

"But that wasn't what happened to Drusus."

"No," I say solemnly. "It wasn't."

Myla steps out of my arms. "There may be something else I can do here." Her eyes light up red as she glares at the greed demon. "Think I can take that bad boy down?"

I scan the demon and frown. "A demon that size? It's a part of him." There's no need to explain the rest to Myla. She already knows that if we kill that demon now, then Charles is dead as well.

Speaking of Charles, he continues to face away from us while staying deep in his conversation. On his call, they've identified twelve different places to run with the story. It's just a question of which one will do the most damage.

My heart sinks. One word keeps rattling around my brain. *Damage.* Charles and Xax are scheming to hurt an innocent researcher. I look to Myla. She's trying to help others as well. Will her fate be the same as that of Penny Brice?

While Charles keeps talking, Myla shakes her head. "There are so many angels like Drusus. To fix this, it's like the wrath coven said: I need my own knights."

"You always have Walker and me." Myla shoots me a sly look. "Not that you can't do this on your own."

Myla's eyes widen. "I've got it. We'll make it a contest. People love contests. And the winners can be part of my knights of the round table."

I grin. "See? You're half way there already."

Across the room, Charles lets out a booming laugh. He's dropped all pretense of discomfort. "You know what?" Charles asks. "I almost feel sorry for Doctor Brice. Almost."

My stomach sinks. Right now, all Charles sees is his own greed. But in the afterlife? He'll be confronted non-stop with visions of every person his actions destroyed. Humans think that Hell is being roasted over a pit of fire. That's rare. More often, it's simply being confronted with the evil you created.

Over and over.

For all eternity.

And this guy? He has no idea of the terrible Hell he's making for himself.

16

MYLA

*S*o *that sucked.*

I had hopes. Big hopes. First with Lucifer's lab. Second with another chat with Drusus.

Talk about your letdowns.

Lucifer's lab exploded, almost killing me and Lincoln. Drusus is clearly not ready to be a guardian angel—or any kind of angel, really—but I've no ideas how to help him.

There's one bright spot, though. I may have figured out a way to fill my own round table. *The contest.* That's got to count for something.

It takes a few hours to get back to Purgatory. Soon Lincoln and I are marching back through our front door. Shockingly enough, the house is quiet, even though it's early afternoon.

Lincoln and I share a long gaze. *It can't be. Can it?* Yes, it's early afternoon and is our son actually … napping?

Sure enough, Octavia tiptoes to the front door while

making a clear *shh* motion with her pointer finger over her lips. In low voice, she addresses us. "What's this I hear about a contest?"

"How did you hear about that?" asks Lincoln. For the record, my guy is really good at derailing Octavia by answering questions with more questions. It's a skill I need to learn.

"Don't avoid answering me, son."

Lincoln fixes her with a silent stare. My guy is also a pro at working his *deadpan look.*

Octavia rolls her eyes. "Fine, I have contacts everywhere. There was a demon in the room when you were discussing the contest. It seems the creature overheard. Hell is not pleased. They like how angels fade."

"Ah," says Lincoln. And that's really all he has to say. We all know Octavia has an amazing spy network. I didn't realize it included Hell, but there you go.

"We are planning a contest," I explain. "Winners will help me solve the whole fading angels thing." Just saying the words out loud takes a weight off my heart.

"Excellent notion." Octavia pulls a card from her pocket and hands it over. "I took the liberty of writing down a list of items in the thrax archives that may be helpful. With Cryptan gone—"

"There's a new archivist," I finish.

"Quite right," says Octavia. If this were someone else, they might be ticked off that I finished their sentence. However, Octavia enjoys it when you're one step ahead of her. Or in this case, at least on par.

I take the card and turn it over. Octavia's listed out a bunch of ancient books and the sections I might find useful. I exhale. "Remy is the new archivist. Dad said she turned up other stuff, too. I'm overdue for a visit." I press the card against my heart. "Thank you."

It's more than just the list of books. Octavia has clearly been scheming overtime to help out. It's appreciated.

"You'll want to leave for the archives now, I assume?" asks Octavia. "I'd planned to take Maxon to the Ryder gardens after his nap."

Lincoln steps to her side. "The three of us can hit the gardens." He looks to me. "What do you think?"

Translation: do you want to do this solo?

"I know my way to the vaults," I reply. Which is my way of saying, *yes, solo would be great.*

Octavia narrows her eyes as her gaze slowly flicks between Lincoln and me. "You're going alone?" she asks slowly.

I lift my chin. "I'm building my own knights of the round table."

"Brilliant," says Octavia. "As I always say, the best way to learn to ride is from the saddle."

Pride warms my chest. This is Octavia's way of sharing her faith in me. The vote of confidence helps.

After leaving Octavia and Lincoln, I go check on Maxon—who's thankfully still asleep—and then change from a human skirt-suit into my dragonscale fighting outfit.

And with that, I'm off to Antrum.

17

MYLA

𝒩o doubt about it; getting around Antrum is a total pain in the butt. There are no cars or unauthorized magic. You have to hoof it everywhere. Not that I mind a little walking, but sheesh.

OK, honestly? I *totally* mind a little walking.

I'm part demon. That means I stay buff without having to hit the gym or eat a carrot. If you were me, would you spend your life exercising?

Thought so.

Once in Antrum, I spend tons of quality time marching through tunnels until I reach a round, safe-style door that's set into a stone wall.

Here it is. *The entrance to the ancient archives.*

The sight tightens my throat with sorrow. Coming here reminds me of visiting Cryptan, the old archivist. Sadly, Cryptan was murdered by Aldred, the evil Earl of Acca.

Now Cryptan's niece runs the vault. A weight of guilt settles in my heart. Cryptan was a good man and a sweet friend. I should have visited his niece earlier.

I huff out a breath. *Oh well. Lincoln did kill Aldred and avenge Cryptan's murder, so there's that.*

Nearby, a guard in full metal armor clears his throat. I look over. "What is it?"

"Did you hear my question?" he asks. The guy has his silver helm on with the visor down, so his voice is a little muffled.

Now, if I were Lincoln, I'd know exactly who this guard was, what house he came from, and perhaps what he even ate for breakfast. But I'm me, so all I know about this particular person is that he's Guard Dude.

"No, I didn't hear you," I reply.

"With all due respect, your Majesty," says Guard Dude. "I asked if you wanted to be announced to enter the vault."

"Yes, that would be great."

Guard Dude spins the vault door. A click sounds before the round portal swings open. "Announcing her Highness Queen Myla of Antrum."

A reedy female voice sounds through the opening. "I welcome a visit from her Majesty."

That's my cue.

Hiking up my skirts, I step through portal and into the room beyond. It looks nothing like I remembered it.

It's still a dark stone chamber. But back when Cryptan ran the place, the place was filled with enchanted books.

Each volume sat neatly atop a tall podium. Now that's all gone.

Along the left side of the room, animal cages are stacked. I'm talking dogs, cats, owls ... and is that a monkey?

Yup, that's a monkey.

In the center of the room, there stands a pile of random medieval junk. Horseshoes. Harnesses. Longswords. Most are broken.

And on the right? A towering labyrinth of boxes. All are labeled with the identical—and not too useful—title of *books*.

All in all, the archives look like a barn, metalsmith, and box company all threw up on each other. It's a little odd, but Remy's in charge now. I'm sure she has her reasons.

Speaking of Remy, the girl in question stands nearby. She wears a simple green dress which highlights her small and frail frame. Even so, she overflows with hummingbird-style energy. Remy also has round eyes and a pointed chin, which further supports her hummingbird look.

For a long moment, we just stare at each other. Thrax are all about protocol. As the queen, I should speak first. But what do you say to someone in this situation? Will she want to know how Cryptan liked reading Julius Caesar in Latin ... or how I almost got him a dog? I decide to go for the traditional statement. If Remy wants to know more, she'll ask.

"I'm sorry about your uncle," I say. "Cryptan was a good man."

"Thank you. I barely knew him."

"He and I were friends. Would you like to know more about him?"

"Cryptan kept many notes here. I'm well versed in his habits."

"Then you know about his dog obsession." Cryptan wrote reams on what kind of puppy he wanted.

"No, did he want a dog?"

I frown. It's strange for Remy not to know about Cryptan's thing with pooches. Then again, the guy spent most of his life inside this chamber. Not like he and Remy could have hung out much.

"He did want a dog," I explain. "But it looks like you're a step ahead of him." I gesture toward the carriers. "Tell me about these animals."

"I plan to keep a pet for company. These are my potentials."

I step past the cages. The monkey screeches as I walk by. "Some of these are wild animals. They're not meant to be pets. And honestly? I'm not a fan of cages for anyone."

"Oh, whichever pet I chose will get to roam around the chamber."

I frown. "Somehow, I don't think the monkey will like that, either." I inspect more cages. "Or the hawk." That last animal makes me pause. "Is this bird from Kamal?"

Remy speed-walks to my side. Leaning over, she inspects the cage. "Why would that make a difference?"

I think back to Lucifer's lab. Something swooped in and grabbed those gemstones. "Kamal hawks are exceptionally well trained. Some even have magically-enhanced intellects. They can be useful in many tasks."

"Oh, of course." Remy blushes. "I suppose I got a little flustered with you visiting and all. Yes, that bird is from Kamal."

In other words, that bird could have grabbed stuff from Lucifer's lab. Now, I'm on a roll. I step over to the pile of metal stuff. "What's the purpose of this?"

"I've no idea. I found it all in the back recesses of the archives. I'm trying to sort through everything. We need to focus on books here. I can't keep stuff that don't belong."

I scan the stack more carefully. Sure enough, there are broken daggers and shields in the mix. Which leads to my next question. "Have you found any magical staffs?" *Like the Staff of Avalon.*

"Not yet," says Remy cheerily. "But that's a huge pile. There may be something in there. Would you like an alert if I find anything?"

"Yes, please." I move onto the stack of boxes. The top one is opened, so I step up and inspect the contents.

Not liking what I see here.

"I thought you said this place should only focus on books," I state. "Isn't that right?"

"It is, your Majesty."

"Then why is this box filled with royal correspondence?" To emphasize my point, I pull out the top sheet and read the title. "Incaenda boat blessing schedule. This is recent stuff."

"Oh, I don't know how I got those, either. They were labelled as *books*, so someone sent them here. I was about to send them over to the royal correspondence archivists when you arrived."

"Right." I know Remy is Cryptan's niece and all, but I'm getting a majorly bad vibe here.

"Don't worry, your Majesty. I know my role. I'm the knowledge keeper. Thrax rely on me to protect and categorize items that are magical or top secret."

I know my role.

Those four words echo through my mind. Because in looking around this chamber? Remy is all over the place. What's she really trying to do?

Remy twists her hands together at her waistline. "I've made a total mess of this. The Queen Emeritus told me what you were seeking. I found some original plans from King Arthur himself."

That gets my attention in a big way. "What kind of plans?"

"How he chose his knights of the round table. He actually gave them detailed tests in math, science, and logic. The ones who scored best were invited to be knights."

"I thought they had to kill things."

"Yes, there were jousts and other tournaments of strength, but I didn't think those would be as useful to you." Remy steps over to another open box and pulls out a dusty book. "Here's what I was thinking. There are some great tests in this volume. We could invite everyone to the

Arena to take the test, grade the results, and that's your contest."

Remy offers me the book; I pull it from her hands. The pages list all sorts of math equations and word games. "You're sure this is what King Arthur used?"

"His stuff was actually a little more basic. I suggest a tougher challenge."

My schooling amounted to tips and tricks on how to serve my ghoul overlords. Long story short, I have no idea if these questions are any good. "I'm not sure."

"Please let me prove myself," says Remy. "You won't have to do a thing. I'll set up the contest, get the enchanted notebooks to grab results, and even hold the test."

Now, most of my *assistant experience* is based around avoiding people who want to ask me a million questions. Not gonna lie. This whole *you won't have to do a thing* offer is pretty sweet. "How long will it take?"

"Only a few weeks. If it doesn't work out, you still have plenty of time to try something else." Her bird-like body almost vibrates with held-in excitement. "Give me a chance. That's all I ask."

I flip through more pages in the book. On the inside cover is written an unusual name. I read it aloud. "The Great Lady Remy Elayna Danae." I tilt my head. "You're from one of the lesser houses, aren't you?"

"Yes, of course." Remy blushes again. "I've had this book for ages. When I wrote that, I was just a kid and doodling. You know how we girls are. Imagining being a Great Lady is part of growing up, right?"

"Perhaps," I say. "My experience with Great Ladies hasn't been too awesome." In fact, one tried to kill me multiple times, not that I'll share such news with Remy.

For a full minute, I scan through more pages and consider my options. There really isn't much to lose if I give Remy a chance. Sure, she made a bad impression, but don't I do that all the time? And I'm trying to learn how to get my own knights of the round table. Having people who can do stuff without bugging me … that's the kind of knight I'd like.

It's one that's definitely worth testing out.

"All right, Remy." I hand her back the book. "Let's give your plan a try."

"Thank you so much, your Majesty! You won't be disappointed."

I picture a sky filled with fading angels. *How many are vanishing right now?* When I next speak, I take care to place extra emphasis on each word. "I certainly hope not."

As I walk away, that smooth voice sounds in my head again.

Do not leave. Keep talking to Remy.

I stifle the urge to punch myself in the face. *Talk to Remy?* I just chatted her up for at least fifteen minutes. The girl has a lot on her mind, including a feral monkey to deal with. I pinch the bridge of my nose. Maybe this is some kind of *girl-cling spell,* because it keeps wanting me to hang out with chicks.

Sure, I'm magically immune, but even that has its limits. I'll have to ask Lucas, the Earl of Striga, to run a few tests on me once he returns from his latest round of travels.

Oh, well. It's not like the voice is telling me to *kill, kill, kill* or anything. I can wait until Lucas is back. Hopefully.

18

LINCOLN

TWO WEEKS LATER

*A*t last, the great day of the contest has arrived. I sit on a stone bench in a balcony of Purgatory's Arena, nervous energy churning through my limbs. Any minute now, the event will begin.

It simply must be a success.

Myla slides onto the bench beside me. "You're sure this looks okay?"

I've found it's important not to give too-quick answers on occasions such as this one. I carefully scan Myla from head to toe, seeing her purple skirt-suit, ivory shirt and black heels. When I next speak, I'm careful to put an extra dose of serious into my manner. "You look perfect."

"Are you absolutely sure? I mean, this is the kind of thing my mother wears. I don't want folks to think of me as a demi-goddess, but does this suit say, *I'm trying to be my Mom?*"

"It says, *competent and in charge.*"

Myla exhales with a long *hoo* noise. She scans the balcony. "Being here alone is weird."

My wife doesn't need to say anything more; I know what she means. Neither of our parents are attending today. Myla's mother and father are off at their Ghoul Reconciliation Convention. Octavia is watching Maxon. And Connor watches over Antrum.

I nod. "It's as if there are parent-shaped cut-outs on the wall, showing where they should be standing."

Myla grabs my hand and squeezes. "Don't look now but the contestants are arriving."

Sure enough, figures step out onto the Arena floor below. I give Myla the side-eye. "Why am I not looking?"

"We need to seem cool." Myla sighs. "Well, you're already cool. I'm a bit of a mess."

I scooch closer to her on the bench. "Do I need to call out the big guns?"

Myla nods vigorously. "Do it."

This is one of our rituals for high-stress situations. I have a special tactic to ensure Myla can do what she does best, which is kick ass and take names.

I lock gazes with my wife. "I bet that you, Myla Lewis, can't give a great speech today about your contest."

Myla lowers her voice. "What are we betting?"

"The usual. One kiss, no conditions." Which means that one of us can call a kiss at any time and the other one must supply the same. It rarely ends with just kissing.

Myla cracks her neck. "All right. I'm on this."

I grin. When it comes to Myla, her natural competitive

instinct trumps just about any level of anxiety. One of the advantages of being her husband is that I get to learn these things.

A low hum of voices fill the stadium. Far below on the Arena floor, more contestants march in through an entry archway. Mostly, those arriving are quasi demons. The obvious giveaway are the multitude of tail types, such as pheasant, squirrel, rabbit, and even stingray. That said, there are some angels and thrax in the mix as well. Few ghouls, though. Somehow, that fact makes my inner cord of unease twist itself more tightly.

What's happening with that Ghoul Reconciliation Convention?

Remy sits beside the entrance arch. Like Myla, she wears a suit. Only in her case, Remy's is green to match her house colors. As each contestant steps through, Remy hands that person an enchanted pen and small notepad while explaining these will be used to record their responses. Folks nod and take their seats. Soon the flow of foot traffic dies down to nothing.

Eventually Remy leaves the table to step into the center of the Arena. In a clear voice, she calls out to the contestants. "Settle down, everyone! We will now have an opening speech from the contest sponsor, Myla Lewis!"

All eyes turn to the balcony in general, and Myla in particular. "You can do this," I whisper in her ear.

Myla rises and strides up to the balcony's edge. The crowd falls silent. Myla grips the stone ledge and calls out to the audience.

"Welcome to the Angelic Assistance Contest! Here in Purgatory, we take sole responsibility for sorting spirits into their best after-life. In the past, souls were sent to Hell unless their hearts were absolutely pure."

A hiss sounds from the audience. Many quasis glare at the few ghouls in the crowd.

"That's over now," continues Myla. "What's important today is that we send more souls to Heaven. However, that isn't ideal for all of them. Some angels fade over time, so I'm looking for a small group of brilliant folks who can help ensure every soul gets its best chance at a happy afterlife."

Myla pauses. All eyes are still on her. I couldn't be more proud.

"Today, you're here because you want to help." Myla gestures across the crowd. "All of you will go through a series of tests. Afterward, a small number of you will be selected to help out Purgatory in this historic effort. What do you say?"

A long pause follows before a grey haired woman raises her hand. "I have a question." There's no missing how her fox tail swooshes behind her.

Myla gestures in her direction. "Please go on."

"Who are you? What have you done with the Great Scala?"

Oh, damn.

At these words, grumbles arise from the crowd. A few voices sound over the din. It's hard to hear exactly what they say, but the question, *Where is the Great Scala?*, comes up quite a bit.

Myla turns and meets my gaze. A mixture of frustration and sadness glistens in her eyes. This isn't the first time the quasi people don't equate Myla Lewis with the Great Scala. It's like the human story of superman, only Clark Kent walks around saying, *I'm the Man of Steel in pants and glasses, get it?* Still, everyone just ignores him.

I give Myla what I hope is an encouraging smile. My wife returns her focus to the crowd.

"I'm the Great Scala's assistant," she announces at length. That seems to settle everyone down. "Remy Elayna Danae will now lead you through the tests."

With that, Myla retakes her seat beside me. I wrap my arm around her shoulders. "Good work."

Myla rolls her eyes. "Liar."

"Look, the people here now know what they're supposed to do. You're building up your identity outside of the Great Scala. That won't happen overnight. Besides, not every speech is supposed to be oratorical fireworks."

Myla grins and I'm glad to see that it's a genuine one. "Thanks." She leans in. "So does that count as a win for yours truly?"

"Absolutely."

Myla winks. "Even better."

Back on the Arena floor, Remy reviews how to write on an enchanted notepad with a magical pen. Turns out, it's just like regular writing, but it still takes a few tries for that concept to sink in. Not that I blame quasis for taking their time. Magic can be overwhelming if you've never used it before.

At length, the test itself begins in earnest. Remy rattles off math equations and asks for folks to write down their answers. She the quizzes them on vocabulary words and history. I'm not sure how this all relates to helping angels, but this process did come from the thrax vaults. There must be some value in here somewhere.

After no less than ninety-six questions, a new figure steps out through the entrance archway to join Remy on the Arena floor.

It's a ghoul, and he's in dark green body armor. Even worse, he also wearing a sash for the Ghoul Reconciliation Convention. About a dozen other ghouls follow behind him, all wearing the same combination of body armor and sash.

Remy turns to the ghoul squad. "Can I help you folks?"

Moving in unison, the ghouls raise their arms high as they cry out one word. "Attack!"

Jolts of alarm race through my nervous system as even more green-clad ghouls rush out onto the Arena floor. And they head straight for Remy.

Double damn.

19

MYLA

ttack?
   Seriously?

Last time I heard that word called out in this Arena, it was from none other than Armageddon. At the time, the King of Hell was invading Purgatory. Now it's a bunch of ghoul renegades from Mom's Convention.

And even worse, one of those ghouls holds a dagger … and he's closing in on Remy.

For a moment, it's all I can do to stare. Sure, my parents have kept quiet about the whole Ghoul Reconciliation Convention. But now, the truth is unavoidable. My parents were protecting me from knowing that there was an insurrection brewing.

Damn. This is bad.

Lincoln rushes for the balcony's edge. His reaction snaps me out of my shock. Rising, I race toward the same spot. Moving in unison, Lincoln and I leap off the balcony to land on the Arena floor below. Another fact becomes clear.

This shit's hard to do in a suit. Just while landing, I lost my heels and shredded my skirt.

Across the Arena floor, Remy screams. Lincoln and I race toward her.

We're not the only ones with the idea to run. Some quasis speed for the exits. But even more of my people hate ghouls. Those folks pour onto the Arena floor and rush toward the armored undeadlies. This scene has all the makings of a civil war. We've lost control.

At last, Lincoln and I reach Remy. A ghoul looms over her, a dagger gleaming in his pale hand. Before him, Remy lies unmoving on the Arena floor. Leaping forward, Lincoln twists the attacker's arm behind his back, making the ghoul drop his weapon. I kneel at Remy's side, taking her hand in mine. A thin line of blood drips from her temple.

"Are you all right?" I ask.

Remy flutters her eyes open. "Who ... What ... Queen Myla?"

I exhale. Remy's in shock, but she seems unharmed. "It's me."

By now, Lincoln has the ghoul restrained, but there isn't much we can do about the rest of the crowd. Fists collide. Someone screams. This could be a bloodbath. Not that ghouls have blood, but still. The whole point of the convention was to mend fences between my people and the undeadlies. A real battle in Purgatory's Arena would definitely count in the *not helping* column.

All of a sudden, the sky darkens. It's my parents, flying right toward us. Dad is in full archangel mode. I'm talking golden armor, matching wings, and a badass attitude. He's not the only one, either. Dad holds Mom in his arms, and she has a scowl on her face that says, *momma bear is not happy.*

The pair land on the balcony. Mom steps to the edge, raises her arms, and goes into her best presidential-mode. "My people. You must return to your seats. This is not a productive way to resolve our differences."

No one listens. More fists pound. Extra cries echo in the air.

My father's face turns dark as thunder. As he takes to the skies, he ignites his baculum as a sword made from angel fire.

"Listen to me!" Dad cries. To accent his point, the sky changes from its permanent Purgatory grey to a single sheet of white flame.

Never seen that before. *Dad is casting a spell, but what?*

The white flames highlight Dad's silhouette. Everyone pauses. My father bellows out again.

"You heard my wife!" Dad cries. "Shut up and sit down!"

Dad whistles and the fire vanishes, only to be replaced by dozens of angels in sliver armor. My eyes widen. So this was Dad's spell. The General of the Angels just summoned his troops.

Part of me is in awe of my father's power. Another part is just crazy-happy this won't be a total loss.

Dad points to the Arena floor. "Take the rebel ghouls away," he commands. Warrior angels fly down in pairs, scooping up each ghoul before flying off.

"Dismissed!" cries Dad.

It's amazing what my father can do with a single word. All the contestants neatly file out of the stadium. The remaining angels wing away. Beside me, Lincoln lifts Remy into his arms.

"I'll take her to get checked out," says Lincoln. "There's a first aid station not far from here."

I force a smile. "Thanks. I'll chat with my parents."

As if on cue, Dad flies across the balcony and scoops Mom into his arms once more. After that, my parents land beside me on the Arena floor. Dad sets Mom down and pulls me into a hug. He's actually really good at giving cuddly embraces despite the whole *I'm wearing armor* thing.

"How's my baby?" he asks.

"I'm fine."

Dad releases me and Mom continues the hug-a-thon. "How's my sweet Myla-la?"

I force another smile. "Still good."

Mom breaks the hug to straighten the lapels on my ruined suit coat. "Today went really well, don't you think? I mean, apart from the ghoul attack which you couldn't have done anything about."

Don't say it. Don't day it. Don't say it.

Fuuuuuuuuuuck, I'm saying it.

"Actually, I might have been able to do something. That is, if I knew about any trouble at the convention."

Mom pats my cheek. "We're only trying to shield you from bad news, baby. We had no idea the rebels would go to the Arena of all places."

"And who cares about rebel ghouls anyway?" asks Dad.

"Precisely," adds Mom. "Of course, you know today was a success, don't you?"

Thus follows a long and expectant stare from my parents. They're just waiting for me to say, *today was a disaster*, so they can tell me everything is perfect.

Which is sweet idea, but totally wrong.

Today *was* a disaster. This was weeks of planning to achieve my first real step on building my own knights of the round table. Instead, the contest was cut short and my parents had to bail me out. Maybe we got enough questions to find the right knights, but who knows? It could be a huge waste, too.

Even so, there's no point having the same conversation over and over.

Me: I suck.

Them: No you don't.

I know my parents. This could go on for hours. So, instead I force yet another smile. "I know it."

"That's my Myla-la," says Mom.

With that semi-lie behind me, I decide that now is the perfect time to go home and hold my baby. After all, it's almost naptime for Maxon. And nothing heals the soul better than a sleeping child and a rocking chair.

20

LINCOLN

*A*n hour later, I find Myla at home, rocking a very asleep Maxon. The house is deserted. My wife looks up as I enter.

"Is Remy safe?" she whispers.

When I speak, I take care to use the same low tone. "The thrax clinic is double checking everything, but Remy seems fine. Only a minor concussion."

"You know, when I first met Remy, I suspected she was up to no good."

"I remember." Myla told me all about the animals, broken tools, and boxes of so-called books. "You were right to be suspicious."

"Now Remy did this whole contest for me, and what happens? She's almost killed by ghouls from my mother's convention."

"There is some good news," I offer. "The magic

notepads worked. Remy says she has enough to find the folks you need."

Myla nods and runs her fingers through Maxon's hair. I notice the gleam of a golden ring on her thumb. I blink hard, not believing what I'm seeing.

"Is that the Band of Epochs?" I ask.

"Abso-freaking-lutely," says Myla. "It was waiting for me when I got home." She nods toward an opened box that sits on a nearby bookshelf. Myla picks up a message beside the container and hands it to me. "Take a look."

I read the words silently.

Dear Myla,

My visions have changed. Your interactions with the fading angels are no longer a cause for concern. Therefore, I have taken the liberty of removing the Band of Epochs from the Heavenly vaults and am returning it to you forthwith.

Sincerely,

Verus

"What do you think?" asks Myla.

"It's more Verus double-speak," I reply.

"Agreed." Myla hands me the ring. "Do you notice anything different?"

I clasp the item in my palm. "Feels lighter."

"It is. When I found the Band of Epochs, it had five trips through time in it. Dad showed me how to check."

"And now?"

"Only four. When you say a certain spell, the ring splits into mini-rings, if that makes sense. One ring for each trip. That's why the band is lighter now. A single mini-ring is gone. Someone can use it to travel though time."

"Or they've already made their visit." I scan Maxon's bedroom, as if the secret of Verus' true intentions will be written on the walls somewhere. But there are only my son's collection of King Arthur posters.

"Any ideas what she's up to?" Myla asks.

I tap my chin and think things through. "Verus insists you hand over the Band of Epochs to the Heavenly vaults, which you do. But the ring comes back minus one trip through time. Verus is clearly scheming somehow. But what her true aim is? I can't guess."

"Same here." Myla lets out a long breath. "After everything that happened today, that letter feels like it's saying, *Myla Lewis is a failure who couldn't start a demonpocalypse anyway.* Which shouldn't hurt my feelings, but..." Sorrow seem to careen off her in waves.

I kneel by Myla's side. "May I say something?"

Myla nods. Unshed tears glisten in her eyes.

"It's not how you fall down, it's how you get up. And you always rise again, Myla."

"Thanks." Myla offers me a genuine, if sad, smile. I take that as a good sign. For a long minute, I just sit beside my wife, watching her rock our son.

Sometimes, the best thing you can do is keep a silent vigil over your family.

21

MYLA

ONE WEEK LATER

I pace a line across Ghost Tower One.
 Left.
Right.
Left.
Right.

All the while, my gaze stays locked on the front doors. Any minute now, the folks who could be my knights will step through that very entrance. Nervous energy charges through my limbs.

I scan the rest of the empty space. Like all ghost towers, this is a tall and rectangular building made from concrete. Imagine hanging out inside a giant chimney and that's the general idea. A small control room juts out from one wall. Layers of clouds drift overhead—they're the magical structures where we store souls before processing for Heaven or Hell.

Lincoln waits nearby. He exudes total calm in his dark human suit. For my part, I'm in my Scala robes. The purple skirt-suit look from the contest? Total bust. Also in the *not-great* column, Remy isn't here today. Sadly, she's still recovering from her concussion at the contest.

And yeah, I feel hella guilty about that.

Across the floor, the main doors finally swing open. Three quasis step in. I stop pacing and move to stand beside Lincoln. My breath catches as they cross the room and pause before us.

At last. Three of the most acclaimed geniuses in all Purgatory are here. In honor of the occasion, I give this trio-o-brainiacs secret nicknames.

First, there's Ginger Girl. Self-explanatory.

Second, I have Old Guy With A Throatbeard. Which I decide to shorten to OGWAT.

And third, it's Bill. I call him that because he's wearing a bowling shirt with Bill written on it. I'm smart that way.

Addressing the trio, I gesture to the concrete walls around me. "Welcome to Ghost Tower One," I declare. "This is the oldest facility in Purgatory for storing souls. I thought we'd meet here so you can see our problems first hand."

I pause and give the group a chance to talk. After all, if a demi-goddess and her hottie Consort just summoned me into the equivalent of a three-story-tall concrete tower packed with ghosts, I know I'd have questions.

In reply, there is only silence. Tapping my chin, I consider this turn of events. Lincoln and I can be a little overwhelming. Maybe these folks are just waiting for some official stuff, like introductions.

I clear my throat. "I am Myla Lewis, the Great Scala, and this is my Consort, Lincoln." Beside me, my husband bows slightly at the waist.

Still nothing. Unless you count the blank stares. *Huh.*

Normally, Lincoln never says much at Purgatory events. Now my guy breaks his normal no-talkie rule. "We need your help." He raises the control pad in his hands. "How about a brief demonstration?"

"Yes," all three say together.

Whaaaat?

My guy and I exchange a pointed look. Speaking only when asked a direct question? That's a total red flag for non-creative dumbassery. And talking in unison? An even bigger warning sign.

Still. Maybe these three just need more information.

"Great idea." I point to Lincoln's control pad. "Let's show these folks what's up."

Lincoln presses some buttons. A holding tank comes down, which is a clear glass-like structure that's filled with souls. Inside, the transparent spirits lay in neat rows on what looks like a rolling hill. All of them are blissfully asleep.

I gesture toward the spirits. "See these souls?"

"We do," they all reply.

Wow. I really wish they would stop speaking in unison.

"Well," I continue. "Some did not live purely good lives. You can tell because if you look really closely, there are black spots where their mortal hearts used to be. Back when the ghouls ran Purgatory, we all know what would happen to spirits like these."

Ginger Girl raises her hand. "Me, please!"

"It wasn't really a question. I said, *we all knew* the answer."

Ginger Girl hops in place. "Right here! I got it!"

She's so not dropping this. "Sure."

"They all got sent to *Hell*!" Ginger Girl says the word *Hell* with a little too much enthusiasm for my taste.

"That is true," I agree.

"So I got it right." Ginger Girl beams. "Do I get a gold star or a cookie now?"

I frown. *Maybe I heard her wrong.* "Did you say—"

"I'd rather a gold star." Ginger Girl holds out her palm.

My eyes widen. "No, you do not get a gold star."

And with that, it's official. I'm supposed to be brainstorming with a trio of brilliant thinkers. Instead, this discussion is as annoying as fighting Papyrum demons, and those minor monsters give out a ton of paper cuts. I should be shocked, but I knew this was possible. After all, the contest ended before all the questions were asked. Maybe we skipped the *independent thought section*.

Ginger Girl stomps her foot. "Then what about a cookie?"

I fold my arms over my chest. "Nope." *Cookies are for creatives.*

In every situation, there comes a time to let go. I am almost there with this particular trio. Still, I'll give one last attempt. Perhaps I need to keep things high level. Sure, these folks may not be able to help with the fading angels, but they could do snack runs or something. Allimari takes forever to find a decent cookie.

One last try.

I clasp my hands together in the motion of pleading people everywhere. "Can one of you help me, your Great Scala, with anything at all?" I ask. "Even a little bit?"

"No," they all reply.

Well, that's honest. I make shoo-fingers toward the door. "You can go, if you like."

Suddenly, deep peals of thunder rumble overhead. My ears pop. Lighting flashes beyond the windows. The Ghost Tower shakes with such force, great cracks tear up the concrete walls. An electric kind of energy fills the air.

Magic.

The three quasis stare around in open-mouthed fear. One thing I've learned as the Great Scala: if I freak out to a level five, then everyone else takes their terror to eleven. So I act super-calm while I whisper-speak to Lincoln from one side of my mouth.

"Do you know what this is?" I ask.

"Powerful magic," he replies.

"Anything more specific on that for me?"

"Ah, no."

Fresh thunder rumbles. More lightning strikes. The sense of magic in the air turns so thick, it's as if stones were weighing on my chest. The bare light bulbs along the walls burst in a flare of light.

Complete darkness surrounds us.

The ghost tower turns silent.

And my odd inner voice takes this moment to come to life again. Once more, she speaks in a voice only I can hear.

You and Lincoln are safe. I protect you both.

My forehead knits in confusion. Protect us? From what? The fact that I still have to wait two hours for a ginger snap?

A moment later, the lights flicker on once more. Only their appearance has changed. This is the first ghost tower ever, so the bulbs here are bare and simple. But now? They look like fancy orbs with multi-colored facets to them. I scan the room, wondering what else has changed.

The three quasis are gone. Not a big shock. They probably ran out in the dark.

Lincoln's data pad has vanished. Okay, he might have dropped it or something.

And the floor is now white plastic instead of concrete. Weird, but pretty minor. Plus there was some heavy duty magic flying around. Floor transformation isn't that big of a deal in terms of spells.

That's when I see it.

All the clouds are gone, which means that the soul storage containers have disappeared.

That's a huge problem. Those hovering clouds were chock-full of spirits. Now they're gone. My stomach drops. What just happened? Who took all the souls?

Thud! Thud! Thud!

I speak to Lincoln from one side of my mouth again. "Is someone at the door?"

"Oh yes," he replies.

Slam!

The front door opens. A demon steps through. The guy is tall and pale with slicked-back hair. He wears a white suit over an open, black shirt. His massive amounts of chest hair are accented by a round medallion while his golden tail ends with an arrowhead shape. My own tail perks up to arch over my shoulder. That settles it. Even my tail knows this isn't just any demon.

Hells Bells.

This is none other than Lester, the Archdemon of Lust. As in, one of the nine archdemons that offset the nine archangels. Even worse, Lester brought back-up singers and dancers with him. And no, I am not kidding.

A pack of twenty minor demons follow Lester into the ghost tower. They're of many different skin tones and ages, but all wear matching white suits that go along with their pale bat wings and white tails. No question about it: Lester is into disco. Not sure how I feel about that.

I take it back. I'm totally freaked out.

My life is one long parade of odd stuff. But this? Next generation strange.

I stand perfectly still, my gaze frozen on the sight before me. An idea appears. Maybe I'm hallucinating.

Yes, that's it.

Magic clouds my mind.

I nudge Lincoln with my elbow. "Psst." I nod toward the hopefully-fake disco guy. "Is that Lester, the Archdemon of Lust?

Lincoln rubs his jaw in a slow rhythm. "Yes, it is."

"Shouldn't he be locked up?"

"Absolutely."

A voice in the back of my head starts screaming, *the demonpocalypse is nigh*! I'm still pulling for some kind of magical hallucination, though.

Lester struts across the floor to pause before me. His dancers stand behind him in a classic V-shape that's popular in music videos on Earth. "Hey, hottie." Lester winks at me before turning to Lincoln. "And Consort to the hottie."

I raise my hand. "I have a name, Lester. I'm Myla." There are some things I never back down on. Calling me Myla is one of them.

Lester sniffs. "Like I care." The archdemon spins about in that disco move than ends with his finger sticking in the air. "I've been sent to talk to you both. Somehow, you survived our demonpocalypse."

"Did you say demonpocalypse?"

Come on, magical hallucination. You can stop any time now.

"Yes, remember a few minutes ago?" asks Lester. "There were *thunder bolts and lightning very very frightening*? That was the demonpocalypse. The Crimson Scourge went back in time and changed history. Now, we're all free."

My blood chills over. I was just adjusting to the concept

of Lester running around. This is so much worse. "All nine archdemons are loose?" I ask.

Lester bobs his brows. "All nine."

"What about the archangels?" asks Lincoln.

"Let's just say they're not in the picture," states Lester. "Thanks to a little change in history, there are no thrax anymore. No angels, archangels, quasis, ghouls, humans … You and lover boy are all that's left. Someone cast a spell that allowed you to survive."

My eyes widen. A spell helped us survive? Was that from my new smooth-talking mental parasite? I thought she was only interested in forcing me to chat with chicks. Now she's somehow saving me from a demopocalypse. Not that I'm ungrateful, but it's one thing to think someone's hanging out in your brain and handing out friendship tips. It's another matter to know you have a megawitch hiding in your unconscious.

Is this the work of the wrath coven? Verus? I got nothing.

Lester twirls, stops, and does that thing where he laces his fingers and makes them into a wave shape. "Great news. I'm here to offer you asylum. You can join my dance troupe. That way, you can remain alive until I tire of you. How's that for a deal?"

I'm ready to tell Lester to stick it, but his demonic back-up singers start singing the refrain of *Staying Alive*, but with new words.

> *Deal deal deal deal*
> *Lester's is making a deal*

Making a deal

My body prickles over in shock. Disco demons are bad enough. But the singing is just over the top, even for my life.

Deal deal deal deal
Lester's is making a deeeeeeeeeeeeeeeeeal
Ohhhhhhh OH!

After a few more dance moves, the back up group pauses. Lester then gestures to me and Lincoln. "Well?" he asks.

I tap my chin, like I'm seriously considering this option. "Wow, that's really tempting."

Lester winks. "Of course, it is."

Lincoln takes my hand. "Myla and I will step outside for a few minutes and talk this over. Can you wait for an answer?"

"You got it." Lester turns to his group of demonic back-up singers. "You know what we have time for now? Disco contest!"

Everyone cheers as the ghost tower floor lights up with colored blocks. The fancy new bulbs cast strobe action around the room. The back-up singers launch into an Abba medley.

Lincoln and I speed walk to the exit. As we rush along, one thought repeats in my mind.

This can't be a real demonpocalypse.

22

MYLA

*L*incoln and I leave the ghost tower. A horrible sight greets us as we step outside. The landscape is a ruin of rubble in every direction. There isn't a soul around. My Purgatory is gone. Probably the rest of the after-realms, too.

Fuck fuck fuckity FUCK fuck FUUUUUUCK.

Notice how I put an extra fuck in there at the end? Things are just that bad.

I turn to Lincoln. "Let me get this straight. Everyone is gone. Our parents, Maxon, Walker, Cissy?"

"It appears so." Lincolns shakes his head. "Sadly, I've no reason to doubt Lester's word. We could do a thorough review of the after-realms, but I suspect this is all we'll find. Ruins."

Lincoln leans back on his heels while rubbing his chin. That's another one of his *thinking-faces*. Meanwhile, I've got an idea of my own and it's to call for supernatural assistance.

Closing my eyes, I summon my igni, AKA the little supernatural lightning bolts that empower me to move souls to Heaven or Hell.

Come to me, little ones. Could use your help.

There's no reply, but that doesn't mean anything. My igni are always flighty. Still, I hope they're okay.

My gaze locks on the barren landscape. With each passing second, my pulse speeds faster.

Everyone is gone.

I picture Maxon jumping on the couch ... my father's white-toothed grin ... Walker lying his ass off ... And Drusus letting out his infectious chuckle. As every image flies through my mind, my heart cracks a little more.

I punch my leg in frustration. "Damn! I specifically did not what this to happen! If I kept the ring, things would have been fine." I turn to Lincoln. "Right?"

"Correct."

Some little part of me says I'm going off on a tirade, but more of me doesn't care. I just lived through a freaking demonpocalypse. I need time to process.

I throw up my arms. "But no, Verus wanted the Band of Epochs put into Heavenly storage. And that's when someone must have stolen one of the mini-rings. And let's be honest, that someone is probably the

Crimson Scourge. Now an evil mage has traveled to the past and caused a demonpocalypse." I plunk down onto my butt, which is an uncomfortable choice, considering how there's nothing but rubble around to sit on. "I'm spent."

Lincoln taps his lips. I've seen this move before. It means he's come to some conclusion. "We've faced the end of the after-realms before, right?"

"Oh, yeah."

"And in each case, we prevailed. So there's no need to panic."

I hold my thumb and forefinger an inch apart. "I might be panicking a little bit."

"Same here." Lincoln sighs. "Let's recap what we know. The Crimson Scourge probably stole one of the mini-rings from the Band of Epochs and started the demonpocalypse. However, your ring still holds four trips through time. That's enough for you and me to travel back to the past and then return to the present."

I bob my head, thinking. "And while we're meandering around history, maybe we can prevent the demonpocalypse from ever happening." A memory appears. "I asked Verus if the demonpocalypse were reversible."

"What did she say?"

"That she's an awesome oracle."

Lincoln's mouth quirks up in a smile. "Which in Verus-speak means yes, it's reversible."

I kick at more rubble and try to rally. Not happening. That's when my tail balls into a fist shape and fake-punches my upper arm. This is its way of saying, *buck up buttercup.*

I give my tail a scratchy-pat, which is its absolute favorite. "Nice suggestion, boy."

"And what's what?" asks Lincoln.

"We need to fight this thing." I rise. "Dad says the Band of Epochs chooses where to best send us. All we need to do is speak the spell, break a mini-ring, and we're off."

Lincoln beams. "I love your spirit."

"In that case, we better leave before Lester gets curious."

Holding the Band of Epochs between my palms, I cast the separation spell like Dad showed me. Soon four thin rings appear. I pass two bands to Lincoln, who grips one in each hand.

"Any reason to wait?" I ask.

"Not that I can think of." Lincoln scans the landscape one last time. "It's not like there are any supplies around."

After setting my first ring on my thumb, I then grip my second ring between my fingers, ready to break it in two. Lincoln does the same. Lifting my chin, I inhale, ready to state the incantation my father taught me.

At that moment, the ghost tower doors burst open. Lester is here.

"What do you say?" asks the archdemon. "Ready to accept my terms?"

In reply, Lincoln and I snap our rings while quickly speaking the spell.

"World and care

Take us there"

The broken halves of my ring flare with purple light. I grin. *This is working.* I look over to Lincoln. His band hasn't broken. There's no light. No magic.

Damn.

I reach toward Lincoln. Before I can touch his skin, purple mist surrounds me. Vapor clogs my lungs and blocks my vision. My legs turn rubbery as I crumple to the ground. My eyes flutter shut; consciousness fades. At this moment, everything I know is gone.

Even Lincoln.

23

MYLA

*T*he next thing I know, I stand on a grassy field beside a dirt road. My head feels like someone's been using it as a bongo drum for six months, minimum. I try to focus, but it isn't easy.

Where am I, anyway?

Stepping in a slow circle, I scan my surroundings. A sunny sky arches overhead. Purgatory is perma-cloudy, which means there's no way I'm back home. So where is this place? I'm certainly not in a cave, cloud, or cemetery. Which rules out Antrum, Heaven, and the Dark Lands.

Only one option remains: Earth.

I glance at my hand. A ring glistens on my thumb. My foggy mind tries to process this. There was something important about this ring and time travel. The answer appears.

The Band of Epochs, that's what this ring is called.

More of to my brain starts to function. For some

reason, I used this ring travel through time. Only question is, now that I know *where* I landed, I need to know *when* I arrived.

A small cart appears on the road up ahead. It's essentially a wooden box on wheels pulled by a pair of horses. On the side of the wagon are painted the words, *Pendragon Academy*.

My eyes widen. I remember that name. There was a book about King Arthur and the Pendragon. *Does that mean I'm back in medieval times?* I scan the skies. No planes soar overhead. In every direction, there are nothing but fields, trees and more trees. Fresh, crisp air surrounds me. Long story short, there's no tech, buildings, or pollution.

Huh. Chances are, I'm in Arthurian times.

My heart lightens a little. The wrath coven was right again. *Evil but accurate.* I've journeyed to the time when I can chat up King Arthur.

A new idea hits me.

Maybe there are more options in the *supernatural assistance column* than just the wrath coven.

I'm talking igni.

True fact: I shouldn't even be able summon my igni on Earth, but I just did some magic ring stuffy-stuff. Rules may not apply. I close my eyes.

Come to me, little ones.

Sure enough, a swirling column of tiny lightning bolts

appears before me. A sense of rightness settles into my soul.

Ah, there you are.

A moment later, a cacophony of screams fill my head, a noise that only I can hear. A million terrified voices screech at once. Normally, only the dark igni yell their little guts out. This time, all of them are upset. Very clear statements of rage and fear echo over the din, namely:

"You're not our Great Scala!"

"NOT OUR GREAT SCALA!"

"NOOOOOT OOOOUR GREEEEEAT SCAAAAL-LLLLAAA!"

"AAARRRRRRGH!"

Once my igni start doing pirate impressions, I know it's time to cut them loose. "Ok, little dudes," I exclaim. "Forget I said anything. Sheesh."

With a burst of brightness, the many lightning bolts vanish. I'm glad to have my sanity back, but the *no-igni-help* thing is a downer. My supernatural powers would have been useful.

At least, that wagon is still approaching. That said, it's rather far away. Thanks to Allimari, I'm now an expert in slow-moving entities. This will take a while. I plunk down by the side of the road.

Guess there's nothing to do now but wait, and hope whoever drives that wagon is friendly.

24

LINCOLN

J can only stare at the place where Myla once stood. Moments ago, my wife snapped her signet band. Afterward, she vanished in a swirl of purple smoke.

Gone.

For my part, I attempted to break the ring while speaking the correct incantation. Yet no matter how hard I tried, my ring stayed annoyingly whole. Instead of snapping, an electric charge of magic would skitter across my fingers.

No question what the issue is here. I know when an otherworldly power is fighting me. Something or someone doesn't want me journeying through time.

Well, this isn't my first round of dealing with quirky supernatural items. I'll get the spell to function. I always do.

The Archdemon of Lust steps closer, his pale face

turning purple with rage. He may not be the snappiest dresser, but at eight feet tall, he doesn't really have to be. Behind him, Lester's minions move nearer as well. Not that I wouldn't enjoy a nice battle—and these dancing demons would be an interesting fight—but the fact remains.

Leaving Myla alone in time is simply not an option.

Focusing my energy, I pull deep into my soul, tapping into my angelic power. A chill pools behind my eyes. No doubt, my irises now glow blue. Channeling my inner magic, I grip the ring once more and speak the incantation.

"World and care
Take me there"

Crack!

This time, the band breaks in two. Excitement and relief wash through me. Purple smoke appears everywhere. An electric sense of power tightens my skin. Violet lights flash. The world fades away under a colored haze.

My body floats upward. More mists swirl around me, creating a wall of cloud that I can't see past. Deep rumbles shake the air. A woman's voice sounds in the mists. Her tone is familiar and not all at once.

"I tried to stop you from following, yet if you insist..."

Although I don't know the speaker, there are some rules of magic that never change. Whoever is speaking, she's casting a powerful spell.

The haze vanishes. Violet lights fade. One moment, I'm floating in a cloud of mist and power. The next, I stand outside a familiar spot, even though it's one I've only seen in books.

Pendragon castle. This is the seat of King Arthur's father.

Turns out, the illustration in Maxon's book is rather accurate. The castle is a blocky structure with thin windows and a wide moat. Reaching out, I touch the familiar pattern of dark and light stone.

I can't believe it. I'm actually in King Arthur's day.

Or am I? There's one way to be certain.

I step around to the castle's front. The red drawbridge is pulled up against the building's facade. A pair of tattered pennants hang from nearby window-holes. Both show a grey dragon sewn on a black background. Latin words appear at the bottom: *the king is gone, the castle sleeps.*

That confirms it. After the Pendragon died, his home was closed up and all serfs were turned into freedmen. I've definitely been transported to the time of King Arthur. More specifically, I've arrived about twenty years after the Pendragon's death. My thoughts spin through everything I know of this era. By this point, King Arthur has locked up all the archdemons under this very castle. Colossus lies in a dungeon under Camelot.

And that's where I need to go. *Camelot.* The other eight archdemons are nothing without their king. Fortunately, Maxon isn't the only one who obsessed about King Arthur. I followed all things Arthurian as well. I even kept detailed maps of this area, so I know Camelot is a few days' journey from here. I can certainly walk the distance, but not in a modern suit.

What a situation.

My life has been one long Renaissance Faire with every kind of medieval trinket at my royal disposal. Now I travel to the *actual* middle ages and I'm wearing a business suit.

Nicely played, fate.

At least, there are a few fashion changes I can quickly make. My jacket and tie get tossed into the nearby moat. Next I roll up my sleeves and untuck my shirt. With any luck, I appear like someone wearing an oddly-shaped tunic.

Bang!

An explosion rocks the air. The ground shimmies. Smoke pours out from every window-hole in the castle. My pulse speeds. Kneeling down, I touch the earth. No question where the blast itself took place: below ground. Which means the dungeons were the target. Did the other eight archdemons get loose?

Before, the drawbridge rested silently against the castle's facade. Now it shivers and creaks. My eyes widen. A realization appears.

Oh, they're loose alright.

I steal around to the castle's side. Careful to keep my body hidden, I peep around the wall's edge. *Perfect.* This spot affords me an excellent view of the front drawbridge.

The rattle of chains sounds as the drawbridge lowers. The massive wooden plank hits the ground with a thud.

A figure in a red fur cloak trots out on a white mare. A

roughly-stitched leather hood is pulled low over the rider's face.

Memories appear. Myla described one of the quilts the wrath coven made. It showed a figure in a red cloak who rode a white horse. The Crimson Scourge. Could this be the same mage? Myla had sent out request after request for any background on this witch or wizard. No one could find a thing.

More figures march out behind the cloaked rider. Sure enough, all eight archdemons file out onto the drawbridge.

There are Null and Rage, the pair that look like knights. Plain and Vain, who wear long cloaks. The skeleton figures of Skyn and Bone. Even Lester's here, wearing his puffy shorts and a wide hat while carrying a lute. And finally, there stands Ximena. She's the Archdemon of Lust and Wrath. Although Ximena can shift into dragon form, she now appears as a petite woman with cocoa-colored skin and long brown hair.

I brace myself, waiting for the wallop of power that comes from being near a greater demon. After all, Armageddon packed a major hit. It's true that Lester didn't have any unsavory side effects from being near him, but these are all eight archdemons at once. Some of them should surely force emotions through me.

Fear.

Rage.

Lust.

Yet nothing happens. I always knew the archdemons got super-charged once Colossus possessed them. After all, that's why they were imprisoned separately from their king in the first place. Seems that *solo weakness stuff* is even more dramatic than I expected. This fact shines as a ray of hope in an otherwise bleak day.

Back on the drawbridge, the archdemons bow to the rider. Ximena rises first and speaks. "Crimson Scourge, we praise you for giving us our freedom."

A knight in rusted armor speaks next. It's Null, the Archdemon of Sloth. "We are incomplete without our king."

Ximena rounds on Null. "*The Seven* are incomplete without Colossus. I suffer no such limitations." She focuses on the Crimson Scourge. "We shall meet again at Camelot."

No question what they plan to do there. *Free Colossus.* I picture all the images I've seen of that archdemon king in action. He revels in any kill that's particularly bloody.

At least, Colossus isn't free yet. I take that as another ray of hope.

The Crimson Scourge takes off at a gallop. Meanwhile, Ximena rounds on the other archdemons. "Who remembers what happened right before we were all imprisoned?"

Lester plucks out a tune on his lyre while singing to the refrain from Greensleeves.

> *A blonde wench was all my joy*
> *Her bosom was my deliiiiiiight*

"Quiet, Lester." Ximena shakes her head. "Seems I must remind you, after all. We angered the Almighty by appearing too often to humans on Earth. Now we're free. But if we use magic or kill wantonly, then the archangels will—" Ximena rolls her hand, encouraging them to think.

My chest tightens. Ximena is a lust and wrath demon, just like my Myla. That hand movement is something my wife does often.

Please, let Myla be safe, alive, and nearby.

"Ugh." Ximena growls. "The archangels said they would fly down from Heaven and kill us all. Therefore, we must hold to the plan from the Crimson Scourge. We walk to Camelot and address King Arthur. There, we make our case that we've all learned our lessons. Along the way, none of us can appear to any humans. No magic. No gruesome deaths. Once King Arthur is convinced, then we'll hold our *special party*, right?" Ximena scans the faces around her.

Blank stares are her only reply.

"Damn." Ximena sighs. "I can not be locked up with you lot again."

Clearly, outside of Ximena, these archdemons are not the sharpest blades in the demonic knife drawer. No wonder King Arthur was able to slap all eight of them into a prison.

It's logical and yet ... I've spent so much time reading the Arthurian legends. It seems impossible that Dalston Rusus the Bard could be so inaccurate.

"Let me try this again," says Ximena. "After we hold the special party, we can take care of the archangels and then free Colossus."

Rage, the Archdemon of Wrath, raises his fist. "COLOSSUS!"

"I want to *be* Colossus." That's Plain, the Archdemon of Envy.

"Will they have food at Camelot?" asks the Archdemon of Gluttony.

Ximena claps her hands. "Attention!" The group quiets. "Here's what happens next. We'll break out into three groups so we don't attract attention from humans. None of us will show our demonic powers. I'll travel by road with Null and Rage. Plain, Vain, and Lester, you journey by river. Skyn and Bone, you take the mountain route. We'll all meet at Camelot in two days."

Null raises his hand. "Why don't we transport now?"

"Because we're repentant, remember?" asks Ximena. "No magic, no kills, no seductions. We follow the rules of the Almighty and do nothing to alert humans about our true nature. They are unable to see our demonic side unless we unleash it for them."

"We will heed your words," says Vain.

"Thank you." Ximena waves to Null and Rage. "Let us set off."

All the archdemons tromp away from the drawbridge. From there, they do indeed split into three parties. No question what group I'll follow. *Ximena's.* She's lust and wrath, just like Myla. I know how the Furor dragon mind works.

A plan quickly takes shape. It's a rough scheme, but it may be a way for me to officially join Ximena's group.

Careful to stay hidden, I follow Ximena, Null, and Rage. As I move along, fresh images appear in my mind. I see Myla's eyes flashing red after we share a fierce kiss … baby Maxon giggling while clasping his toes … And my people lining up their boats on the Incaeneda river, eager for a blessing. Right now, those memories never truly existed.

My plan has to work.

I can't lose them.

MYLA

he wagon rolls along the twisty road. It's heading in my direction, it's just taking for-freaking-ever to get here. I spend the time picking lint off my Scala robes and trying not to freak out.

At one point, there's a boom that sounds a lot like thunder. But no clouds show up, so I can't even get distracted by the weather. Unfortunately, the waiting gives my normally-hyper mind a chance to go into overdrive, imagining all the horrible things that might be happening to Lincoln right now.

What I wouldn't give for a deck of cards at this point. All this thinking is making me twitchy.

At last, the wagon rolls to a stop beside me. An old man and woman sit at the driver's bench. They're both pale, stooped and white-haired with sparkly blue eyes and clothing that can only be described as *rags*. I quickly catalog the threat level.

They're cute.

Definitely slow moving.

In fact, I'm surprised they aren't dead.

All in all? Harmless.

One drawback: I have no idea if my version of English will make any sense to them. So I decide to speak in small sentences and with over-the-top hand motions. Hey, it works for Tarzan. Why not me?

"Me Myla." I tap my chest. "Come from far away in future." I gesture toward the horizon.

There. That was perfect.

The couple stare at me for a moment. Actually, it's more like five long seconds, and I'm starting to wonder if I should do my Tarzan speech again. At last, the old woman speaks.

"You were the one with the vision." She elbows the guy next to her. "Why must we meet her at this moment? Who is she?"

The old dude gestures at my head. "Look at her hair. This wench is none other than the Crimson Scourge, sent here to free Colossus and end the world."

Now that was a lot of blah-blah and hair shaming. Even so, there are two important pieces of info. First, if these two think I'm the Crimson Scourge sent to *free* Colossus, then the archdemon king is still locked up. *Nice.* Second, the lady said the guy got visions. He must be a mage. Maybe she is, too, but one thing at a time.

"Let me get this straight," I say. "Did you two have a premonition to roll over here and check me out?"

The old guy now speaks in what I consider to be an exaggerated warble. "I don't know what you mean, child."

That's a *yes*.

And that false voice raises a good question. If the old-guy accent is a fraud, then what else is bogus? An idea appears. I've seen my share of illusion charms at work. I even know a good trick for sussing them out. Tilting my head, I scan the edges of the wagon. Sometimes basic illusions can't stand up to close inspection against direct sunlight.

Ha! Sure enough, the top of the wooden wagon is semi-transparent.

"You—" I point to the guy "—are a mage who's sees the future. Ergo, you can understand me perfectly well. Let's talk." Let the record show I'm especially happy with my use of the word *ergo*. It sounds vaguely medieval.

The pair stare forward in silence. *So irritating.*

"Hey, I've got all day." To highlight that point, I fold my arms over my chest. "Show me your true selves so we can have a real conversation. If you're magical, then you know I am as well." Never one to miss an entrance, my tail arcs over my shoulder to wave at the couple.

"Fine." The woman raises her hand while whispering an incantation. Within seconds, blue smoke surrounds both her and the guy. When the mist vanishes, the old couple are gone. The wagon is toast, too. Instead, I look upon a young couple. Both can't be more than teenagers, although with magic users, it can be tough to tell.

"I'm Nimue," says the girl. Without the obfuscation

spell, I catch the hint of an accent in her voice. I'm no expert in languages, but her cadence reminds me of Mandarin. Her face holds the permanent look of a smile. In terms of clothes, she wears a blue silk robe that's tied at the waist. There's no wagon anymore; now she's riding a gray horse.

And her name is Nimue.

Huh. There was a water nymph by that name who lured Merlin out of Camelot. She's a big villain in the stories of Dalston Rusus the Bard. Can this Nimue be the same person? I frown, considering. Then I come to a conclusion.

It's probably her. This is my life, after all.

The guy beside her speaks next. "I'm Merlin."

Like Nimue, this Merlin is tall, lean and wearing a silk robe that's tied at his waist. Both of them sport long braids that swing down their backs. Merlin's robe is black, which is the same color as his horse. The big difference is that Merlin has flecks of gray at his temples, as well as a permanent squint to his expression. It's like someone's about to hit him in the face with a baseball bat, and he is forever awaiting the blow.

"I'm Myla, by the way. And are you two *the* Merlin and Nimue?"

"Do you mean the ones sung about by Dalston Rusus the Bard?" asks Merlin.

"Bingo." The pair eye me with what can only be called deadpan stares. "You do know what *bingo* means, right?"

"We understand the modern way of speech," says

Nimue. "It goes with the power to see the future. There is something else that concerns my brother."

Getting his cue, Merlin points at my face. "You are not the Crimson Scourge! Even that fiend knows better than to listen to Dalston Rusus. That bard has twisted our sagas beyond repair."

Merlin may not be an old guy, but he certainly acts like one. I throw up hands. "That's what I was trying to tell you." I gesture to my face. "My name is Myla. My-la. Not the Crimson Scourge."

Merlin turns to the girl. "Come sister, let us depart."

"Whoa, there. You're brother and sister?"

In reply, Merlin and Nimue shoot me stares that can only be described as, *are you freaking kidding me?*

"Okay, I take it back. Total family resemblance here."

"We are holders of truth," states Merlin. "Unlike that bard."

"Hey, I get what it's like when your story is warped. Case in point. Two months ago, I got this big zit on my nose." Some part of me knows I'm babbling, but I can't seem to stop. "I know, gross. But the *Purgatory Enquirer* ran a front page story saying I had an alien parasite on my face. It was a whole *thing*."

"Sounds awful," says Merlin. He lifts his horse's reins. "Yet my sister and I must still depart."

"Wait, my brother," says Nimue. "Whoever this stranger is, perhaps she can be helpful."

"Spot on, Nimue. I traveled through time so I could stop Colossus from getting free. See, in my reality, there's been a big demonpocalypse. Nothing's left, unless you count the evil-doers. So I'm here to keep all the archdemons locked up."

"Most of them are already free," says Nimue. "Did you not hear the explosion before?"

"Yes," I reply. "But I thought that was thunder."

Nimue shakes her head. "That was the eight archdemons escaping their prison below Pendragon castle. Now we're off to see the Pendragon himself, so we can seek his advice."

"Isn't the Pendragon dead?" I ask.

"Not exactly," says Nimue. "Would you like to meet him?"

I tap the center of my chest. "Me?"

Three things about this. First, it's pretty fucking awesome to meet *the* Merlin and Nimue, even if the whole world and all of history is at stake. Second, these two pack a ton of power, so they could totally be useful later. And third, I'd love to meet the Pendragon. Mostly because he has a badass name.

Nimue nods. "You."

At the same time, Merlin glares at Nimue in a way that says, *I hate this idea.*

"Count me in," I say.

"Can you change forms and fly?" Nimue gestures toward my tail. Which takes the opportunity to wave again because, *of course it does.*

"Oh, I'm not a dragon shifter, if that's what you mean."

Nimue launches into a little bippity-boppity-boo

action. After some incantations and blue mist, I have myself a bluish horse of my own. It reminds me of Nightshade, my own mare from Lincoln.

Don't think it. Don't think it. Don't think it.

I think it.

Nightshade is now gone, same as everyone else, including Lincoln. Or maybe my guy is just being tortured somewhere instead of dead. Talk about awful.

My horse springs into action to trot behind Merlin and Nimue. Now that I'm in motion, my morose mood lightens a little. Thoughts of downing archdemons now come to the forefront of my mind.

Revenge, that's the ticket.

Since Merlin isn't Mister Chatty, I address Nimue. "What do you know about the Colossus' dungeon?"

"The archdemon king lies confined beneath Camelot. He is held inside a prison-crypt that's guarded by seven seals."

An odd sound comes from Merlin's mouth. I'm pretty sure he's grinding his teeth. "And those seals could easily be broken now that the other archdemons are free," he grumbles.

"If you can't point out positive things, it's better to be silent," counters Nimue.

Next the siblings prove they are truly related by launching into a long back-and-forth about who is really the downer of the family. There aren't any juicy magical details, though. Only bickering. After a few minutes, I tune them out. Our goal is clear anyway. After visiting the

Pendragon, we're off for Colossus and Camelot. That's all I care about.

As we ride on, I catch a tiny cloud in my peripheral vision. It's small, white, and moving faster than anything else in the sky. However, when I turn to look, I don't see anything.

"Fluff?" I whisper. "Is that you?"

Nothing happens, unless you count the ongoing spat between Nimue and Merlin.

Oh, well. It would have been nice to have a familiar face along, even if it is a renegade snow imp.

LINCOLN

Ximena, Null and Rage march along the road. I follow along through the underbrush, careful to keep myself hidden. Eventually, the archdemons find an obliging town with a stable full of horses. Ximena keeps to her word—no spells get cast—but that doesn't stop the archdemons from getting horses the old fashioned way. *Stealing them.* Soon, Ximena and company are trotting along on the main road to Camelot.

Fortunately for me, there are faster ways to King Arthur's castle. Long story short, if I cut across the open lands, I can bypass the archdemons, even if they ride on horseback. My goal isn't to beat them to Camelot, though. Instead, I plan to cook them a meal of roasted rabbit.

Yes, that is correct.

Me.

Three archdemons.

Rabbit dinner.

This is happening.

Once Ximena and company are out of sight, I hike across a countryside of rolling hills and towering forests. After a half-day's march, I find myself back at the main road once more. Soon I discover a clean and dry spot that's not too close to the road. There I set up camp.

Next comes what I call *the amazing all-purpose baculum display*. I do these demonstrations for warriors in training, but it's rare I get to execute them in the wild.

This is how it works. When I ignite the baculum, I can command angelfire into whatever shape I wish. Here I begin by conjuring myself an angefire axe to chop up some firewood. Next comes an angelfire knife to fashion a roasting spit. After that I summon a hunting bow. Within a few hours, I have a crackling fire and roasting rabbit.

My trap is set.

All that remains is my prey.

By the time the archdemons appear, the sun has fallen close to the horizon line. First, I see Ximena. She wears a silk overcoat that laces up-front, hiding the battle leathers she dons underneath. The knights behind her appear like a standard guard for a lady of means.

As they close in, I rise and wave. "Ho, there!"

Ximena raises her hand. All the horses stop. "Who are you?" she calls.

"Someone who knows that dragons hate the cold and love meals of roasted rabbit," I reply. "My name's Lincoln."

Rage leans forward in the saddle. "Should we kill him?"

Ximena rolls her eyes. "I shall not dignify that with an answer."

Null punches Rage's upper arm. "Told you she would say no. You should not have wasted the energy in asking."

Ximena slips off the saddle and takes her horse by the reins. She saunters over in my direction.

Perfect.

Ximena pauses just outside the circle of firelight. "How did you know I'm a dragon?"

"The short answer is this," I reply. "I'm part angel and can see your tail while you're in human form. The longer response is that I know you're Ximena, the Archdemon of Lust and Wrath."

Ximena steps closer. "My comrades wish to kill you. Why shouldn't I give them what they want?"

"Other than the fact that you'd have a sky-full of archangels after you?"

Ximena's eyes widen a fraction. "Yes, that."

"Why, it's obvious." I grin. "Never fight a dragon until you see the color of their scales." It's an old Furor saying which means, know your opponent before going into battle. It's a nice way of pointing out, *you've no idea what I'm capable of.*

Ximena eyes me from head to toe. "Fair enough." She turns to the knights. "Tie up the horses. I have business with this stranger." She seats herself on a large rock beside the fire. "You wear odd garb."

"I'm from the future." I hold up my hand, showing off the ring that encircles my finger.

"The Band of Epochs." Ximena clicks her tongue. "Not sure why Lucifer played around with such trinkets. Time travel causes nothing but trouble; I never dabble in the stuff." She tilts her head. "What do you want?"

"You're headed for Camelot. Once there, you shouldn't storm the gates. King Arthur must accept you peacefully."

Ximena shrugs. "We archdemons have changed, you know. We're no longer evil. King Arthur will welcome us with open arms."

"And that's your story," I state. "With me along, you can make that tale believable. Wish to enter Camelot? Have me make the introductions. I'm part angel, same as King Arthur."

"And why would a part-angel wish to help archdemons?"

"Two reasons. First, I came to this era in order to seek my fortune. King Arthur has plenty to spare."

Ximena nods. *Treasure is always a great motivator for dragons.* "And second?" she asks.

"You've no choice. You need my help. Present company excepted, these archdemons are a rather pitiful lot."

Ximena sighs. "True, but that's why we need Colossus. The other Archdemons aren't built to think or fight for themselves. Colossus must empower and guide them."

Speaking of Null and Rage, they stand twenty paces away, arguing about how to tie up the horses. I shake my head. "That's a sad sight, right there."

"They'll be better once our king is free."

"Yet you're still clever, even without Colossus."

Ximena's nostrils flare. "I'm a dragon."

"True." I offer her my hand. "Do we have a deal?"

"You're part angel. I probably can't trust you."

"You're all demon. I *definitely* can't trust you. Does it really matter so long as I get you inside Camelot?"

Ximena chuckles. "No, I suppose it doesn't."

"Excellent." We shake hands.

"I'll talk to the others."

Rising, Ximena paces over to where Null and Rage are arguing about horses. I can't hear all of their conversation, but my name seems to come up quite a bit. While they chat things through, I prod the fire's embers once more. As fresh waves of sparks rise up, the points of light seem to drift into the shape of different faces.

Myla.

Maxon.

My parents.

My people.

Another pang of longing twists up my rib cage. I've spent years with my Angelbound love at my side. No matter what the problem, we faced it together … and laughed.

Now, I don't even know if she's alive or safe. Saving the world just got a whole lot harder.

MYLA

*R*ide, ride ,ride.
Bleugh, bleugh, bleugh.

Merlin, Nimue and I spend hours trotting along forest paths in search of this Pendragon fellow. Supposedly, the Pendragon will know how to fix any Colossus-related jailbreaks. All along the road, the siblings quarrel about whose turn it is to cast cleaning spells on the horses' gear. Or record new incantations into their grimoire. Or add fresh power gems to their secret casket of mage goodies.

I now appreciate being an only child.

Eventually, the pair halt at a deserted pond. A line of pine trees surround the water's edge. Green needles cascade from the branches to make odd patterns on the water. The setting sun casts a yellow glow over the scene.

Huh.

What do Nimue and Merlin want with a pond? I'd ask, but every time I try to make conversation, it somehow turns into another *sibling battle* over chores. So I hang back and watch.

The pair approach the water's edge. Holding hands, they whisper incantations over the pond. I've seen mages link fingers before. It helps focus and enhance their spell.

Blue mist surrounds Nimue's right arm. *Magic.* The colored haze elongates. When it solidifies, the magical mist takes the form of a silver staff. The instrument stands tall as Nimue and is topped by a metal square lined with blue jewels.

As Nimue and Merlin continue whispering spells, the azure stones of the staff light up. Blue beams reach out onto the pond, making the waters bright as a summer sky. Next the mist tumbles from the staff to roll over the entire pond. *More magic.* The haze glitters for a moment before seeping into the water itself.

Thanks to the magic, the pond's surface turns as transparent as a window. And through that clear pane, I see a golden castle. Under the water. Just hanging out.

My mouth falls open with shock. A castle hidden in a lake? Sweet.

Nimue and Merlin raise their joined hands. The gleaming castle rises up to settle on the surface of the pool. The building is a small-ish affair made from pure gold. Bits of seaweed and lichen cling to its gleaming surface. A few fish flop about on the long walkway that stretches from the front gate to the shoreline.

Nimue and Merlin lower their arms. The castle's front

gate swings open. Moving in unison, the pair step across the water and into the castle itself.

Guess that's all the invitation I'm getting.

I hustle across the walkway and through the still-open front gate. Inside the castle, there's a small reception room. Two knights in golden armor lean against the wall, totally asleep.

Yes! It takes everything I have not to cheer. This is an *enchanted castle situation*, just like in fairy tales. A word pops into my brain.

Avalon.

Isn't that where King Arthur ends up? He gets enchanted along with his court and chucked to the bottom of a lake or something until he's needed again. Anyway, I'm pretty sure that's the story. Maybe this gold building is something similar.

I find Merlin and Nimue in the next room, which is a sizable hall. The walls are lined with shelf after shelf of leather-bound books. A huge round table fills the center of the space. A man sits there, his torso slumped over the tabletop. His shoulders rise and fall in a slow rhythm. *That settles it.* More enchanted sleep action. This is getting good.

Nimue and Merlin cross the room to kneel before the resting figure. The pair holds hand once more. "Arise, Pendragon," they say in unison.

The stones in Nimue's staff flare blue again. Tendrils of mist roll out from the gleaming rocks. Cords of magic wind about the resting man. For a moment, the sleeper is surrounded in an azure cloud. Then the mist enters the man's body. Light flares beneath his skin.

The spell is cast.

Yawning, the man sits up and opens his eyes. He's an older fellow with sage-dark skin, a thin face, and a wiry body. Despite being asleep for *who knows how long*, his chin and head are clean-shaven. Like Nimue and Merlin, he wears long silk robes. After blinking a few times, he stares at the siblings.

"Ah, Nimue and Merlin," he intones. "My favorite students."

The brother and sister bow their heads. "Pendragon. We are honored to be children of your academy."

I scan the walls of books with a new appreciation. This place must be a school. And considering how it turns out mages, I'm betting it's an academy of magic.

The edges of the Pendragon's mouth curl up into a sad smile. "It is good to see you, son and daughter of my heart. Yet, I doubt this is a happy visit. You're here regarding our school's most famous son, Arthur."

Nimue is first to speak. "It is indeed the reason we are here. Trouble looms with King Arthur."

Merlin balls his hands into fists. "Why did you choose him to lift Excalibur?"

"We've been through this many times," states the Pendragon. "I needed to lure out Colossus in order to capture him. That's why I set up the sword in the stone. As an extra enticement, I magically tied all my students to forever serve whoever removed Excalibur."

As the Pendragon speaks the words *forever serve*, Nimue and Merlin visibly shiver.

"It had to be done," continues the Pendragon. "By possessing the owner of Excalibur, Colossus could lead the human world without appearing to break any Heavenly rules. The archdemon king then possessed Arthur, giving that human enough strength to pull out the sword. So it was Colossus who chose King Arthur, not me."

Nimue and Merlin nod while staring at their feet. Not exactly a ringing endorsement of the Pendragon's plan.

"You have made a great sacrifice," adds the Pendragon. "It has changed history forever. No matter what a bard may sing, it was the three of us who ultimately trapped the archdemons in their prison-crypts with the *Opus Magica*."

Whoa. Now that's some heavy stuff.

All this time, I've been hanging back by the entrance archway. Now I step forward and raise my hand. "Hello there, Mister Pendragon. Myla Lewis here."

The Pendragon eyes me from head to toe. "You're the Great Scala from the future, come here to try and prevent Colossus from escaping."

Nimue and Merlin round on me. "You're the Great Scala? Why didn't you tell us?"

"Technically, I'm not the Great Scala in this particular era. Someone else has the gig and my igni won't talk to me. Well, they do make pirate noises, but I don't consider that speaking. Anyway." I step closer to the Pendragon. "You're right; I'm here to stop Colossus. And to do that, I need to be one hundred percent sure I understand things. You—" I point to the Pendragon "—aren't really King Arthur's father. You're his spiritual dad through this academy."

"Yes," says the Pendragon.

"And King Arthur didn't lock up Colossus and the other archdemons in some prison-crypts. It was you, Nimue and Merlin using a book called the *Opus Magica*."

The Pendragon nods. "Also true."

Nimue turns to me. "You're from the future. How do your people think Colossus and his minions were locked up?"

"Well." I wince, knowing this won't be a popular revelation. "Here's the honest truth. In my era, everyone thinks King Arthur invented the roundtable and imprisoned all the archdemons. We also think the Pendragon is Arthur's biological father."

"Lies!" cries Merlin. "The three of us imprisoned Colossus. The Pendragon created the round table. All the students here acted as equals. And it was the followers of Pendragon Academy who created the first thrax."

Nimue's mouth thins to an angry line. "And what about us?" No question which *us* she's talking about. *Herself and her brother.*

There's no point sugar-coating this. "We think you two ran off and left King Arthur hanging. And we also might think you're an old guy—" I gesture to Merlin for this part "—and you're an enchantress who lives in a lake." I point to Nimue.

The siblings turn silent. Both stare at me with opened mouths and bugged out eyes. No way will this quiet last for long, though. These two can chatter for hours over chores. Being framed as villains in history? That could take days for them to process.

The Pendragon must have the same idea. He stands and raises his hands, palms forward. It's a clear motion that means, *no chitchat.* "You did not come here to discuss such things. What has happened?"

Nimue and Merlin still look stunned, so I decide to take the lead. "Eight archdemons have escaped from under your castle. Now we need to stop Colossus from escaping his prison under Camelot. Since you three locked him up before, I'm feeling pretty good that we can nail this puppy. Not that I'd ever hurt a puppy, but you get the idea."

"This time, we *must* convince Arthur to help us," says Nimue.

The Pendragon sighs. "We all know Arthur is unreliable."

"We do?" I ask. "Because I'd like a little more on that."

"There is no time to speak of Arthur's failings," says the Pendragon. "We must empower a new *Opus Magica.*"

The Pendragon presses his palms atop the table. Blue power and light flow between his hands. The energy quickly congeals into a leather-bound book that holds two seals on the cover, one white and one red. "And here it is. A new *Opus Magica.*"

Merlin frowns. "The last *Opus Magica* took hundreds of years to charge with power, not to mention thousands of mages. The other archdemons are headed to Camelot right now. We don't have time to start a fresh book."

"Uh, guys?" I gesture to the *Opus Magica*. "Not sure how this thing locks up Colossus. You've got a book with two colored disc things glued to the top."

"They are magical seals," says Nimue. She looks at me as if to say, *duh*.

"Right." I look to the Pendragon. "So how does *all that* work?"

The Pendragon rests his hands atop the volume. "Mages write their names in the book. That action pulls some of their soul and magic onto the page. Over time, enough power builds up so that the book can pull the eight archdemons into the first seal—" here he touches the white disc "—and Colossus into the second. They all can not be imprisoned together. Otherwise, Colossus is too powerful to contain."

I tilt my head and look at the two round discs. Not a lot of real estate there. "And the seals are portals to a dungeon or something?"

"Precisely," replies the Pendragon. "And a rather secure dungeon, if I may say so. I have built failsafes into the fail-safes. It won't be fast or simple for Colossus to escape, even with the other archdemons loose."

I'm about to ask for more details on the whole *failsafe thing*, but Nimue jumps in first.

"Merlin and I were the final mages to write our names in the last *Opus Magica*." Nimue stares at the new book like it's covered in flesh eating bacteria. "We were hoping for something that we could use today."

"This is what I have to give you." The Pendragon yawns.

"And now I must continue my rest. You may summon me again when the Staff of Pendragon recharges."

A memory appears. Nimue and Merlin just raised this very castle with a silver staff. Now that thing has a name: the Staff of Pendragon. Another thought knocks around the back of my head. *Something about mage staffs is important, but I can't place what it is.*

"It will take months to charge the Staff of Pendragon again," says Nimue. She runs her fingers over the the gems along the staff's top. Before, those stones looked blue. Now, they're pure white.

"The time will pass more quickly than you think," intones the Pendragon. He rests his head onto the table once more.

With that motion, the castle begins sinking into the lake. Water rushes through the entrance archway. Chilly liquid curls around my feet. Merlin grabs the new *Opus Magica*, then he and Nimue race for the exit. *Great idea.* I follow them out of the castle and across the thin bridge to shore. The moment I set foot on dry land, the castle sinks beneath the pond to a symphony of gurgling noises.

Merlin and Nimue stand nearby, chatting about all the mages they know who might sign the new *Opus Magica*. They seem to think there aren't many.

From the corner of my eye, I see another white puffball flit into a nearby pine tree. My breath catches.

Could that be Fluff?

I scan the nearby line of pines, but there's no sign of Captain Fluffbottom. A splash sounds behind me. I step up to the water's edge, wondering if Fluff fell into the pond. Yet there's no sign of a snow imp in the water. It's just my own reflection.

And it winks at me.

That's a shocker because I didn't wink. *Only my reflection did.* I lean in closer to the water. Maybe it's some kind of magical leftover from when Nimue and Merlin raised the Pendragon.

My reflection smiles. Again, I'm not grinning. At all. Then she speaks.

There is still time to save Drusus.

I've heard that voice before. It's the one that sounded in my head back at the wrath coven. That time, she told me to turn around and talk to Allimari. Then later, she wanted me to chat with Remy, the new archivist. I thought this was some kind of spell to force me into making new friends or something.

So that theory is a bust.

Now, this person isn't just a voice. She looks like me. And she's giving pep talks about Drusus?

This is too much.

Ignoring this entity has gotten rid of it in the past, so that's just what I do now. Merlin and Nimue are busy conjuring up stuff to camp for the night. I help them as best I can.

And I avoid going anywhere near the water.

LINCOLN

For the rest of the evening, I sit by the fire and keep careful watch. Ximena, Null, and Rage don't need to sleep, so I've extra incentive to stay awake. Still, Ximena is my main source for any company during the night. She reviews in detail the archdemon plans for a party, and explains exactly what my role must be.

The scheme seems solid enough. The archdemons will say they have changed their ways and wish to hold a celebration in the magical castle of Avalon. The archangels will be invited to the event. In Ximena's opinion, said invitees will be gullible enough to attend. Once the celebration begins, the archangels will get locked up in Avalon.

I point out the obvious: the archangels will expect a trap. However, Ximena maintains that the Crimson Scourge has an unbeatable plan in place. And I cannot argue with the work the Crimson Scourge has done so far. The eight archdemons are loose now. And in my future,

Colossus definitely got free. So that's another success for the Crimson Scourge.

Now it's my job to figure out how that last part happened … and then stop it before it begins.

At last, the horizon lightens. Ximena volunteers to give me her horse to ride while she takes dragon form and flies the rest of the way. We take to the road (or in Ximena's case, to the skies) and arrive at Camelot by late morning. It's a boxy structure with a few towers. A steep wall surrounds the main building.

To be honest, my childhood imaginings of this castle were rather more grand than this reality. Most thrax palaces could consume multiple Camelots and still have room to spare.

I frown. *If I've been misinformed about the appearance of Camelot, what else don't I know?*

We approach the front gate. Ximena has retaken her human form and once again resembles a lady of means in a riding coat and breeches. Null and Rage flank her. All three archdemons hang back while I step up and knock.

"All hail!" I call.

A small guard window slides open in the wooden door. "Who goes there?" Although the door-hole isn't a large one, I can see that the guard has the mismatched eyes of a thrax. *Good.*

I step closer to show off my own irises: one blue and one brown. "I am a traveling knight who wishes to offer my services to King Arthur."

"And those three behind you?" asks the guard.

"Part of my company."

The guard sniffs. "You're dressed strangely."

"I'm here with important information for your king. That should count for more than my attire. *In thrax sic hunt.*" This Latin phrase is a thrax password from Arthurian times. We still use it in the modern day.

The guard nods. "Enter."

The door slowly swings open. It takes an effort, but I hide my look of surprise. Back home at Arx Hall, my guards would rather die than allow a stranger onto our grounds without my expressed permission. King Arthur is the one who supposedly built up all those rules in the first place.

Has something happened to the king?

The guard allows me to step through without even locking the gate behind him, so I take that duty on my own.

"This way," says the guard. "I'll show ye to the reception hall."

"Thank you."

As we step toward the castle proper, I carefully scan the open grounds between the main structure and the surrounding wall. There are no other guards nearby, at least not that I can see. *What a disaster.* This is quite possibly the worst castle security I've ever witnessed.

The guard guides me into Camelot proper. We pass through a series of stone corridors and finally, into a grand reception hall. The vaulted ceiling is lined with multi-colored pennants. I spot ones for my favorite knights of the round table. There are the Sirs Lancelot, Gawain, and Galahad. Percival, Tristan, and Kay. Of course, there's no mention of Nimue or Merlin, but that's to be expected, considering how those two magic users deserted their king.

The hall takes on a dream-like sheen. *I can't believe I'm here. Camelot.*

The center of the room is filled by a large round table. Knights sit about it. Well, *sit* isn't the right word. *Lounge, perhaps?* Lancelot even has his feet up on a nearby bench. I must have caught them all at a festival for relaxation. We thrax have one every five years or so.

The guard clears his throat. "Announcing a visitor for the king."

That's when I notice the star of this particular show: King Arthur. He sits on a raised platform at the far wall of the chamber. His golden throne is adorned with curlicues.

That's unexpected. King Arthur is supposed to sit at the table with his knights. *A first among peers*, as the bard sings.

The king himself looks nothing like his picture in books. He's a small and round fellow who wears wears a too-small tunic and pants. The clothing can only be described as *overdue for the laundress*. With Arthur's every breath, the scent of stale alcohol wafts across the chamber. His skin looks so pale as to be unhealthy. A thinning mop of brown hair covers his head.

"Well," says Arthur. "What do you want?" He accents his question with an exceedingly loud belch.

I blink hard, not believing what I'm seeing. This is King

Arthur, the very thrax who rescued us all from *the brutal time*? The man who transformed our people from a ragtag bunch of part-angels into an elite fighting force?

Another bodily noise follows up the belch. Foul scents assault my nose. Evidently, Arthur had beans during his latest meal.

I shake my head. *This is awful.*

Still, Arthur locked up Colossus somewhere in this very castle. He's my key to preventing the world's end. He may be a gaseous rogue, but I'll deal with it.

"My king," I begin. "I've come to you with dire news. There are archdemons outside."

King Arthur jams his finger in his nose. *Honestly.* Maxon has better manners. "You don't say." Thankfully, the king chooses to remove the offending digit from his head. With any luck, the *bodily function roundup* is over for now.

"The archdemons have changed from evil to good," I explain.

"Which ones?" asks Arthur.

"All eight. They've been released from their prison under Pendragon castle. In honor of their change to goodness, they wish to hold a party here at Camelot."

These words have an unexpected effect on the room. All the knights stand at attention. Arthur rises from his throne.

"A celebration in my honor?" he asks.

I frown. "Your honor? I don't follow."

"Think, man," bellows Arthur. "It was my imprisonment of the eight archdemons which changed their ways." He stomps his foot on the floor. "And I've still got Colossus locked up right under here. Without their king, the other archdemons aren't much to worry about."

It takes considerable self-restraint not to launch into a lecture on castle security. Leaders simply do not bellow out the location of key prisoners, even when under torture, let alone at the promise of a party.

For the first time, I wonder if the Crimson Scourge is a diabolical genius … or if King Arthur is merely supremely gullible. In either case, the demonpocalypse began here somehow.

"Bring the archdemons in!" cries the king. "Let's hold a festival to celebrate all the wondrous things I've done." He turns to the knights. "See? I'm so marvelous, even the archdemons come to honor me."

The guard shrugs and marches off to allow archdemons into Camelot. *This can't be happening.* And by that, I mean, there must be another explanation. King Arthur simply is not this daft.

Arthur turns to his knights. "Galahad, summon my bard. Lancelot, go fetch Merlin and Nimue." At these orders, the knights in question rise and leave the chamber.

That's yet another surprise. *Summon Merlin and Nimue?* I thought the two ran off, never to be seen again. Arthur makes it sound like the greatest magic users of all time are nothing more than buttons left in the back of a drawer— something to grab the moment when needed.

There must be an explanation for all this.

Time to do some exploration around Camelot.

I bow to the king. "If you don't mind, your Majesty, I should like a change of clothes." *And to see if this castle is under a spell.*

"Aye." King Arthur gestures toward the exit archway. "Find a servant. Or a wench. Do what you want, just don't miss the celebration of me."

"I shall attend. Of that you can be certain."

All my life, I thought humans were the ones who didn't really know King Arthur. They had the wrong castles, history, everything. Now I suspect that none of us truly understood the man. Turning, I leave the reception hall with one goal in mind.

Find out what's really happening here ... before Colossus is set free.

29

MYLA

G *rrrrrrr.*

It's late morning, and Nimue and Merlin stand under a tree, chatting about mage stuff. They conjured a pretty mean breakfast, but now they're still sipping some kind of magic juice from huge mugs and making small talk. There's no sign that we're actually packing up camp and taking off any time soon.

Looks like some folks need extra motivation.

I sashay over to the tree in question. "Do you guys need help packing anything so we can leave? After all, we're off for Camelot. Tick-tock."

"It is a fine morning," says Nimue. "Slow down and enjoy it."

I stare at her and count off a good five seconds. "Wow, that was a nice break. Let's get going now."

Merlin cracks a smile. "That was no time at all."

"I disagree. Back home, I'd have reviewed a million

souls by now. Not to mention all my work with the fading angels." I really drag out the words *fading angels*, hoping that will grab their attention.

Nope. The *fading angels line* does nothing. Nimue and Merlin keep yammering away. Something about crystals storing power. Whatever.

I clear my throat. "Guys?" They turn in my direction. "Honestly, all this sitting around is making me nuts. Can we go already? I haven't been this bored since high school." *And that's saying something.*

"We are preparing ourselves," says Nimue. "Magic users require extra time."

"Well, everyone I know might be erased from all history unless I figure some things out, fast. Plus my husband is missing and may be running around here somewhere. So anything you can do to actually get your magical asses in gear? That would be most appreciated."

"Point made," says Merlin. And he turns his back on me.

I come to a major revelation. *Merlin is a total dick.*

Looking away from Merlin and Nimue, I scan the road that I'd very much like to be traveling on. That's when it happens.

A little black blob appears on the horizon.

Can it be? *Yes, it is!*

A trio of figures have appeared on the road ahead. Yay! If nothing else, I can hitch myself another ride out of here.

Nimue and Merlin notice the newcomers as well. Both frown so deeply, I worry that they'll permanently crease their faces or something.

"Oh, no," whispers Merlin.

"What is it?" I ask. "Archdemons?" Because I've been hoping to fight one or two of them along the way. It's better than sitting on a rock and watching mages.

"No, it's some knights of the round table," sighs Nimue. The way she says the words *knights of the round table*, it's the way I might say, *annual vaginal exam.* Not fun.

The knights close in and sure enough, it's none other than Lancelot and some other medieval dudes I don't recognize. My heart speeds. *The* Sir Lancelot! Amazing. Not that I'm the type to *fan girl,* but come on. Lancelot is Mister Romance. Anyone could get a little starry eyed.

The knights show up on their oversized white horses. Up close, I can see that Lancelot has a swoosh of blond hair under his helm and one of those pinch-lipped expressions on his face. "Bonjour," he says in his cute French accent. "Your presence eez demanded at Camelot."

Merlin nods. "We'll be there within the hour."

Lancelot and his dudes turn and gallop away. My mouth falls so far open, a bug flies into the back of my throat. *Yuck.*

Unlike before, Nimue and Merlin are now all action. They head over to their horses and mount up.

"Hey!" I call. "What was that?"

"A summons," says Merlin. He doesn't add a *duh* on the end of his statement, but it's totally implied.

"So you'll just go." That's what I say, but what I'm thinking is something else entirely. The statement goes along the line of, *didn't you desert King Arthur?* That implies no more summoning ever, or at the very least, lots of ignoring such summons.

This world is a really freaky place.

"I think I understand," says Nimue.

"Good," I snark. "Because I don't."

Nimue raises her hands. Fresh bits of blue smoke whirl around her palms.

Then they slam into me.

One moment, I'm standing in my Scala robes. The next, I'm back on my blue horse.

"Better?" asks Nimue. "Not everyone is comfortable mounting."

Without another word, Nimue and Merlin take off at a gallop. I flick my horses reins and follow. Who cares if I don't understand much of what's going on? At last, the moment is here.

Camelot, here I come.

30

MYLA

amelot, what a shit show.

Once we arrive, Merlin and Nimue shove me into a tower room. The chamber is a small and round with one skinny window and a mattress stuffed with straw.

"So." I eye the pair carefully. "What's with this?"

"We must raise Avalon," intones Merlin. "On order of the king."

"Huh. Like you did the golden castle with Pendragon?"

"Yes," replies Merlin. "We are magically bound to serve King Arthur."

At this point, a rude-ish question pops into my head. Which I should just allow to pass by. No need to pry into personal stuff.

Don't ask the question. Don't ask the question. Don't ask the question.

Fuck it.

"If you'd sworn to serve, how come you were roaming around the countryside in a fake wagon?"

Nimue lifts her chin. "We were exiled from the castle."

I'd question this some more, but Nimue's chin is wobbling a little bit. Merlin's eyes glisten with tears. Clearly, whatever happened with King Arthur really upset them both.

"We must take our leave now," says Merlin. "You should rest."

"Hey," I counter. "It's like I told you before; I don't need any more sleep." I step toward the door. Nimue holds up her arm with her palm flat and facing toward me. The meaning is clear: *Stay in the freaking tower.*

"We can't have you roaming the castle," declares Merlin.

Pausing for a moment, I consider the situation. I could protest, but these are magic users. If I don't play along, they might cast a nasty spell. As I recall, turning people into frogs was a big deal during this era.

I don't want to be amphibian.

And I've broken out of worse situations.

So I lie my ass off.

"Oh gee golly." I raise my arms and let out an extended yawn. "I am so darned sleepy."

Not sure why this lie means I have to talk like I'm on a children's TV program, but whatever. I'm rolling with it.

"We shall return when we can," says Nimue. With that, the two mages step out the door. There's the familiar snick of a lock being turned. I give them a full minute to take off before I try the handle.

Yup. Totally locked.

Giving up on the door, I head over to the window. There are a list of ways I could escape now, but one option is my favorite. I cross my fingers and call outside. "Fluffbottom?"

Nothing happens.

"Come on Fluff. I know you've been following me. I need your help here."

My new best friend appears on my shoulder. "Hi, hi."

I smile my face off. "Hi yourself, little guy." I scratch his tummy with my pinky. "Why didn't you appear before?"

"Shy, shy. I flew away when trouble came. Won't do that ever again."

"Don't worry about the lab. Anyone can get scared when a mountain's about to explode. You can do me a favor now, though."

"Yes, yes."

"Get me a key, will you?"

"Bye, bye." Fluffbottom spreads his furry wings and takes off through the window.

Huh. That bye-bye wasn't exactly conclusive. Fluffbottom may just take off at this point. He did before, after all.

Happily, Fluff returns in a few minutes. A large bronze key is held tightly in his little claws. "Back, back!"

"Well done, Fluff!" The imp drops the tiny bronze treasure onto my palm. "Ooh, it's a skeleton key, too. Even better."

I cross the room and set the key in the lock. *Snick.* Sure

enough, the door opens with ease. Fluff marches across the floor with his ears and tiny tail in the air. So proud. He pauses to face me, his tiny chin raised. "Help, help. Fluff-bottom is the best."

"That you are."

"More help?"

"Well, if you want to be super useful, go around and look for anything that might give details on how to stop Colossus from getting loose."

"Failsafes and failsafes," says Fluff.

I tilt my head. "What does that mean?"

"From Lucifer's book. Prison-crypt has tricks and traps. Must break through seven seals to set Colossus free. It's hard to open. Gives us time."

"The Pendragon talked about that. Are the seals like doors?"

"Yes, yes," repeats Fluff. "One for each deadly sin and its archdemon. I find more for you." With that, the imp vanishes and does whatever Fluff thinks would helpful in this kind of situation.

Yay, Fluff.

I slip out of the room and head down a curly flight of stairs. The next floor down is empty. I figure that's a good spot to start. Stealing out of the stairs, I find a wooden room lined with twelve doors and as many mirrors. Pausing, I wait for the inevitable rumble of servants.

No one shows up.

This floor lies deserted, which is odd. Even dumpy little castles like this one need tons of serfs to do even the most basic stuff. Believe me. After being married to Lincoln, I know these things.

Ah, Lincoln.

Once again, the thought of my husband fills my heart with unease. Is he safe?

Shaking my head, I focus on the task at hand, namely opening doors and snooping around. I open the first door. It's a long and thin dressing room filled with boots.

Wait, boots?

Scrunching up my face, I think this though. Medieval folks are always organizing stuff into a single spot. Like a buttery, a creamery, or my favorite, the chocolaterie. Maybe this is a boot-ery or something?

Meh. Whatever it is, it isn't helping me figure out how to stop Colossus from escaping.

I move on to the next door. Once again, the skeleton key works perfectly. This is a larger space and it's nothing but crowns. Before, I thought the boot-ery might be a place to benefit everyone. But keeping tons of crowns around is for one person only, King Arthur.

Interesting. That might explain why there are no servants around. This must be the king's private dressing area. Once the drama of getting ready is over, everyone moves on with their day.

Only ten more doors to go. I try the next in line.

It's a chamber of underwear only. All onesie cotton thingies, too. As a matter of fact, this is the same exact style that I'd put on baby Maxon.

Whoa. King Arthur in a onesie. Can't unsee that now.

Moving on.

This door opens to a larger space that holds a bunch of leather armor.

Even better, it also holds my half-naked husband. A knot of worry unwinds within my soul.

Oh, Hells yes.

31

LINCOLN

*A*fter I snuck away from the reception chamber, it took me twenty minutes and two helpful servants to find where King Arthur stores his extra battle gear. For a time, I tried on various armor options. Then the door opens.

Which brings me to the present moment.

"Myla?" I ask.

Without saying a word, the woman rushes in and kisses my face off.

That's my Myla, all right.

There are a million things I could say now. How much I've missed her. The secrets I learned about archdemons, the Crimson Scourge, Colossus, and the upcoming party. But all those thoughts vanish as her mouth moves across mine. I slide my hands down her thighs, grip the folds of her Scala robes, and pull the fabric upward.

Myla pauses. "The world's about to end, everyone we

know could vanish permanently, and Colossus might escape any minute … but we're about to have sex?" Her pupils are flashing red, which means she's all for the carnal option here.

As am I.

In reply, I hoist her robes higher. "I believe we are."

Footsteps sound from outside the closet. We pause. After another kiss, I drop Myla's robes, steal closer to the door, and listen. It's hard to hear much, but I catch the odd word.

"What's going on?" whispers Myla.

"Some servants are here; it seems Arthur demands a change of clothes." My eyes widen as I hear the last bit of news. "And Xavier is on his way."

Myla's irises keep flashing red. "So no sex."

"Not yet. In a matter of seconds, this place will be overrun with servants."

She grumbles as she straightens her Scala robes. "Humans … end of the world … pain in my ass. GAH!"

I couldn't agree more.

Myla eyes the leather armor. "My robes won't change here. I should probably grab some battle gear."

Which is logical. Myla can get replacement robes made, given enough time. She quickly finds a decent set of leathers.

"Where is Xavier?" she asks.

I press my ear to the door once more. "Can't tell. We'll need to actually leave this chamber to discover that fact." I finish pulling on my leather breastplate. "To bad there aren't any weapons in here, but I do have my baculum."

"Me, too." Myla pats the pockets of her body armor. "All set. Now how should we work this?"

"Meaning?"

"We're clearly strangers in a strange closet."

I hook my arm about her. "We walk out like superstars and demand to know where your father is."

"What can I say?" asks Myla. "I love this plan."

Together, Myla and I step out of the closet and into a whirlwind of activity. I march over to a nearby servant.

"Excuse me, my good woman. Where are the archangels gathering?"

"On the southern courtyard, sir." She gestures out the thin window. Sure enough, I see a small gathering of white robes and golden wings. Although his back is toward me, I'd know one particular outline anywhere.

Xavier.

Myla sighs. *I must imagine that it's good to have your archangel Dad around, even if he doesn't know who you are.*

"Thank you." I bow my head. "If you'll excuse us."

As Myla and I step away, my wife speaks to me in a low voice. "Well done, sir."

"Thank you, milady. Now let's get in some trouble."

32

MYLA

*a*s Lincoln and I navigate through Camelot's halls, I catch the outline of someone someone lurking in a far-off alcove. A slice of light illuminates the man's face.

I stop.

Look.

Rub my eyes.

Look again.

No doubt about it.

Drusus is here.

And I'm not talking about the angelic version of this guy. Before me stands the walking, talking, living Drusus. A little younger, but still him. I mean, the angelic Drusus wouldn't tell me *when* he'd been alive, but I'd assumed it was about a hundred years ago. Still, there really isn't any reason Drusus couldn't be living now.

Lincoln draws his brows together. "Why have we stopped?"

I nod toward the shadowy guy. "That's Drusus," I whisper.

"Are you certain?"

Good question.

I clear my throat and then speak in an extra loud voice. "Excuse me, are you Drusus?

The man steps out of the shadows. "I haven't been called that name in years. These days I'm known as Dalston Rusus the Bard." He bows, a movement that shows off the extra-huge feather in his mega hat. "At your service."

I carefully scan the dude. Sure enough, he's wearing the *puffy shorts and tights combo* that's popular with minstrels of this time. He even carries a lute.

The question tumbles from my mouth, seemingly on its own. "What are you doing here?"

Drusus takes off his hat with a flourish. "I shall sing for King Arthur's court. By my songs, shall all learn the greatness of Arthurian rule."

I smack my lips. "I really wouldn't do that if I were you."

"Why not?" asks Drusus. "I only take the deeds my king describes and place them to music."

"What if I told you that you single-handedly erase the true nature of the Pendragon, Merlin and Nimue from history?"

"That's not possible."

"It's more than possible," says Lincoln. "In fact, I predict your songs will be turned into books that children will love —and be misled by—for centuries to come."

"Here's the thing," I say. There's not much time here, so I'm cutting to the point. "You need to change, honey."

"What do you mean? I serve my king."

I wag my finger at him. "Don't play dumb with me. You know what I'm talking about. Your songs about King Arthur are total lies. Now you're all, *hey I'm just doing my job*, while I'm the one stuck watching you sit on a cloud and mope."

"Mope?"

"Your angel self acts all droopy and sad for eternity. Only you don't last for eternity. You start to fade because it's horrible to watch how your lying songs ruin people."

"Ruin," says Drusus.

I set my fist on my hip. "You keep repeating what I say."

Drusus shrugs. "You are strange girl who has cornered me in a hallway. Verily, it is much to comprehend."

"Fine," I say. "I'll try to speak more plainly."

"I thank thee."

"If you do the wrong thing here—" I point to the ground "—Then you will suck at being an angel up there —" I gesture to the sky "—and eventually you will die. Forever."

"Verily?" asks Drusus.

"Soooooooooo verily. The time to stop all your angelic suffering isn't *after* you're on a cloud and look like you've listened to break-up tunes for ten years solid. The moment to change your eternal fate is now. You're on a bad path, friend."

Drusus pales. "I shall go to Hell?"

"Depends how you define Hell," says Lincoln. "You don't have to be roasted over a fire to be tortured."

Drusus takes a half-step backward. "I'm not certain of what you speak."

Sure, he isn't.

"Look," I say. "Let me give this one last try. You need to get off the Sucksville Road and travel something that leads to Happy Forever Town. That way, when you're hanging on your cloud, you can look down and go, *wow, my shitty offspring isn't a slimeball who's killing sick people, he's actually a good person who gives a crap about someone besides himself.* You know what I'm talking about."

Drusus stares at his slippy-on leather booties. "Perhaps. But what must I do?"

"Just go out there and sing the truth," I state. " You have gifts; they're given to you for a reason. You're supposed to use them for good."

Drusus bows so low, his super-floppy hat falls off. "I thank thee for thy wisdom." After putting on his hat again, Drusus marches off into the shadows. *At double-speed.*

I look to Lincoln. "What do you think the chances are that he'll listen?"

"Fifty-fifty," says Lincoln.

I sigh. "We'll see."

33

MYLA

*a*fter the chat with Drusus, we quickly find the southern courtyard. I'm used to the castles in Antrum, which basically require a magical GPS to find where they hide the snacks. It's super-easy here. Soon Lincoln and I step out onto a place of cobblestones, grass and trees that stands behind the castle proper. And there he is.

My father.

Or rather, my Not-Dad. It's my father from a previous time before he met my mother.

Weird.

Not-Dad stands in golden armor, conversing with the other archangels. I scan the yard. There's like, one guard around. No knights or King Arthur.

Weird-er.

I whisper to Lincoln. "The security around here sucks. You and I are total strangers and yet we're waltzing around, asking questions and stealing supplies. I got chucked into a tower bedroom like forever ago and no one noticed I snuck out."

"Tower room?"

"Long story." It's actually not that long but I'm really getting into this now. "I mean, it's one thing when it's only King Arthur hanging around or whatever. But now, my Not-Dad is out on the freaking lawn with no one to greet him and a guard who looks like he's sleeping off too much mead and wench-time."

Lincoln nods. "I met King Arthur. If that guard is anything like his king, then that is precisely what he's sleeping off."

I open my mouth super-wide in what I consider to be my *mega drama shock* face. This is one of the situations which calls for its use. "No. Way. King Arthur *knows* about this crappy guard situation?"

"He does. And I hate to break this to you, but King Arthur is a bit of a disappointment. I searched the castle for a time before we met up. I'd hoped there was some reason for his behavior such as say, a compulsion spell. Unfortunately, I think King Arthur is just a medieval douchebag."

I stare at Lincoln for a long moment, my mouth still hanging open. "That's a shocker, but I do see a silver lining here."

A smile quirks Lincoln's mouth. "So what's your plan?"

And yes, I do have one.

"There's no guard or whatever to stop us here," I state.

"That's a bonus. I'll just walk up to Not-Dad and start talking. My father has a thing about politeness. Remember when that lady kept petting his angel feathers and he wouldn't stop her?"

"I do," replies Lincoln. "And, if you don't mind my saying so, Xavier has a soft spot for women." Lincoln lets the thought hang out there.

I know what my guy means. It's not that my father is a dude-hater, but he is a capital-G General. If someone's in armor and asking questions, my father's personality goes, *shields up.* But if I walk up all solo and sweet—well, as sweet as I get—then there's a better chance Not-Dad will spill some intel.

I crack my neck. "On it."

Lincoln kisses my cheek. "Go do your thing."

Marching forward, I pause behind Not-Dad and tap his golden-clad shoulder. He turns around and damn. *Does he ever look miserable.* There's a hollowness to Not-Dad's eyes that just cracks my heart.

That's when it hits me. This Not-Dad misses Mom, even though he doesn't know her. I've heard, *it's better to have loved and lost than never loved at all.* Now I get it. My real father always has a fire in his soul. Even when Dad was suffering; he had a purpose. Mom. They truly love each other.

And that realization makes my eyes kind of watery.

"Can I help you?" asks Not-Dad.

This is a moment for verbal fireworks. Leadership. Glamour. I take in a deep breath.

"Hey, so I'm your daughter."

Not my best opening.

"Are you now?" Not-Dad looks at me like I'm insane. "And who is this demon on your shoulder?"

My brows lift. My snow imp is back?

Sure enough, the little fuzzball materializes on my shoulder to salute my father. "Captain Fluffbottom."

"You have a demon imp as a pet?" asks Not-Dad.

"Buddy, buddy."

"This is my friend, Fluff." I scratch his tummy with my pinky. "He's been secretly stalking me for a while, it seems. How did you see him?"

Not-Dad grins. "I see many things. Just as I see how you are a quasi-demon."

This is a classic situation, by the way. My father has a list of unique super-powers a mile long. For a lot of them, he doesn't even know they're special until another archangel or whoever can't do them. Like seeing supposedly-invisible imps.

Never one to be ignored, my tail swoops around to wave at Not-Dad as well. I roll my eyes. "My tail also says hello."

Not-Dad bows slightly at the waist. "Greetings to you, your imp, and tail."

A sparkle lights up Not-Dad's blue eyes. I've seen my father when he's done with people. There are glaciers that seem fiery when compared to my father's glare. But now? Not-Dad is interested.

"Greetings back at ya," I reply. "So, uh, what's going on?"

A small smile rounds Not-Dad's mouth. He's totally humoring me, but whatever. As long as I get intel, I'm a happy girl.

"A joyous event," replies Not-Dad. "The archdemons have learned the error of their ways. Merlin and Nimue will soon raise Avalon so we may have a proper celebration of their change."

"Wow, is that ever a bad idea."

Not-Dad shrugs. "My fellow archangels have flown out to inspect each archdemon. None have used magic or committed any sins. They appear legitimate in their transformation."

"Only because Colossus is still locked up. Not sure if you're aware of this one, but the archdemons are totally *meh* without their leader. Plus Merlin and Nimue are raising Avalon? I saw one of these underground castle things. Everyone was trapped in an enchanted sleep."

"It's rather easy to raise an enchanted castle," says Not-Dad. "The sleeping enchantment is a different matter. There's only one way to activate it. You must wield a special staff loaded with charged gemstones."

A memory appears. Back in Lucifer's lab, Lincoln and I found an empty box labeled for gemstones to the Staff of Avalon. Gears in my mind churn, aligning this old recollection and Not-Dad's new words. "I've got news for you. The gemstones for the Staff for Avalon have been found."

Not-Dad shrugs. "The gems won't function without the staff itself."

"Hah." Now I'm on familiar territory. Real-Dad and I have this verbal battle all the time. "Did you actually *see* the thing get destroyed?" Not-Dad opens his mouth to reply, but I keep going. *Here comes one of my fave arguments.* "This is like a story where the evil dude falls off a cliff ... but you know he's coming back. Unless you saw that staff thing broken up before your own eyes, I wouldn't believe it was gone."

Not-Dad gives me a dry look. "I *did* see it broken up before my eyes."

"Oh." I debate walking away—this is turning into a whopper of an embarrassing conversation. Yet I can't. My family, my people, and my entire world are all at risk. I lift my chin. "I take it back. Who cares what you saw? It is hella dumb to party with a bunch of archdemons in an enchanted castle."

"All the archangels voted; the majority wish to cele-brate." Not-Dad sighs. "Yet I know your argument would have been accepted by Lucifer."

This. Is. Awesome.

True fact: I've spent hours chatting with *real Dad* about the rules of archangel life. I totally have this one covered.

"I've got an idea," I announce. "Let's hold an official archangel revote. I'll stand in for Lucifer. Maybe the results will be different." Most archangel votes are close. They rarely agree on anything.

Not-Dad's blue eyes glow with intensity. "You know about that rule? How?"

The words just tumble from my mouth. "I'm your daughter from the future. You're blabby."

Not-Dad eyes me carefully. I know my real father enough to realize this is his assessing gaze, the one which silently asks, *is she full of crap?* Before Not-Dad can come to a decision, a voice echoes across the open grounds.

"I, King Arthur, have arrived! Let my celebration begin!"

I should stay focused on convincing Not-Dad to hold a re-vote. Yet I can't. King Arthur just showed up and announced himself.

The real King Arthur. Wow.

Some small part of me screams that was lame protocol. Kings just don't announce themselves. Even so, I can't help but feel little medieval butterflies take up residence in my stomach.

Did I mention this is the real King Arthur?

The king steps closer and whoa. Lincoln was right. I mean, I knew my guy wouldn't lie. Even so, it's one thing to *hear* that King Arthur is a hot mess. It's another thing to see a royal shit-show in full color. He's all potbelly, filthy clothes, and wobbly gait. Plus, he's got eight archdemons marching behind him as well as a figure cloaked in red. No question who that is.

The Crimson Scourge.

I suck in a quick breath. This is so very, very bad.

34

MYLA

King Arthur meanders onto the grassy field. Although Lincoln and I only stand a few yards away, we can still smell the *regal booze breath*. The king stumbles over to a wooden bench, leans over, and grips the top. His entire body sways as Arthur tries to hoist himself up.

Once.

Twice.

Three times.

It's the fourth time that Arthur finally hauls himself to stand atop the bench. By now, everyone has stopped chatting. All eyes are focused on the so-called king. So there's no reason for Arthur to set his pinkies into either side of his mouth and let out a loud whistle. Yet that's what he does anyway.

"First of all," says the king. "Have the rascals arrived?

Merlin and Nimue, show yourselves!" He scans the crowd and grins. "There you are."

Sure enough, Merlin and Nimue lurk at the fringes of the grassy field. The siblings don't seem to notice me, but that's probably because they're too busy glaring hot death in Arthur's direction. I'm starting to understand why they might truly loathe the guy.

"You are bound to serve me," announces Arthur. "I am the true king who drew forth the sword in the stone."

"Aye," say Merlin and Nimue in unison. That may be the word they say, but all the hatred in the universe is locked into that single syllable.

Arthur pipes up again. "Now these traitorous mages shall raise Avalon! Then we'll begin our celebration."

The siblings clasp hands and whisper incantations over the ground. Blue mist rolls out from their palms to fill the forest beyond the grassy field. Soon there's enough haze that the colored cloud rises above the far-away treetops.

The ground rumbles. A silver castle breaks through the grass and forest. The earth splits. Trees snap. Animals screech as they run for it. Little by little, a silver castle shoves its way up to the surface.

So that was badass.

Like Pendragon castle, this structure is compact and boxy. A ring of jagged stones encircles the roof, reminding me of a jawline with so many missing teeth.

I recall my chat with Not-Dad. He said that any mage could raise this castle without wielding the Staff of Avalon.

Sure enough, Merlin and Nimue had no staff. They just held hands and had it happen.

Whew.

Some tension unwinds from my shoulders. Looks like Not-Dad was right about raising Avalon. Perhaps he's right about other things, too. Namely, that only Staff of Avalon can cast a sleeping enchantment inside the castle itself.

Arthur points to Merlin and Nimue. "Be Gone. Return to exile."

What a prick.

For their parts, Merlin and Nimue step away so quickly, you'd think they cast a speed spell.

"Let us enter the castle," announces Arthur. "There you will formally meet my new companion." He gestures toward the red-robed figure. My breath catches.

His new companion is the Crimson Scourge.

I scan the grounds, waiting for someone to cry how they are not stepping into an enchanted castle with the Crimson Scourge.

No one says a word.

I wave at Not-Dad. He glances over in my direction. I point to the red cloaked figure and mouth the words, *no, no, no.*

Not-Dad sighs and looks away. I can almost hear his words in my head. *We voted.* When it comes to archangel stuff, all versions of my father follow the rules.

Which leads to a big decision. I give Lincoln's hand a gentle squeeze. Our gazes lock. I glance between the forest spot where Lin and Nimue stepped away … and then to

Avalon. I lift my brows. The question is there if not asked, *which way should we go?*

Lincoln tilts his head toward the castle. *Avalon.*

I nod. *Agreed.*

"Let us begin!" announces Arthur.

With that, the king marches inside Avalon. Everyone follows. Archangels. Archdemons. Knights. The obvious *Crimson Scourge person.* Lincoln and I go as well.

Inside, the castle resembles the one I saw with the Pendragon. Like before, there's a small reception chamber and a huge mead hall. The larger chamber isn't lined with books, but it still holds a circular table at its center. Arthur goes to stand before the hearth.

"Welcome, archangels and archdemons!" he cries. "On this historic day, we shall all celebrate my brilliance." He looks over to the Crimson Scourge. "And we have a special guest. Huzzah!"

Arthur pauses, waiting for a response. Most likely, he's waiting for a cheer. It doesn't come.

"Now," continues Arthur. "I'm not one to sing my own praises. That is far better done by Dalston Rusus the Bard! Come forward!"

Sure enough, Drusus steps up. Unlike Arthur and his *special guest* speech, the bard's appearance actually causes some polite applause. Drusus takes his place beside Arthur. After swinging his lute out before him, the bard begins to play. The tune he plucks out is gentle and haunting.

I cross my fingers behind my back. *Don't be a creep here, Drusus. Tell the truth.*

The bard's voice echoes out through the hall, the tone lyrical and sweet.

> *A young boy of no means*
> *becomes king of all the lands*
> *King Arthur did it all*
> *King Arthur did it all, all, all*

Sorrow presses in around me. Drusus is *not* telling the truth. Lincoln wraps his arm about my shoulder. He knows what a bummer this is. Drusus sings on.

> *Locked up archdemons*
> *Set Colossus in a cage*
> *King Arthur did it all*
> *King Arthur did it all, all, all*

> *The demonic learns a lesson*
> *And so we celebrate*
> *King Arthur did it all*
> *King Arthur did it all, all, all*

The words aren't much, but add in the sweet lute playing and Drusus' magnetic voice? The song becomes nothing less than haunting. Within a minute, no one is looking at the drunk king anymore. Instead, we're all entranced by Drusus.

Memories appear. I'm back with Drusus and Charles. No wonder Drusus got so upset about his extended son.

Drusus spent his life lying for King Arthur. Those musical untruths hurt people, starting with Merlin and Nimue. Centuries later, Charles is doing the same thing.

The song ends. This time everyone claps enthusiastically, myself included. It makes me feel a little sick to my stomach, but Drusus is just that good. Which is incredibly evil.

Arthur turns to the figure in red. "Come forward, my friend!"

Here we go. Crimson Scourge time.

The mage seems to move in slow motion while stepping to stand beside Arthur. Once before the hearth, Arthur pulls back the hood covering the Crimson Scourge's face. I can't believe my eyes.

It's Remy.

Helping with the contest Remy.

Stuck in the bowels of Antrum with lots of odd boxes Remy.

Stole part of my Band of Epochs Remy.

Remy Elayna Danae, whose initials spell the word RED, which must be how she got the *crimson* part of the Crimson Scourge.

What a bitch.

Remy lifts her arms. Red mist appears around her right hand. *Magic.* A moment later, a staff materializes in her fist. This instrument looks like the one Nimue wielded to raise Pendragon Castle, only Remy's version looks like someone welded together broken bits.

My heart sinks. Remy had that pile of smashed up metal

junk in the archives. Chances are, the broken staff of Avalon was in there. And the gemstones? Remy must have sent her falcon in to get them from Lucifer's lab.

More memories appear. Remy also kept boxes of royal correspondence. The thrax are positively obsessed with all things Lucifer-related. One of Lincoln's people might have reported the lab's discovery. Remy read our freaking mail. She could easily have intercepted that info.

I want to face-palm myself. Remy was so helpful. She almost got killed at the contest. And it was all a scam. I think back to her inscription. *The Great Lady Remy Elayna Danae.* I get that thrax culture doesn't make it easy to move up in the world. But this is an extreme way to handle things.

Remy whispers an incantation. The jewels of the staff flare with golden light. Yellow mist bursts from the stones, filling the room with a heavy haze. When the enchanted cloud fades, all the archangels are asleep. Including Not-Dad.

I open my mouth, ready to scream my lungs out. Mostly, I want to yell at Remy.

Lincoln pulls me into a hug. "Don't." His touch helps me stay calm. Barely.

Remy strolls over to us both. "Aren't you going to thank me for keeping you awake?"

I round on her. "Two words. You. Suck."

She grins. "All I wanted was to be a great lady. Now I'll be the most important ruler of all time. And you can't stop me. In fact, you have to watch it all unfold."

I smack my lips. "Yeah, I got that."

"I chose a horrible contest for you," continues Remy. "Picked the worst winners. You never suspected a thing. I hunted down the ghouls from your mother's conference and paid them invade the Arena. Even gave extra gold to whoever fake-knocked me out. Still you were oblivious. Now you'll witness my success. I will lead and shine where both of you have stumbled and failed."

"This won't work," says Lincoln. "If you turn yourself in now, Myla and I can protect you."

"Not a chance. Instead, I'll raise Colossus while you two watch." Remy steps out the exit. Eight archdemons march along behind her. None force Lincoln and me to follow. I shake my head. *Damn.* Remy knows us too well. My guy and I won't run when someone's about to raise Colossus.

We'll try and fight this somehow.

LINCOLN

*T*urning to Myla, I cup my beloved's face. "Do you wish to run?"

No matter what, I won't risk Myla's safety. For me, there is no world without her. If my wife wants to escape, I'll protect her with everything in me, body and soul. We'll figure the rest out somehow. We always do.

Myla's eyes flare with blue light. "No running. More ass kicking."

I smile. "Excellent."

With that decision made, Myla and I leave the silver palace. Once the last archdemon steps outside, the silver castle lowers into the ground once more. The soil piles back into place. Trees and grass retake their old positions. If I hadn't seen Avalon rise, I wouldn't have believed it was ever here.

And yet the archangels are still inside.

I hate to think of anyone as buried alive. But

archangels? And to have Remy—one of my own people—be the cause? Even more loathsome.

With the enchanted castle gone, we march through the corridors of Camelot. Along the way, I can't help but notice how the floor's dotted with muddy boot prints. Many rooms are ransacked.

Evidently, the staff left in a hurry, including all the not-too-effective guards.

A wise choice, actually.

At last, we enter the main mead hall. It's a long rectangular room with an arched ceiling. An empty fire-place lines one wall. Hefty wooden tables cover the floor.

Remy scans the room, cataloguing as she goes. "We're all here. Eight archdemons. The esteemed King Arthur and his knights of the round table." She glares at me and Myla. "And a pair of unfortunate adventurers. Now it is time for the Crimson Scourge to fulfill her destiny!"

Remy raises the Staff of Avalon once again. "Today, we shall free Colossus!" She pounds the instrument against the tiled floor. The golden gems flare with yellow light once more.

Slam!

All the tables whip away to careen into the walls. The floor tiles crumble into dust, revealing a pair of seals set beneath them, one red and one white. They're small—perhaps the size of my palm—but that doesn't mean they aren't powerful.

Myla whispers in my ear. "I saw those seals before. They're from the cover of a book called the *Opus Magica*."

She nods toward the two discs. "They keep Colossus locked up."

"How do they work?"

"There were two prisons, so I'm guessing that's why there are two seals. And it's all lousy with failsafes. You can't just open the door to Colossus. The prison-crypt is built in a way that stalls his release."

All of a sudden, I'm really wishing Merlin and Nimue hadn't departed so quickly. Is there anyone else here who may be able to give us more information?

My gaze locks onto Ximena, the archdemon dragon. She leans by the exit archway, an unreadable look on her face. Ximena has always been her own person. Would she aid us in stopping Colossus?

Remy points at Arthur. "Come forward!" she cries.

If there's one benefit to this moment, it's that Arthur seems to have sobered up. "Yes, lady?"

"You must call me the Great Crimson Scourge."

Myla and I exchange a dry look. Remy clearly wanted to be a Great Lady. Now she's given herself a title with Great in it.

"My apologies." Arthur leans over in a sloppy bow. "What do you wish, oh Great Crimson Scourge?"

Remy gestures to the floor. "Your so-called father designed this."

"Yes," replies Arthur. "The prison-crypt below us is the Pendragon's work."

"How does one start opening the seals?" As Remy asks this question, her face is the definition of *gloating*. She knows how to work the seals. Remy's just setting Arthur up.

"Oh." Arthur looks around the room. "Must we do that now? I thought there was to be a celebration."

I can almost see the rusty wheels of the king's mind begin churning. Clearly, he hasn't thought beyond the fact that there'd be a great party in his honor. The idea that Colossus is getting loose right now appears to be a shock.

"To open the prison-crypt, you need a blood sacrifice," continues Arthur. "After that, there's the chance to battle within the prison-crypt itself. That can slow Colossus from escaping." His face brightens. "Is that what you wish to do? Slow the crypt from opening so we may have our celebration?"

"Perhaps," says Remy. "But who shall fight? You?"

"Not me," answers Arthur quickly. "My knights will do battle. That's what they're trained for."

Myla laces her fingers with mine. We don't need to say a word. Both of us know what will happen next. Remy's been setting some kind of trap for King Arthur. Now she'll spring it.

"Agreed," says Remy. "In that case, you'll be the blood sacrifice." Flipping her staff ninety degrees, Remy hoists the instrument onto her shoulder like a spear.

For a moment, the gems atop the staff glow gold with power. Then the instrument flies out of Remy's hand to skewer Arthur right through the chest. He slumps over, dead.

"Ow," whispers Myla. "That was cold."

The king's blood oozes across the floor to cover the seals. For a moment, the discs flare with light and power.

Then they vanish, only to be replaced by a three-foot wide hole in the floor. I eye the new pit warily.

Should I jump in? It may be the only way to slow Colossus from escaping.

The seven archdemons also transform. Where their bodies were once solid, they now turn shiny and gelatinous. Red light flares around them as they become liquid. The crimson fluid seeps across the floor to cascade into the new pit. No doubt, they're heading to the prison-crypt of Colossus.

On reflex, I look to Ximena again. She wasn't one of the ones who seeped into the floor. And with the other archdemons gone, Ximena now does what she'd been planning all along.

The Queen of the Dragons walks away.

No help to be found there.

If Remy cares that Ximena took off, then the so-called Great Crimson Scourge doesn't seem concerned. Instead, Remy raises her arm and opens her palm. The staff breaks free from King Arthur's chest and flies back across the room. A second later, the instrument lands right onto Remy's hand.

All the room now looks over to the knights, who seem to have been spending the last few minutes trying to escape. Not an effective plan. They all twist in place while pulling at their armored boots. Yet the knights cannot move their feet. *More magic.*

"Sorry, boys," says Remy. "Your king already promised you to fight the archdemons." She slams the staff against the ground once more. Golden light flares around the knights. Like the archdemons, the warriors turn gelatinous before oozing across the floor to drip down into the pit.

Remy shoots a quick glance at me and Myla. Pure evil lights the Crimson Scourge's eyes. No question what that look means. Once Remy is through with the knights, it will be our turn.

We don't have much time.

I give Myla's hand a gentle squeeze. "I'll try to slow it as much as I can." There's no question what *it* is in this scenario. Colossus's escape.

"I'll get help," says Myla.

After giving my wife one last kiss, I race toward the pit.

Three yards.

Two yards.

One.

I jump into the darkness. Icy cold bites into my skin as I tumble down. Above me, the round opening grows smaller and smaller. Beyond the hole, I can make out a tiny section of the chamber above. The last thing I see is Myla's beloved face before all becomes dark.

MYLA

*M*y guy can sure haul ass when he needs to. One second, Lincoln stands at my side, our hands entwined. A few heartbeats later, my husband leaps into a nasty pit. A pang of worry moves through me.

Be safe, Lincoln.

I'm not the only one getting the feels here, either.

Remy rushes to the pit's edge. "How dare he leave?" She rounds on me. "You both were supposed to watch Colossus crown me as the Great Crimson Queen."

Wait, WHAT?

I take a little *mental time out* to review this new bit of news. Then I round on Remy.

"Let me get this straight," I say. "My husband just tossed his sweet self into a hole in the floor ... which leads directly to some prison-crypt and almost certain death. Meanwhile, every person I've ever known—or cared about —has been erased from history. And all so you could become a Great Lady. But that won't be enough. You have even bigger plans. Once Colossus is free, you think he'll make you his Queen?"

"Obviously," says Remy. "It's all in the prophecy."

At this point, it's important to note three nice things about this other-wise crappy situation. One, Remy is chatting me up, which is always a dumb move for any villain. Two, all the guards and knights are long gone, so it's just her and me in this room. And three, I have a kick-ass plan to escape and find help.

My tail arcs over my shoulder. I pretend to inspect the scales on the arrowhead end. "And who gave you that prophecy, exactly?"

"I found it in the archives. *Whoever frees Colossus can be his bride.* It's a vision from the Heretic."

As prophets go, the Heretic is a loser. Not that I'll share this insight with Remy. Clearly, she's had the archivist job for all of two months and knows everything.

"The Heretic, wow." As I keep fiddling with my tail, I saunter a little closer.

Pro tip: When closing in on someone, it's always good to be doing something with your hands. Makes them less likely to notice your feet. This is something Remy would know if she'd taken any battle training.

But she hasn't.

So this next bit will be awesome.

I make my move.

"Go get her, Fluff!"

My favorite snow imp now materializes in the air

between me and Remy. Fluff essentially transforms into a fur rocket as he zooms right for Remy's face. His little limbs extend forward, highlighting the tiny talons on his hands and feet.

Remy stands completely still, her features slack with shock. Fluff slams right into her face, making Remy scream in terror. It's a beautiful thing.

Now, I'd love to watch Fluff scratch up Remy, but there isn't time. This is my chance to escape and I'm taking it. I race from the mead hall and hustle over to the stables. As I speed along, I hear Remy's whiny screams echo through the air.

Damn, I sure hope she doesn't hurt Captain Fluffbottom.

In no time, I'm riding a nice spotted mare in a little direction I like to call, *away from Camelot*. Or more specifically, it's toward my last camp with Nimue and Merlin. I need their help and that's the best place to look.

After all, Lincoln can't slow down Colossus forever.

I gallop across a dirt road and onto an open field. In fact, I'm starting to feel pretty good about my bad self when a shadow crosses overhead.

It's not a cloud.

A moment later, a big-ass red dragon plunks itself down before me. My horse rears on its hind legs and generally freaks out, but I'm able to calm the animal. For a moment, my mind is a blank of shock.

Who is this, anyway?

Then it hits me. That's right. Seven seals. Seven archdemons. Ximena is number eight and she covers two sins, namely lust and wrath. She isn't part of any prison-crypt plan.

Only now she's blocking my path while looking super pissed off.

Uh oh.

LINCOLN

*N*ot sure how long I tumble. To my mind, the descent takes hours. No doubt, there's an enchantment around this prison-crypt and it alters my perception of time. I could be falling for years or moments.

At last, I hit solid ground. My body curls into a crouch with my hands braced on the floor. Round orbs of red light flare to life around me. They materialize at the seam between the wall and the floor. After hovering for a moment, they rise into the long and dark tunnel above.

Standing up, I survey my surroundings. I've reached a long and rectangular chamber made from what appears to be polished black stone. At one short end of the rectangle, the wall holds a large white seal. The disc stretches about ten feet high. Numerals 1 to 7 are written in a swirling line that ends at the seal's center.

No doubt about it. This is the same seal that was set

into the floor of the mead hall, only now it's ten feet tall. This must represent the seven archdemons.

On the chamber's opposite side, the wall holds the red seal, which has also swollen to become ten feet fall. The disc is adorned with a line carving of Colossus's goat head. Between the two seals there stretches a golden pathway. Oh, and the knights of the round table are also here, cowering in a far corner. I try not to look at them too closely, though. So depressing.

How can these be the same knights I obsessed about in my youth? I spent hours reenacting their battles, starting at the age when I could barely toddle about. Now their so-called achievements were actually done by the Pendragon, Merlin and Nimue.

As I said, it's quite the disappointment. And a lesson in the value of bards.

The white seal spins, ending with the numeral one up top. Every muscle in my body goes on alert.

The game is about to begin.

A liquid sheen rolls over the white seal. One moment, the disc seems made of stone. The next? It's as if a pool of still water were set into the wall, existing in its own whacked-out gravity. A fist pushes through the water's vertical surface. There's no missing how the gauntlet is covered in rust. Only one archdemon wears such armor.

Null, the Archdemon of sloth.

Sure enough, Null steps through the water-like seal and onto the golden floor. He looks just as he did when we travelled with Ximena: eight feet of rusted metal armor.

Null sets his fist on his chest. "I am Null, the Archdemon of Sloth. I shall go to the seal of Colossus, add my power, and help set my master free."

I step onto the center of the thin golden path that connects one seal to the other. "No." Out of the corner of my eye, I glance to the knights.

Still cowering. Unbelievable.

Null marches toward me. Or rather, he is no doubt moving toward the far wall and the seal of Colossus. Strangely enough, Null doesn't even pull out his rusty sword from its scabbard. His metal boots clomp noisily on the floor as he gets closer.

I pull my baculum from their holster at the base of my spine. Holding the pair of silver bars in my fists, I order them to ignite into a longsword made of white flame.

Null pauses before me. Although he's rusted out and slow moving, there's no denying he's still an archdemon. And he stands eight feet tall, let's not forget that part. Raising his arm, Null moves to punch me in the ribs. I swoop my blade down, ready to block the strike.

That's when Null does something I've never had happen in a battle before.

The Archdemon of Sloth tumbles forward, careful to ensure my blade slices right through his chest. I step back, yanking my weapon free.

What was that?

I return to battle stance. The archdemon must be playing games. Null is only pretending to die so I'll lower my guard.

Null lands on the floor with a thud. His body takes on the same gelatinous sheen that I saw before in the mead hall. Only this time, Null doesn't change into liquid. Within seconds, his body transforms into a swirling mist. I suck in a shocked breath.

Oh, no.

I should never have fought sloth at all. Killing him only saved the archdemon the hassle of walking across the golden pathway.

Before me, the red haze that once was Null now flies across the room to merge with the opposite seal.

Colossus.

The red disc spins. When the motion ends, there is no longer the line image of a goat's head on the seal's surface. Instead, a moving mural blinks out at me.

"Hello, Lincoln," says the King of the Archdemons. His voice is a deep rasp. His next five words send a tremor through my soul.

"Soon, I'll come for you."

I can only hope Myla arrives first.

38

MYLA

A massive creature looms before me.

Dragon-Ximena.

Mother of all Furor.

Badass of badasses.

Small horns encircle her head, reminding me of a crown. Heavy plates arch up from her back and tail. Her massive talons dig into the ground before me.

I wince. She probably plans to chomp my face off. Or try, anyway.

"Let me by," I say simply. It's not the best opening line ever, but I'm winging it here.

"And why would I allow that?" growls Dragon-Ximena.

My tail takes this moment to pop over my shoulder and wave at Ximena. Her heavy dragon brows quirk with interest.

"Down, boy." I guide the arrowhead-end behind me and

refocus on Ximena. "I'm part Furor, as you know." I hitch my thumb behind me. "You've got a fan."

In reply, Ximena says *zip*.

"So, back to why you'll let me go," I say. " You've been trapped in a supernatural prison with the other archdemons for a long time. I've met Lester, by the way." I make my *eek face*. "That couldn't have been fun."

Ximena huffs out a breath. That's not exactly a ringing endorsement of my theory. But I know Lester. I hated spending two minutes with him, let alone centuries.

"And what got you locked up with Lester and the others?" I ask. "Colossus. If Mister Misty gets out of prison, he'll cause big trouble. Sooner or later, that means you and the other archdemons will spend too much quality time together in a dungeon."

Or at least, that's my story and I'm sticking to it.

Ximena purses her lips, which is an odd look considering the length of her dragon's jaw. "We buried all the archangels. They can not hurt us now."

Here's the thing. Ximena's words say she's unconcerned. Yet that worried lilt in her voice says otherwise. I go in for the close.

"Last time I checked, there's more up in Heaven than just archangels." I point to the sky for emphasis. "All of them would love to capture you and your buddies."

"The other archdemons are *not* my friends."

It's on the tip of my tongue to say: *Ha. Knew that would get you.* Yet I'm able to hold back. My guy needs help.

"No offense," I continue. "But it doesn't seem like

Heaven got that memo. And they totally warned you that if you pulled any crap again, the punishment would be worse next time."

Ximena narrows her dragon eyes, which also entails her vertical pupils thinning as well. Not gonna lie. It's terrifying. "What do you propose?"

"Let me pass your dragon-ness." I pat my horse's neck to emphasize the transportation part. "Once I find Merlin and Nimue, the three of us will go back and destroy Colossus."

"That is a terrible plan," snarls Ximena.

"Look, Miss *Judgy Von Judgerton*. There are mages nearby and a horse under my butt. Either you get out of my way or…"

Ximena sniffs again. "Or what?"

"I'll think of something. I always do. Just consider yourself warned." I flick the reins on my horse.

That's when it happens.

Ximena opens her massive dragon's jaw and lets out the mother of all roars. I'm talking eardrum splitting, heart pounding, dragon-gonna-chomp-you terror.

My horse falls over. Dead.

Thank goodness my reflexes are still good or I'd be trapped under a dead horse. Even so, I shouldn't have to be avoiding falling land mammals. I round on Ximena. "You totally killed my stolen horse."

"That I did. I need a snack before we take off." Leaning forward, she starts chowing down on the horse in question. I turn around and pretend to find the nearby trees super-fascinating. A lot of crunching and slurping sounds follow. It's gross.

"Are you done?" I ask.

Ximena burps. "Yes. Now I'll take you tofind Merlin and Nimue. But on one condition."

"Name it. "

"I want to be free while all the other archdemons are locked up. Colossus included."

"Deal."

"Good. Now climb aboard my back."

I slowly turn around to face her. This is Dragon Ximena, after all. I pat my tail. "Hey, boy."

My tail flips up so the arrowhead end points toward my face. That's it's way of saying, *what's up?*

"Should we trust her?" I ask. This is far from the weirdest thing I've done today, by the way.

The arrowhead end flips between looking at Ximena and focusing on me. After a long minute of this, it bobs in an up and down motion. *Yes.*

Fluff takes the opportunity to materialize as well. "Trust, trust," he says.

I grin. "Yay, you made it!"

With that resolved, I scramble up Ximena's front leg and get myself situated on her back.

"Ximena? It's not a hundred percent clear where I put my hands. Should I—"

But before I can even finish the question, Ximena has taken to the skies.

And I scream my head off.

39

LINCOLN

$\mathcal{M}$y battle with Null was a failure. The Archdemon of Sloth wanted to be killed. The faster Null died, the more quickly he was reunited with Colossus ... and the sooner the King of the Archdemons got free. A word appears in my mind's eye.

Failsafe.

This is all part of the Pendragon's design. I count three failsafes so far. First, the other archdemons were imprisoned apart from Colossus. Second, the archdemons must rejoin with Colossus' seal for the archdemon king to get free. Third, a golden path slows down that reunion.

Bottom line? My goal isn't to kill the archdemons, but to delay them. Destroying them is a last resort.

Which shouldn't be a problem. Perhaps.

I've spent years training thrax for demon patrol. The entire goal during these sessions is to keep my sparring partners alive, upright, and fighting for as long as possible. Straightening my back, I lock my gaze on the white disc.

I can do this.

Suddenly, the pale seal spins once more. This time, it stops with the numeral two at the top.

Next archdemon, coming up.

Again, the disc takes on the look of liquid. Just like before, a gauntleted fist presses through. Only this armor isn't rusted; it's black and spotless. The entire warrior follows next.

It's Rage, the Archdemon of Wrath.

Unlike Null, Rage grips short swords in each hand. For my part, I ignite my baculum into a long sword. Footsteps sound behind me. Turning, I see an unexpected sight.

The knights of the round table.

"We shall aid zee in zhy battle," says Lancelot. It's a little hard to understand him through his French accent, but I get the general idea.

I stifle the urge to groan. When it looked like fighting archdemons got you killed, then these warriors hid in a corner. I didn't even get so much as a *fare thee well* when I stood my ground. Now that it seems the fights are rather easy, they're all lined up to help.

Our group stands about half way between the Archdemon of Wrath and his goal: the seal of Colossus.

"Here's the plan," I state. "We are not to kill the archdemon, only slow him down."

Lancelot raises his sword. "For king and glory!"

"No glory," I say quickly. "We're here to prevent that

guy—" I point to Rage "—from merging with *that seal*."
When I speak the words *that seal*, I gesture toward the red
disc of Colossus.

"Zeee foul demon shall not triumph," says Lancelot.
"Come along, men. Destroy zee Archdemon of Wrath!"

I pinch the bridge of my nose. "What part of *slow down
but don't kill him* was unclear?" Shaking my head, I stay in
battle stance. Twelve men are already attacking a single
foe. This isn't the largest chamber ever. Not sure they'll all
have room to raise their swords.

At least, they aren't at risk. If the Archdemon of Sloth is
any indication, the knights will deliver the slightest of
attacks and Wrath will self-destruct.

Lancelot raises his blade high, ready to fight. Wrath
swipes his short swords through the air with such speed,
the blades become nothing but a dark blur.

A moment later Lancelot still stands before the
Archdemon of Wrath.

Only difference is, the knight is without a head. His
lifeless body collapses onto the floor.

A stunned silence follows. All the knights stare at
Lancelot, their faces pale with shock. They aren't alone.
Unlike Null, Rage wants to fight. Which makes sense, only
it leads to a conclusion that makes my heart sink.

Each one of these archdemons will have their own way
of battling over to reach Colossus.

This will be tricky.

As if to emphasize that point, Rage goes after the
knights. His massive body is a blur of motion as his short

sword wheels through the air. Within a matter of seconds, Rage has killed every last warrior.

Then the Archdemon of Wrath turns to me. Pulling a dagger from his armor, Rage tosses the weapon at my heart. I leap out of the way, but not fast enough. The blade lodges in my side. I crumple to my knees. Pain radiates through my torso.

Rage pauses before me. I yank the dagger from my side and toss it to the ground with a clang. Warm blood oozes along my skin. Fresh jolts of pain cut through me. Rage doesn't bother with a battle stance as he raises his short-swords high. Clearly, the Archdemon of Wrath doesn't think I have the strength to fight back.

That's my only advantage.

Rage swoops down to strike me. I always knew some deadly sins were related. In this case, wrath and sloth. Now that Rage thinks he's beaten me, he no longer bothers with supernatural speed. That's just plain lazy.

And it's a big mistake.

As the blade lowers, I leap aside while splitting my own weapon into short swords. Rage moves to strike again while I lift my blades. Our weapons connect. We strike and block. Lunge and dodge. Neither of us connect another body strike. One of Rage's short swords gets sliced in half by repeated hits from my angelfire blade, but beyond that? It's a stalemate.

Minutes pass. All my angelic power focuses on meeting Rage blow for blow. Still, my wound seeps blood. Although I can follow the battle, spots of white appear in my vision.

I'm passing out.

Rage slams me against the wall. His left hand grips my throat, choking me. The archdemon raises his broken sword, ready to plunge it into my throat.

With that, the truth is unavoidable.

This needs to end.

I will my baculum to take the form of a dagger and plunge it into the demon's belly. Rage crumples over, dead. I fall to my knees as well, gasping for breath.

Sure, I bought some time, but I paid a heavy price for it.

And there are five more demons to delay.

Beside me, Wrath's body disintegrates into a red mist. As with Null before, that vapor flies across the chamber to soak into the seal of Colossus. For a moment, nothing happens. Then the mural of Colossus' face transforms. Before it was a shallow image. Now a full three-dimensional head pops out from the red seal. The King of the Archdemons focuses on me again. The yellow eyes in his goat-like head shine with light and power.

"You won't last one more battle, let alone five," declares Colossus.

And sadly enough, the archdemon king may very well be right.

40

MYLA

I've never ridden a dragon before. The experience isn't a barrel of laughs. In five steps, here's what's been happening.

One. We fly along. I work hard *not* to look down. After a few minutes, I relax a little.

Two. All of a sudden, Ximena goes in a loop-de-loop.

Three. Lots of screaming from yours truly.

Four. More screaming while I grab onto Ximena's back plates for dear life.

Five. Ximena straightens out, claiming she saw Nimue and Merlin and had to loop around to double check. But her statement is undermined by her low chuckle.

Methinks Ximena is toying with me.

Enough already. This dragon needs to stop goofing off and find Nimue and Merlin. Any second now, my guy could get flattened.

I knock on her back plates. "Ximena?" I ask. "How's it going?"

"Still no sign of Merlin or Nimue." Ximena's got dragon-sight, so I trust her take.

My mind whirs. Where would Nimue and Merlin go? Then it hits me. After getting kicked out of Camelot again, perhaps the siblings wanted to visit their happy place. I knock on Ximena's plates once more.

"Do you know the lake where the Pendragon sleeps?" I ask.

"Ah, yes," says Dragon-Ximena. "That is a fine place to check."

Dragon-Ximena spreads out her wings, arcs through the sky, and speeds off in a new direction. Since she's no longer scanning the ground, we're now hitting new levels of *holy shit* when it comes to speed.

And I thought the loop-de-loops were bad.

Not that I'm complaining. In a way, it feels better to be racing off somewhere versus the previous rhythm of *slow-slow-slow*-holy-fuck-we're-upside-down.

Soon we're landing by a familiar lake surrounded with pine trees. I exhale.

And there they are.

Merlin and Nimue sit by the water's edge. They're in almost the exact same spot where they summoned Pendragon castle.

I slide off Dragon-Ximena, straighten my leather armor, and get my head in gear. *I need help; here's where I can find it.* After all, I talked Ximena into aiding me. How hard can these two be?

For her part, Dragon-Ximena plops onto her belly, curls her long tail around her torso, and waits. Her serpentine pupils thin as she focuses on me. Her words are there if unspoken.

You're on your own, Myla Lewis.

Which is fine. I am solo girl anyway. Plus Dragon-Ximena is more than a little distracting.

I lift my chin. *I can do this. Lincoln, Maxon, my family, and my world—everyone relies on me.*

My pulse decides that now is a great time to skyrocket. Guess the whole *it's all on me* pep talk wasn't my best.

Ah, well. It's not like I can sit by a lake and mope. I need to get me some mages.

I saunter over to the water's edge. The siblings don't look up as I approach, so I plunk down beside them. I rub my palms together and hope an awesome speech appears in my head.

Nothing.

The siblings stay silent, so one fact is clear. If anything will happen here, it's coming from the Myla Lewis side of the lake.

A question pops into my mind. What would I usually do? Because that stuff is mostly a failure, so I can just suck those words back into my mouth before they're even spoken.

I picture Alli-somebody. If this were her, I'd just order her to help me save Lincoln and then run from the room.

So that's out. No commanding Nimue and Merlin to help me.

Next I imagine Lincoln and Walker. We work together on stuff all the time. Mostly, it just sort of happens, though. We're aligned on what to do and the rest follows from there. Not practical.

Another memory appears. This time, it's me chatting with my real father about visiting the fading angels. I knew he couldn't resist my eye-batting and please-please-please routine.

Maybe that could be something.

I twirl my hair and think things through. I manipulated Dad for good when it came to the fading angels. My father can't resist my pleading. But what drives Merlin and Nimue? I glance over in their direction.

Sure enough, the pair stare at the still water. Shoulders slumped. Eyes glistening. There's one topic that's super powerful for them. The Pendragon.

A plan forms.

I take in a long breath and hope for verbal fireworks. "The Pendragon was your hero."

The siblings don't look in my direction, but they do move their heads in the barest of nods. I'm counting that as a win.

"The academy must have had many students."

"From all over the world," explains Nimue. "Arthur would never have met the academy's standards, but ... you know the story."

"That I do. You're right about King Arthur being awful.

But the Pendragon's a super-powerful mage who could have done anything with his life. Yet he chose to teach and help others."

For the first time, Merlin and Nimue swing their gazes in my direction. I take that as a win, part two.

"Right now, I'm fighting for my future. So is my husband. There's no time to find enough mages to power the new *Opus Magica*. The Pendragon can't wake up and help us. But if he could, what would he say right now? You two are the most powerful mages alive. Yet you're sitting by a lake and boo-hooing instead of using the tools he taught you."

The siblings stare at me and damn, I wish I could read the looks on their faces.

Will they help or not? Because if the answer is *no*, then I need to high-tail it back to Camelot and do whatever I can. Which, let's face it, is probably to die fighting at Lincoln's side.

The ground beneath me rumbles. Small orbs of red light appear around me. *Magic.* A few feet away a small pit forms in the earth. My inner wrath demon stirs.

A battle is coming.

Dragon-Ximena lifts her long neck and gazes between me and the dark opening. "That pit will draw you into the prison-crypt of Colossus."

I hop to my feet. *Fighting stance.* "So I'm off to battle the archdemons?"

"Yes," replies Ximena. "Only when it comes to archdemons, fighting isn't always what you'd expect."

Eh, fighting-shmiting. It's all the same. Besides, big speeches aren't my thing. The whole *Pendragon would be ashamed of you* talk isn't a clear winner, that's for certain. But slicing up some archdemon with Lincoln at my side? That's exactly what I need.

The pit grows wider until the ground beneath my feet falls away. I tumble through the darkness and smile.

41

MYLA

otal blackness surrounds me as I fall through space.

And fall

And fall.

It's getting a little boring, to be honest.

The next thing I know, I've landed on my feet. Woot. A small pool of light surrounds me. Beyond that, it's all pure blackness in every direction.

Weird. But that's my life.

Misty voices echo through the darkness. I tilt my head, straining to hear. Could that be Lincoln speaking? It's hard to tell—the words sound as if they're spoken through water. I don't catch everything, but I do hear the words *not Lincoln* and *enchantment*.

Yet none of that matters. Lincoln himself steps into the pool of light. He's naked from the waist up, wearing leather pants and nothing else. Every inch of him is gleams as if he's made from gold. Waves of power seep from him and encircle me.

Now, I'm a lust demon myself, so I can tell when someone is sending sexy-time mojo my way. So I steel myself from this vision. Lincoln is part angel. This version simply can't be real. It's a demon Lincoln and that pisses me off. My inner wrath demon roars. Heat and rage stir my soul.

Fake Lincoln moves in to kiss me. So I do the only natural thing in such a situation.

I knee him in the balls.

42

LINCOLN

I hadn't been worried when I saw how my next battle would pit me against Lester, the Archdemon of Lust.

There were no concerns when Lester seeped out of the white seal. After all, the archdemon still wore his bard's ensemble.

Lester then transformed into a golden version of me. Still, I wasn't too anxious. Lester-Lincoln stood bare chested and carried no weapons.

Then Myla appeared.

My attitude changed.

This was my real wife, keeper of my heart and mother of my child. And Lester pulled her in here for a reason. It wasn't a good one. Alarm rattled through my nervous system. I wanted to slice Lester through, yet I forced myself to stay still.

Remember, Lincoln. This is about every person in the after-realms. You're here to slow Lester down.

Besides, Myla's an Arena fighter. She can handle herself.

As Lester-Lincoln stepped closer to Myla, I called out to my girl over and over.

"This isn't real!"

"That's not me!"

"See past the enchantment!"

Then Lester-Lincoln tried to kiss her. Big mistake. Myla fought back with a quick knee to the groin. However, Lester must have encountered this move before. He didn't flinch, let alone back away.

Which brings me to now.

Lester-Lincoln pins my wife against a wall. All rational thought fades from my brain. A primal drive wraps about my soul, taking over every cell in my body.

Myla is my wife. My angelbound love. No one else touches her.

Igniting my baculum into a longsword, I race toward Lester-Lincoln. In one stroke, I slice him through from head to heel. The archdemon instantly dissolves into mist. Dead, or as dead as things get in this prison. Once again, the colored haze that was once Lester's body now speeds into the red disc. The essence of the Archdemon of Lust rejoins Colossus.

The red seal transforms.

The round stone now becomes an empty circular window. Colossus sets his hands on the lower edge and hauls himself out. Now his head, arms, and torso are all free. The rest of him is still trapped behind the wall and seal. All the while, Colossus's skin stays as smooth and firm as red stone.

I should be enraged.

Terrified.

Scheming.

Yet all I can focus on is Myla. I reach toward her. "Are you all right?"

"Lincoln!" she cries.

What happens next only takes seconds. Even so, every aspect of Myla gets seared into my memory. I watch as the floor crumbles beneath her feet. A pit opens. Myla sinks into the ground.

I reach for her.

Our fingertips almost touch.

Then she is gone.

43

LINCOLN

*C*olossus focuses on me once again. "Three archdemons have rejoined me. Four more remain."

The archdemon king grins. I've seen this smile before. It's the kind that happens right before a major demon goes in for the kill. Colossus enjoys annihilation. The more beautiful the target of his destruction, the happier Colossus becomes.

Behind me, fresh voices echo through the chamber.

"We are Envy and Pride. Our magic is second to none."

Turning around, I find two new figures standing before the white seal. Both wear long cloaks with the hoods drawn low. The fabric of these robes appears to be molten steel. For Envy, that metal is tinged green. Meanwhile, Pride's cloak shines golden.

For a long moment, I can only stare at the pair. Two

archdemons at once. Makes sense. After all, envy and pride are dual sides of the same emotion. We envy that which hurts our pride; we take pride in being greater than those we might envy. Still, fighting one archdemon at a time was tough enough.

Pain spikes into my side. It's the wound I received from the Archdemon of Wrath. Blood still seeps from the cut.

My thoughts spin through this next battle. Once again, I must delay these two archdemons from reaching Colossus ... all without getting myself killed.

That won't be easy.

Before me, the archdemons speak in unison again. "We shall enter the seal of Colossus, add our power, and set our master free."

I reignite my baculum as a pair of short-swords. With two foes coming at me, I'll need the extra weapon. Setting my legs shoulder-width apart, I angle my body toward my opponents. Battle stance.

Seconds pass. Envy and Pride do not attack.

Instead, the pair raise their arms. Red smoke surrounds them. *Magic.* Light flickers as their metallic cloaks expand and billow with an invisible wind. Colored steel winds toward me, then elongates into tall panels. One second, I stand on the golden path between the archdemons and Colossus. The next?

I'm in a maze of mirrors, all of which show different versions of me.

The spell is cast.

Spinning about, my attention is caught by a younger incarnation of myself. I wear my royal best as a prince: dark tunic, leather pants, and matching boots. Within the reflection, I stand inside a cabin made from rough-hewn wood—and it's one place I'll never forget. This building is part of the camp where my people stayed when we first visited Purgatory.

This is all before I met Myla.

The unmistakable twinge of green colors the image. It's the same hue as the Archdemon of Envy. A sinking feeling moves inside me. I've a suspicion who this mirror image really represents.

An envious version of me.

"I was raised to wed for political gain," says Envy-Me. "My parents don't believe in love, yet they share a bone-deep connection. It isn't fair."

Emotions flood through my soul. That version of me feels so foreign, and yet I still carry that man's envy. For years, I was taught that marriage was nothing more than a signature on paper. I almost missed out on the most important part of my life.

My Myla.

Another mirror image arrests my gaze. It's a different version of me from this same era. This time, the mirror is tinged red.

Pride-Me.

"Demons are all evil," proclaims Pride-Me. "Females included. Thrax are superior in every way."

Hearing my own words again sends a foul taste into my mouth. I said these things before I met Myla. How I wish I could erase them now.

Still, I can't help but reply to this prideful version of my own soul. "Before living in Purgatory, we'd never met a quasi demon. Once we saw Myla, things changed. *We* changed."

Pride-Me frowns. "Yet you still hurt the demon girl."

"Her name is Myla. And whatever I did, it was only to protect her."

Yet even as I speak the words, they ring hollow. Back then, I pretended to loathe Myla in order to keep her safe. But I'll never forgive myself for causing her pain. There should have been a way to keep my girl safe without hurting her.

Smash!

Both versions of me break through the mirrors. Each carries a long sword made from white flame. I've fought many adversaries, but never myself.

Let alone myself twice over.

I reignite my own baculum as a pair of short swords. Fresh pain digs into my side. My gash from the Archdemon of Wrath is still open and seeping blood. Normally, I'd have put on a field dressing by now. But here, I've no charms or med kits.

That said, this might not be too bleak. These versions of me may know about battle in general, but not my particular fighting style.

Long story short, there's still a chance to stall them.

Envy- and Pride-Me both move right into attack. One goes for a high strike; the other low. I block both thrusts.

Sadly, those are some of my best battle moves. It seems Pride- and Envy-me aren't only conjured to resemble my appearance. They fight in my style as well.

That makes this tougher.

Crouching down, I try sliding past the two versions of me at a low angle. With any luck, I'll get behind them both, where I can cut their Achilles' tendons. That'll slow them down.

The other versions of me see this move coming. One kicks at my ankles. The other punches my throat. Within seconds, I'm flat on my back. Bits of broken mirror slice into my skin. All the breath is knocked from my lungs.

Envy- and Pride-Me raise their longswords, holding their baculum pointed down. They're ready to strike.

I've no choice now. There's no more time that I can buy here. It's kill or be killed.

Still gasping for breath, I reignite my baculum as two small daggers. Flicking my wrists, I toss the fiery blades into their chests. The other versions of me transform from three-dimensional figures into two-sided mirrors. Those metal reflections then shatter into small pieces.

The archdemons are down.

The mirror shards dissolve into red mist. *It's happening. Again.* The colored haze flies over to opposite wall.

Into the seal.

Joining with Colossus.

Once more, the King of the Archdemons changes. This time, Colossus steps right out of the seal. My breath catches. Colossus turns, pulling at the heavy cord that still connects him to the wall behind him.

He isn't free yet. But it's close.

44

MYLA

J was almost-not-quite touching Lincoln's hand. That's when I saw it: the bloom of blood along his leather armor.

My poor Lincoln.

Then I get yanked into this *dark tumbling situation* again.

As I fall through black and empty space, images flicker through my mind. I see my parents ... Cissy ... my sweet baby Maxon ... and Lincoln, bleeding.

My heart thuds so hard, I'm shocked I don't crack a rib.

At last, the darkness vanishes. Once again, I stand by Pendragon lake. Nimue, Merlin, and Dragon-Ximena all wait nearby. *Huh.*

"That was speedy," says Merlin.

"Really?" I ask. "It felt like I was tumbling for hours."

Merlin grips the *Opus Magica* against his chest. "Twas only a matter of minutes."

"What happened?" asks Nimue.

"I saw Lincoln. He isn't well." I shake my head. "Any news here?"

Dragon-Ximena drums her claws against the grass. "Your disappearance gave us all a chance to think."

A spark of hope lights in my chest. I just finished that speech about what the Pendragon would really want. At the time, I thought it was a little *meh*. But maybe combining those words with a quick disappearing act made a difference.

"And?" I prompt.

"My sister and I will help you," says Merlin.

"Yes," I punch my fist in the air before turning to Dragon-Ximena. "You're still in, right?"

"A dragon never breaks her word," says Dragon-Ximena. "Unless it suits her."

"Cryptic," I comment. "But I'll still take that for a *yes*."

Merlin fiddles with the end of his long braid. "What's your plan to defeat Colossus?"

"I'll tell you." I fold my arms over my chest in what I hope is a confident pose. "Once I think of something."

Nimue gasps. "You don't have a plan?"

I hold up my arms, palms forward. "Hey, now. Give me two minutes here. I was just pit-sucked into almost playing tonsil hockey with a fake husband, okay?"

Fluff materializes nearby. He hovers in the air, his own little mousey-arms folded across his chest.

"Wait, wait," squeaks Fluff.

Even my tail gets into the act, arcing over my shoulder. The arrowhead-shaped end points ominously between

Nimue, Merlin, and Dragon-Ximena. Appreciate the support.

No one says anything else, so I figure I've bought myself a little time. Turning away, I head toward a nearby line of forest.

The Great Scala needs to focus.

Pacing under the pines, I start a little internal inventory. Here's what I have on the *plus column*.

Merlin.

Nimue.

Fluff.

Dragon-Ximena.

An empty and useless magic book.

An injured Lincoln.

Honestly, the *good stuff* here is a mixed bag. I segue to the negative side of the equation.

Seven archdemons.

Their king.

Remy the traitor.

Sleeping archangels, including my father.

All the humans Colossus can possess when he escapes.

I stop cold. Not only is this second list hella depressing, the word *possess* rings through my soul in curious ways. Locations spin through my mind. In this era, Antrum isn't even founded yet. The Dark Lands and Purgatory won't have anything useful for me, either.

But Earth? That's another story.

A plan forms. It's a long shot, but it still exists.

Energy and hope charge through my body. I launch

into an internal debate about how best to hand out marching orders when that smooth female voice sounds inside my head.

Make a circle.

For once, I get what this loony voice is saying. It isn't enough for me to order people around here. A new approach is needed. With that realization, something snaps inside me. Connections form. Ideas spark. I feel as if I could sprout wings and fly.

Racing back to the group, I raise my arms. "Field goal!"

"What?" asks Dragon-Ximena.

"It's a human saying from my time," I explain. "It means I have a scheme for how to re-imprison all the archdemons. Colossus included."

Merlin twists his braid in more complex knots. "Verily?"

"So verily," I confirm. "Let me show you." I step to a clear patch of ground and wave the group over. Soon Merlin and Nimue stand before me. Fluff hovers above. Dragon-Ximena plunks her massive head closer.

We're ready to begin.

"Here's the deal," I say. "We need to get Colossus back in his *forever-prison*. But to do that, we must release him first."

Merlin frowns. "We can put Colossus back into prison … without the *Opus Magica?*"

"I'll get to that," I counter. Picking up a stick, I draw

circle into the brown earth before me. "This is our round table. All five of us sit about it as equals."

"Me, me," squeaks Fluff.

"Yup, you too, Fluff." I tap the circle. "King Arthur turned the idea of Pendragon's round table into nothing but a song. Now I want to make it real."

I get another round of nods. *Progress.*

That serene voice fills my head once more.

Circles include and envelop.

In a shocking turn of events, that's some decent advice.

"Here's what we'll do," I state. "I'll go through my plan, then we'll go around our virtual table, and each one of us will make it better. How's that?"

A long pause hangs in the air. This time, I didn't shove the proverbial map-quilt onto someone's hands and run away. We're now a team of equals that battle problems together … like the fellowship of the ring or the Bangtan Boys.

Still no answer from my *team of awesome.*

I clear my throat. "Honestly, what do you think?"

"Annihilation awaits us," sighs Merlin.

"I shall die a virgin," adds Nimue.

"And Colossus will flay me once he finds out I helped you," intones Dragon-Ximena.

"Danger, danger," chirps Fluff.

Then again, maybe *team of awesome* is a stretch.

45

LINCOLN

Colossus rounds on me. The archdemon looms nine feet tall with hefty limbs and skin like polished red stone. His two sets of extra-long arms hang loosely at his sides.

"Only two seals remain," announces the archdemon king. "How I'll enjoy watching you die."

Behind me, new voices sound once more. I force myself to turn, but it isn't easy. My back sears with pain, adding to the hurt from my hip wound. On reflex, I check my pockets. Normally, on demon patrol we have charms for times like these. Some heal. Others stop the pain.

But I'm wearing strange armor. There are still no healing charms here.

Gritting my teeth against the agony, I face my enemy. Across the long space there stand a pair of skeletons: Skyn and Bone, the Archdemons of Gluttony and Greed. For gluttony, Skyn is a dried-out husk whose papery flesh stretches over his skeletal frame. No matter how much he eats, Skyn is never filled. As for greed, Bone is a bare skeleton covered in gold. In other words, Bone is the poster child for the concept of, *what can the dead do with money?*

"We are Skyn and Bone," they say in unison. "We shall enter the seal of Colossus, add our power, and set our master free."

Two foes at once.

I can delay them.

At least, I must try.

The towering skeletons march toward me. Their rasping voices call out a low chant. "Desire. Tear. Own. Destroy."

Scooping up my baculum, I ignite them into short swords again. The skeletons close in. Both hold bone blade daggers.

Snap!

Great cracks form in the golden path beneath my feet. Skeletal arms reach up from breaks, gripping my ankles. I kick those off, but more fissures appear. Massive skeletal arms burst through the ceiling and walls. All the many undead hands have one goal.

Me.

I fight back, slashing my blades in every direction. My pulse races. All around me, skeletal hands shatter and break. Skyn and Bone screech with an otherworldly rage. Adrenaline pumps through my veins. All thoughts of hurt move aside as I keep slashing through skeleton after skeleton.

Yet there are too many of them.

Bony hands clutch at my arms, legs and neck. Their grip turns fierce as they pull me to the floor. I writhe against the broken marble. It's no use. I'm held too firmly.

Bone looms over me, raising his curved dagger high. "You are my kill," says the archdemon.

I stop thrashing. If the end is all there is, I won't have it come while I'm twisting away. Instead, I hold still and focus on the empty, golden eye sockets in the archdemon's skeletal head. "Then do it."

Bone lowers his long blade.

I grit my teeth, steel my spine, and prepare for the end.

Crash!

The ceiling implodes with a flash of blue light and magic. Through the new hole above me, a figure drops onto the nearby floor. I exhale. It's Myla. And she embodies the concept of *pissed off*.

"Back off, skeleton bitches!" cries Myla.

I grin. Things are looking up, quite literally.

MYLA

Oh my freaking Hell.

About a kabillion nasty skeleton arms press my guy down. That golden greed skeleton holds a bone dagger above Lincoln's head, ready to cut his throat.

Not happening.

My inner wrath demon goes berserk. Power charges through my limbs. My eyes flare bright red with demonic energy. Suddenly, the world narrows to nothing but the skeletons and what must happen here.

Slice.

Break.

Crush.

So that's what I do. My body becomes a flurry of rage and action until my guy is free. And sure enough, the moment Lincoln is loose, he leaps into the battle. His baculum short swords become a flurry of white fire as my guy slices through more of the skeleton horde.

Not sure how long it lasts, but soon we're standing back to back with a pile of shattered bones around us. My first instinct is to twist about and wrap my guy in a hug, but something else happens first.

Skyn and Bone have held back all this time. Now the archdemons stomp closer. A shock of awareness skitters across my skin. The pair speak in unison. "Desire. Tear. Own. Destroy."

Lincoln and I move to stand side by side. My guy reignites his baculum as a long sword. I arc my tail over my shoulder.

Bring it on.

The two step forward. I look to Lincoln. "Spears?" I ask.

"Spears," he states.

We reignite our baculum into long spears and chuck the weapons at the archdemons' heads. Both get skewered and fall over. I'm surprised they're so easy to down, but then again, the Pendragon said his prison-crypt was filled with failsafes. Maybe easy archdemon deaths are one of them.

Spinning about, I frame Lincoln's face with my hands. "Are you all right?"

He gives me a lopsided smile. "Nothing a few healing charms can't cure."

"Where are you hur—" My question gets halted by a stunning sight. All the busted skeleton bits now dissolve into red haze.

"What's that?" I ask.

"Skyn and Bone," replies Lincoln. "They're about to reunite with Colossus."

My stomach sinks. Colossus? All of a sudden, I feel the press of eyes staring into the back of my neck. Little by little, I spin about.

Oh. My. Fuck.

On the other side of the room stands a giant demon. Colossus. The goat-y features, extra arms, and yellow eyes … it's all there. The only bright side? The King of the Archdemons seems to be tethered to the wall by a long rope of red power. So that's good.

Then the red mist from Skyn and Bone seeps right into Colossus's torso. My breath catches as his body expands even larger.

Snap!

The tether that ties Colossus to the wall breaks. Captain Fluffbottom materializes before me.

"Trouble, trouble," he squeaks.

"I know, Fluff," I state.

"Risk, risk," adds Fluff. "Plan, plan."

My eyes widen. My snow imp *must not* blab our schemes right in front of Colossus. "Stay quiet and hidden," I warn. The snow imp vanishes.

But it still doesn't change the truth. Fluff has a point: if our scheme doesn't work, I risk not only my own life, but the existence and history of everyone I've ever known and loved.

47

LINCOLN

y brain absorbs every aspect of this moment: Myla standing at my side, her body tense as a coiled spring … the silent chamber … and the towering form of Colossus, glowing red against the black stone wall.

"Time to come out, little pets."

Colossus looks like polished stone, but if you stare more closely, it's clear that he's actually formed from a churning mix of small red particles. Right now, the archdemon king reaches through those particles, jamming his fist inside his own chest.

One by one, Colossus removes the seven archdemons from inside himself.

Soon all seven figures take their places behind Colossus. Add in the archdemon king, and that makes eight enemies against me and Myla.

Not great odds.

Colossus stares at me, his yellow eyes flaring with light and interest. "I have use for you, little king." He waves dismissively at Myla. "But this creature? She means nothing."

Myla just got told she was *nothing* by Colossus. Even so, my girl radiates calm. Usually, being insulted would rile up Myla's inner wrath demon.

Which means she was expecting this from Colossus.

And it's likely all part of a plan.

I stifle the urge to grin.

When the pressure is highest, so are my wife's abilities to scheme.

Colossus steps over to Vain. Or rather, he steps *into* Vain. Normally, Vain is a tall figure in a metallic cloak that seems made of gold. As Colossus enters Vain, the archdemon cries out in agony. A moment later, Vain's golden cloak becomes accented with swirls of red.

Colossus has possessed Vain.

My thoughts swirl through everything I know about the Archdemon of Pride. Like the Archdemon of Envy, Vain is a powerful mage.

Colossus must be planning a spell.

Myla and I need to get out of here. I scan the walls. The seals have closed over. No exit there. Myla burst through the ceiling, but that was with the aid of magic, possibly from Nimue and Merlin. We've no spells left. Beside me, Myla calmly takes in the scene.

I steel my spine. *Myla has a plan.* I simply must wait.

Sure enough, low whispers sound from under Vain's hood. Although I can't catch what's said, the archdemon's voice has the unmistakable sing-song quality that marks an incantation.

Red smoke billows from what is now Colossus-Vain. *Magic.*

Tendrils of colored mist wrap about my wrists and ankles. More loops around Myla's hands and feet as well. The haze solidifies into colored manacles.

We're both locked up now.

Still more red mist pours forth from Colossus-Vain, filling the entire room in a red haze. The air becomes thick with the enchanted mist. The floor turns rubbery beneath my feet. I've been through this before.

Transport spell.

The cloud of magic fades. Little by little, the air clears. I now find myself standing on the courtyard behind Camelot. The good news is that Myla remains at my side. The negative aspect is, obviously, all the archdemons. My gaze locks onto the nearby forest. Under that ground are all the archangels. Surely, someone in Heaven will notice they've been taken. After all, archdemons aren't supposed to use obvious magic on Earth.

Then again, I know how long it took last time. According to my many Arthurian books, it took a thousand years of archdemon nastiness before Colossus and the others were locked up. The Almighty sometimes operates with a different definition of *speedy punishment.*

Long story short, I can't hold my breath for a Heavenly intervention here.

Manacles bite into my wrists. It's painful and not ideal for fighting. I look to Myla, raise my hands, and mouth one word. *Plan?*

My wife knows me well enough to realize there's a whole statement hidden in that single word. Namely, this is my way of saying: *I know you have a scheme here. Are these chains part of the plan?*

In reply, Myla winks. Good news.

For his part, Colossus turns to his archdemons. "Where are the archangels?"

"All imprisoned in Avalon," says Rage.

Colossus tilts his head. Sure, the guy has goat-like features, but some gestures are universal. This particular look says, *I don't believe you.*

And Colossus is right to be wary. Without their king around, the archdemons couldn't leave through a door that's clearly marked *exit*.

"We'll see," says Colossus. He strides over to the edge of the forest and kneels, ready to set his hands into the earth. Not sure if he plans to dissolve his way into Avalon, but with Colossus, it's a possibility.

"Wait!" calls a new voice.

Oh, no. Remy is here.

The so-called Great Crimson Scourge marches out onto the green. "I heard what Rage said. He didn't imprison anyone in Avalon. *I did it.* I am the Crimson Scourge! And my bard shall explain everything."

Beside me, Myla's body stiffens. She whispers a few choice cuss words under her breath.

Evidently, Remy and Drusus are not part of Myla's plan.

48

MYLA

rusus is at it again.

My Drusus.

Wrinkly-old-dude-on-a-cloud Drusus with his sparkly sandals and mopey attitude. The angel who was vanishing before my eyes. The man whose entire bloodline seems bound to the same mistakes, over and over.

I almost punch myself in the face. Hell, I have enough to worry about without focusing on Drusus right now. The guy's doing his Dalston Rusus the Bard thing. There's no need for me to get involved.

But I feel him behind me, staring at me with his big watery eyes.

Not looking. Not looking. Not looking.

Fuck, I looked.

Why am I such a sucker? Here is Drusus again, ready to make life Hell for himself and his offspring for all eternity. Even so, it's not too late. Drusus can take a stand now and sing how Remy's a fraud. Then he'll have all eternity to be an awesome and super-happy angel.

And Drusus is still staring.

Angling my body, I meet his gaze. It's not easy with manacles, but I set my hands at my shoulders and twiddle my fingers in a style that should remind him of angel's wings. My words are there if unspoken.

Don't be a dick. Do the right thing. Make yourself a happy angel.

Remy rounds on Drusus. "Well, are you going to sing about my accomplishments or aren't you?"

Drusus slumps. "Yes, oh Great Crimson Scourge." He flips his handy-dandy lute around so he's ready to play.

"Wait," orders Colossus. Drusus doesn't need to be told twice. The bard swings the lute so it presses against his back once more.

Colossus focuses on Remy. "So you were the one who put all the archangels to sleep in Avalon?"

Remy sets her fist on her hip. It's a motion that's the definition of *swagger.* "That was me."

Colossus steps closer to Remy. Even though the girl is on my *Goes To Hell List* right now, I can't help but feel a little bit worried. She should not be talking to Colossus. It won't end well.

"Then you have the Staff of Avalon," states Colossus. His eyes flare yellow when he says the words, *Staff of Avalon.*

"Sure," replies Remy.

"May I see it?" asks Colossus.

I can't help it. I fake cough, and it sounds a little bit like, *run bitch.*

But Remy's beyond cough-hints at this point. "Of course." She looks up to Colossus through her lashes. "If I prove that I freed you, will I be your queen? That's what the prophecy of the Heretic foretold."

"Yes." Colossus places all four sets of hands on his chest. "Forever."

Frowning, I take a moment for a little mental recap. Colossus is a ten-foot tall demon with four arms, backward legs, and a goat's head.

Goat's head, I tell you!

Where is it a good idea to marry this person?

Oh, Remy.

Even so, Remy raises her arm and whispers another incantation. Within seconds, the Staff of Avalon is gripped in her right fist.

Fast as a whip, Colossus swipes the staff from Remy's hand. With another free set of arms, the archdemon king grabs Remy's head in one hand; the other grips her feet. Remy's so shocked, she doesn't even scream.

Now, I've witnessed my share of disgusting kills on the Arena floor. I've a pretty good idea what's coming here, and there are some things I just don't need to see.

I close my eyes like a boss.

There's some nasty noises of the ripping variety. After a few seconds, I nudge Lincoln.

"Is it over?" I whisper from the side of my mouth.

"Most definitely," says Lincoln.

I open my eyes in time to see Drusus start to run. Colossus takes the Staff of Avalon and points it toward Drusus.

I close my eyes again. Hey, I'm not proud. A nasty squish sounds. "Is it—" I begin.

"—so over," ends Lincoln.

My heart cracks. I mean, I always knew Drusus was dead. After all, I met him as an angel. Still, being present for his nasty end is a different type of awful.

There isn't time to mourn.

Colossus now rounds on me. His long forked tongue flickers out across his lips. "Your turn." The archdemon king slowly stalks closer.

On reflex, I take a half-step backward. Not an easy move with these ankle chains.

Colossus crouches down on his backwards-style animal legs. I've seen this attack before: the old *jump and kill*. My heart thuds with such fury, blood whooshes in my ears.

A shadow passes over the sun. Wincing, I look up to see Dragon-Ximena wheel through the sky to land on the ground between me and Colossus.

I exhale. *Damn, that was close.*

Colossus spider-walks closer to Dragon-Ximena. "Where have you been?"

"Occupied," snarls Dragon Ximena. She's working a definite *you can't possess me* vibe.

Colossus' eyes narrow. It's not a comforting look on him. The archdemon king gestures toward me. "She's one of yours, isn't she? Some Furor blood in there?"

Dragon-Ximena shrugs. "Obviously."

Colossus crawls over to me. His body is a furnace of heat and menace. The archdemon king leans in toward me, stopping when his not-a-nose is an inch from mine. "Then kill her."

My body chills over with alarm. *This is really happening.*

49

LINCOLN

The world around me seems to slow. The green behind Camelot fades to black and white. All breath leaves my body. The words of Colossus echo through my soul, each syllable chilling and final.

Kill Myla.

I take a quick mental inventory. *Am I battle ready?* Blood still seeps from my hip wound … My back is sliced up from metal mirror shards … I'm bound in manacles … And my body armor is shredded. My condition?

More than prepared to fight. The manacles will hamper me, but I've trained for such limitations.

No one touches Myla.

I grip my baculum, ready to reignite them as a longsword.

Myla gently touches my shoulder, stopping me. My breath catches. Turning, I face my wife once more. A mischievous gleam shines in her eyes. Myla's got a plan. I shake my head, thinking through this turn of events.

Myla's bound and supposedly about to be murdered by the Queen of Dragons. And yet my wife is still working her scheme. Adoration pours through my soul. *How I love this woman.* After lowering my baculum, I tap my chest with my left hand. The meaning is clear. *Do you need my help?*

Myla shakes her head and winks. Her reply? *I've so got this.*

Relief and concern battle it out in my soul. I'm pleased Myla has a scheme here, but that doesn't stop my protective instincts from spiraling ever higher. This is my wife. I want her safe, period. Somehow, I'm able to press those worries aside.

This is also my Myla. She can do this.

After Colossus threatened Myla, time seemed to halt. Now the world moves at regular speed once more. In my heart, it feels as if hours have passed since Colossus ordered Myla's execution. In reality, only a few seconds have gone by.

"Hey, Colossus." Myla raises her cuffed hands, a motion that makes her chains jingle. "Kill me and you won't find Lucifer's laboratory."

The King of the Archdemons backs away. It's a ballet of movement, considering how he uses all six limbs. Once again, he strikes me as a spider with a demon's body and goat's head. "And why would I care about that?" he asks.

A grin rounds Myla's mouth. I know how my wife

thinks. The fact that she's not getting killed right now? That means Colossus is interested ... and Myla knows it.

"Lucifer might be a little obsessed with you," explains Myla. "He built a set of armor for you in his laboratory. Super-special stuff."

"Why would I need armor?" To illustrate the point, Colossus bursts out into a misty field of red particles. A moment later, he reforms into his spidery self. "No blade has ever pierced my flesh."

"That's a little limiting, isn't it?" asks Myla. "Lucifer built armor to contain your misty-ness. You'd be able to cast spells or kill on your own, versus having to possess other people all the time."

Colossus lifts his chin. "Not possible."

Myla moves to stand directly at my side. "Lincoln here is my partner in crime. We can take you to the lab. There you'll see the truth for yourself. Imagine the evil you could cause with magic at your command. Picture the joy of killing someone with your *own* hands."

Colossus tilts his head. He's considering this. Excellent. I scan Myla's face. Her mouth thins to a determined line. I've seen that look before. It can only mean one thing. This is the crucial moment.

Will Colossus take the bait and go to Lucifer's laboratory?

My pulse speeds. I don't know all the specifics of Myla's plan, but it must involve that frozen lab. A single thought overtakes my mind.

Please let this work.

Colossus rounds on the dragon queen. "Kill the girl," he orders. "Now."

Stepping forward, I set my body between Myla and the dragon. "You'll need to finish me off first."

"No," states Colossus. "I've another plan for you, little king."

Raising my arms, I prepare to ignite my baculum. Once again, Myla gently rests her hands on my shoulders. "Trust me," she whispers.

Bands of sorrow tighten around my throat. "I can't. Not in this."

Myla moves to stand before me. There's no avoiding her gaze. Everything beautiful and strong shines in her eyes. "Yes," she whispers. "Especially in this."

At that moment, Ximena's claws come down on Myla from behind, spearing my wife though the chest. Blood lines her mouth as she speaks five final words. "Get him to the lab."

Myla falls over.

My world shatters.

50

LINCOLN

My legs turn watery as I kneel by Myla's side. Every corner of my soul is heavy with grief.

She's not breathing. My Myla.

Reaching forward, I gently brush my fingers through her long auburn curls. How many times have I inhaled the cinnamon scent of her hair ... wrapped her locks about my fist as we kissed ... or brushed a few wild strands behind her ear?

Myla can't really be gone.

Odd things happen in mourning. I've seen it with others, but never felt anything like this. It's as if part of my consciousness breaks free. A ghostly version of myself hovers above my own living body. It's that spirit that now watches while the world transforms around me.

Colossus rises to stand. Normally, his hind legs stay half-bent. Now he straightens fully. His gangly body towers above Camelot itself. The King of the Archdemons looms tall like some living red vine that stretches up to the Heavens.

Then Colossus dissolves into mist.

A low red haze covers the courtyard behind Camelot. This is no natural cloud; it's the misty form of Colossus on the prowl. The King of the Archdemons seeks out his next target to possess.

All this while, the seven archdemons have stood along the outer wall of Camelot. A memory appears from when Myla and I first entered Lucifer's lab. We found the red alcove with tiny dolls, one for each archdemon. That's how the seven appear right now—lifeless and stiff as they lean against the stone wall, awaiting possession.

They won't remain motionless for long.

The red essence of Colossus seeps across the castle green. Soon the colored mist crawls up the bodies of each archdemon, wrapping around them like a translucent cloak. After that, the haze soaks into their skin. For a moment, all seven archdemons hiss and writhe in pain. Then they stand tall, their eyes blazing with the same yellow light that shines in the irises of Colossus. Red patterns swirl across their bodies.

All seven are possessed.

The archdemons then launch into a flurry of action. Red light flares as spells are cast. The forest behind Camelot vanishes, replaced by a vast plain covered in human soldiers. In turn, these mortal warriors are divided into seven divisions, one for every archdemon. Each shield shows their symbols of the seven.

A golden skeleton for greed.

A bare skull for gluttony.

The bard's lute for lust.

A green shield for envy; a red one for pride.

Rust for sloth; silver for wrath.

Where once stood a forest, there is now nothing but armies as far as the eye can see. The archdemons march off to stand at the head of their particular column of warriors.

The skies darken. Roars fill the air. The dragon horde wheels overhead. Dragon-Ximena didn't summon them. Some part of me cries that fact is important—Ximena must have alerted her horde beforehand to arrive—yet I can't summon the strength to care.

It's all I can do to keep looking upon Myla. How can someone who contains such light and life be gone?

I barely register the red mist as it surrounds me. Colored haze swirls across my skin. It's Colossus. He wishes to possess me and I almost welcome that fact. Perhaps if the archdemon king controls my consciousness, this pain will become his as well. The red haze seeps into my flesh. For a moment, it's as if every inch of my body were on fire.

I'm becoming possessed by the King of the Archdemons, and for the life of me, I don't care.

Power zooms through my body. My muscles coil with hidden strength. My thoughts focus in a new direction. One phrase repeats.

Lead my army.

It's Colossus, and he's commanding me to act. I don't even bother to fight back. Fresh blasts of red light appear around me. *More magic.* Beneath my feet, the ground rises up into a pillar. My simple battle leathers transform into white steel armor. Now I have been literally raised up above all others. Moving in unison, the humans turn to focus on me. Words tumble from my mouth. They aren't mine.

"Time was, you followed King Arthur," I call. Magic makes my voice carry across the countryside. "Through deeds of strength and valor, I have proven myself a worthy warrior. Now, I am your new king."

The armies cheer. It's a deafening sound, filled with hatred. Thousands of human eyes flare demon red. My gaze falls on Myla.

Still lifeless.

Yet, she said to trust her. My wife's plan was to lure Colossus to the lab. There is no question what to do next. I must follow through on that wish.

More words try to leave my mouth. It's Colossus. He wants me to talk about pillaging all the unworthy humans who were not chosen for his army. I lock my jaw and keep every syllable inside.

It's a battle with Colossus' mind.

The King of the Archdemons fights back.

The burning sensation I felt before now returns with

extra force. Every cell in my body flares with pain. I stay focused on Myla.

I must follow through.

Past the agony, I bite out one phrase. "I will never bow to Colossus."

Red mist seeps from my body to coil on the ground nearby. Within seconds, the haze has taken the form of Colossus. The King of the Archdemons rounds on me, his yellow eyes blazing with rage.

"How dare you?" he asks.

My thoughts turn back to Myla. What would my Angel-bound love do in this situation? The answer appears in a flash of understanding.

My girl would find a soft spot and push.

"Sad, sad Colossus," I declare. "So much power, yet unable to do anything without possessing another. And if that other refuses possession? You're nothing."

Colossus turns to Dragon-Ximena. "You know where this laboratory is?"

Ximena bows her massive head. "I do."

"Take us there," orders Colossus. "And bring the thrax."

"Yes, your Majesty," says Ximena.

Colossus points to me. "Once I will have that armor, you'll be my first kill."

I channel more of my inner Myla. "You can try."

Colossus stomps away. With a flare of red light, the white armor I wear returns to the shape of torn body leathers. At the same time, the pillar I stand upon collapses.

More flares of red magic appear around me. The armies disappear; the forest comes back.

Dragon-Ximena slashes through my chains with her razor-sharp claws. She nips the collar of my leathers, pulling me onto her back. Once I'm in place, Dragon-Ximena spreads her great wings and takes to the air. As we speed away, I carefully scan the ground below us.

There's no sign of Myla's body.

MYLA

I'm alive. *Go me.*

But I'm also soaring through the air clinging to Ximena's back claw because FALLING.

Sure, Ximena's a big enough dragon that her curled-up claw makes for a nice sitting place. I won't build a summer home here, but you get the idea. For the record, I could definitely hang out on this dragon-claw and be a happy girl. But that would mean leaving Lincoln all alone and sad.

Not acceptable.

Which is why I try to scale my way up Ximena's back. Not easy. Did I worry at one point about side-stepping along a mountain ledge? Ha! That's *nothing* compared to crawling up slithery scales while flying along at high velocity. And Ximena still has that love for loop-de-loops.

Ximena did slice through my manacles before leaving Camelot, so a little climbing should be possible. While grabbing onto her leg, I'm able to get myself into a couch-stand …. Aaaaaaaand that's about it. I knock on her scales.

"Ximena?" I call. "Need your help here!"

"You're awake," says Ximena, Dragon Mistress of the Obvious.

"I was always awake, just magic-ed up to look dead." Which means I watched Lincoln in misery. I couldn't even blink, let alone breathe. The spell wouldn't allow it.

And yes, this is all part of the plan to defeat Colossus.

Merlin and Nimue cast the spell to create the illusion of Ximena killing me. At the time, it seemed like a solid scheme. And I did plan to tell Lincoln everything before it happened.

Unfortunately I only shared two words with Lincoln—*trust me*—before I got fake-murdered by a massive red dragon. It wasn't enough. My guy spent what felt like years patting my head and looking miserable.

All of which is why I'm not giving up here. I must connect with my guy, like *now*.

"Ximena!" I cry.

A few minutes ago, I saw how Dragon-Ximena can do her momma-cat move. Namely, she grabbed Lincoln by the collar and then hoisted him onto her back.

I'd like that action, pretty please.

The dragon queen doesn't respond to my cry, but Lincoln does. He leans over Ximena's barrel. For a moment, the sharp lines of his cheekbones and jaw are slack with disbelief. Then his face softens into the biggest smile I've ever seen.

"Myla?"

"It's me, Lincoln. I'm fine!"

In a few swift movements, Lincoln ignites his baculum into a pair of ropes. After that, he levers the cords around Ximena's neck spikes—dragon skin's immune to fire—and creates a kind of pully system to swoop down, grab me, and then hoist me onto Dragon-Ximena's back. I've heard about this way of using baculum over super-short distances. I'd try to pay attention to how it works, but that's impossible because LINCOLN.

My guy faces forward on Ximena's back. I straddle his lap with my legs wrapped about Lincoln's waist. Our mouths meet in a fierce kiss.

"Myla." Lincoln presses his forehead to mine. "Is this real?"

"I'm so sorry. I didn't get a chance to give you the full plan before I got—"

"Pretend-killed by Ximena?" finishes Lincoln.

"Yes. That."

Lincoln wraps his arms more tightly around me, pulling our bodies flush against each other. I rub my hands down his spine and find ...

Fresh blood.

I lean back and gasp. "Lincoln, are you all right?"

He shrugs. "I fought seven archdemons."

I reach into a pocket of my battle leathers and pull out a thin vial. This is another part of the plan, by the way. Merlin and Nimue created some potions for me. I open the small vial of pink liquid and hand it over to Lincoln along with two words.

"Healing potion."

Lincoln gives me a crooked smile. "So, we're not kissing anymore?"

I sigh. "Much as I'd love to get busy with you on a dragon's back while flying along at top speed, this isn't the best place for sexy time." I wink. "Not that I don't appreciate the thought."

He rubs his nose along the length of mine. "With you, the thought is always there."

"Take your healing potion and let's scheme."

"Agreed," says Lincoln. He pops the cork off the small vial, downs the contents and winces.

"Too bitter?" I ask.

"No, too sweet," he replies. "You know how I am."

Which is true. While I love sugar in all its forms, my guy would rather eat a green leafy vegetable any time. *I know.* But I love him anyway.

I brush my fingers long his back. The wounds have all healed over. Even so, I carefully scan Lincoln's face, searching for any lingering signs of pain. "Feeling better?"

"Yes, thank you."

"Any time."

"Now, tell me about this plan of yours."

"Colossus and the other archdemons were imprisoned using a magic book called the *Opus Magica*. Long story short, Merlin and Nimue now have a new *Opus Magica*, along with the super-happy news that it would take another thousand years to charge the thing up enough to lock everyone up again."

"That's rather grim." Lincoln presses his palms against my hips. It's a rather yummy sensation. "Yet you have a plan."

"That we do." I bob my brows.

"We?"

"Yes, it wasn't just me. Nimue, Merlin, Fluff, and Ximena all helped."

"Excellent." Lincoln's mismatched eyes sparkle with pride. It's a great look on him.

"We can't wait for a thousand years to charge up the *Opus Magica*, but guess what could do the job for us super-fast?"

A slow smile winds across Lincoln's mouth. "The crystal clock in Lucifer's lab."

"Oh, yeah."

Lincoln purses his lips. "We need to be careful. There were signs before the bomb went off. Specifically, we heard a whirring sound followed by what Fluff called the *tick-tick-boom*. What if Colossus and the seven archdemons hear either of those noises … and guess what we're up to?"

"Well." I scrunch up my mouth and think this through. "Then Colossus could focus the energy of the crystal clock into himself. That would give him some crazy-ass power."

"Every plan has risks," says Lincoln. "We just need to know what they are."

"Sure," I say.

Even so, that word comes out as more of a question. In

all my excitement about re-locking up Colossus—and saving everyone in the after-realms—I didn't think through how this plan could actually backfire.

Oops.

Lincoln glances about. This is one of my favorite of his *thinking-faces*. "If my memory is right, we'll have two minutes and forty three seconds between the first whirring sound and the actual explosion."

"I knew you'd have the right countdown." I reach into my pocket. "And guess what I remembered for this trip?" I pull out a pair of thin rings. "Merlin and Nimue gave me these charms to keep us warm." I slip mine on my pointer finger.

Lincoln slips his band onto his pinky. "Thank you."

Dragon-Ximena swings her head in our direction. "We're landing."

I pull out another vial from my pocket. "This potion will make me invisible to everyone except our team. Nimue and Merlin already drank some. Fluff can make himself invisible at will, so he didn't need any."

"Prepare to jump," cries Dragon-Ximena.

Uncorking the vial, I down the potion. My body vanishes just as Dragon-Ximena swings past the entrance to Lucifer's lab.

Lincoln and I jump, landing right into the mouth of the dark passage that marks the lab's entrance. Dragon-Ximena then wheels toward the cavern's mouth as well. At the last moment, she transforms into her human self and lands beside us. Ximena's cocoa skin and long brown hair positively glow against the pale landscape. The dragon queen wears a red riding coat over her battle leathers.

Voices echo in from inside the passage. Colossus and his archdemons are already here. Our group takes a few steps deeper into the corridor to Lucifer's lab.

That's when we hear it.

Low rumbles sound from outside the mountain. The passageway around us vibrates from this hidden force. We pause.

"What's that?" I ask.

"No idea," offers Ximena.

Lincoln frowns. "Same here."

Little by little, all three of us turn about. The outside landscape gleams before us, a bright scene that's framed by the passageway's dark mouth. Moments ago, the mountain range was colored in shades of white. A red cloud now rolls out over the land.

Magic.

It's same shade of power Colossus wielded while possessing Vain. A realization hits me. That's what the voices inside the laboratory could have been doing— casting a spell. My pulse speeds. This isn't good.

For a moment, the scene shimmers with crimson light. The passageway around us shivers more violently.

The landscape changes.

Explosions sound as the mountain range collapses. Peak after peak implodes, leaving plumes of white smoke behind. Snow and dust fill the air. Within seconds, the jagged landscape has flattened out. Now, we look upon a snowy plain that stretches off in every direction. A fresh red haze rolls out over the ground.

Another spell begins.

The colored mist solidifies into seven massive armies. Like before at Camelot, all the humans hold the colored shields for their archdemon. Above it all, hundreds of dragons wheel and fly.

Tension zooms through my every muscle. This army also appeared at Camelot. Only now? It's double the size. *Colossus isn't wasting time.* Once the archdemon king gets his armor, he'll move out over the world.

"Damn," I grumble. "Let's hope we didn't make everything worse."

Lincoln nods. "Quite."

LINCOLN

*C*olossus' voice echoes through the corridor once more. Bands of worry tighten around my chest. The archdemon king is off doing *who knows what* in Lucifer's lab.

No time to delay.

Turning, I face the shadowy passage. "Let's move out."

Myla shoots me a thumbs up.

Ximena nods.

Our trio rushes off into darkness until we reach the lab itself. The chamber appears identical to when Myla and I first entered it in our own era. There are tables covered in sheets, round walls lined with shelves, and the small red alcove of statues.

The big difference this time is *who* waits inside the lab. To the right, seven archdemons line up against the wall. Their eyes seem pale and lifeless; Colossus isn't possessing them right now. They remind me of so many toy soldiers, unmoving until someone turns the key in their backs.

On the far left of the room, I find Merlin and Nimue. They appear semi-transparent to me, just like Myla—which means they're invisible to everyone else. The golden clock looms beside them; it's still covered in a white sheet. Merlin grips the new *Opus Magica* tightly against his chest. The pair hold hands as they prepare to begin casting.

Both mages scan the room with anxious stares. They'll need to wait until just before the explosion in order to cast their spell and channel the crystal clock's power into the *Opus Magica*. Otherwise their spell will be visible too early. Colossus and his archdemons might see it ... and then where would we be?

And in the center of the space, there crawls Colossus. He moves spider-style on all limbs, pacing a circle while staring up at the ceiling.

Or to be specific, at the armor suspended there.

Colossus glares at me. "Get me *my armor*, thrax."

I steal a glance toward Myla. The words are there but unspoken, *Is this part of the plan?*

She nods; I move.

Crossing the room, I step to the waist-high lever that juts up from the stone ground. Grasping the lever's top, I yank until it now stands perpendicular to the floor.

The red metal armor slowly lowers.

Beside me, loop after loop of chain rises to the ceiling as Colossus' prize comes down. With a great clunk, the armor hits the floor. It's a segmented affair made of concentric loops that fit over Colossus' long limbs. I can only hope the King of the Archdemons must apply each loop separately. That would take time.

No such luck.

Colossus slides into the armor the way I might drag on my favorite battle leathers. Not that I'm shocked; Lucifer is a rather talented craftsman.

But I am alarmed.

Myla waves to Merlin and Nimue. She's giving them the signal to start. The ghostly mages lower their heads to mouth silent incantations. A light layer of blue mist surrounds the nearby floor. For now, that haze is hidden behind the draped tables. Still, that can't last for long.

Whir.

Across the room, the crystal clock launches into action. To me, the sound seems deafening. Thankfully, Colossus is letting off a chorus of metallic clinks as he slides on his armor. His archdemons watch in rapture.

None of them notice that a countdown has begun.

Every nerve ending in my body goes on alert. That's when it happens. Merlin drops the *Opus Magica*. He scoops it back up quickly, but is it too late?

Myla mouths a curse word. I couldn't agree more.

Moving in unison, all the archdemons turn to scan the left-hand side of the chamber. Their gazes lock on the tall object covered in a white sheet.

The crystal clock.

Myla hugs her elbows. Even though she's partially

invisible, there's no missing how all color has drained from her face.

Colossus stares at the draped clock. "What was that?"

Half-dressed in armor, the King of the Archdemons marches across the lab floor, using his limbs to dart up and over any obstacle, spider style.

With every step closer to the clock, my heart kicks harder against my ribs.

The King of the Archdemons pauses before the covered clock. For a long moment, nothing happens.

Colossus sniffs, shrugs, and turns away.

I exhale. The archdemon king isn't inspecting the clock. Colossus walk-crawls back to the rest of his armor pile. As he steps along, one loop of wrist armor clangs to the floor.

And that sounds scares the crap out of Captain Fluffbottom.

Damn.

The snow imp flies right out from under the clock's tarp, zooms across the room, and cowers against Myla's shoulder. My breath catches. Throughout the scene, Fluff remained invisible, but his affect on the covering sheet wasn't.

Colossus pauses. Little by little, the King of the Archdemons swivels about to face the hidden clock once more. When he next speaks, he accents each syllable.

"What. Hides. Under. That. Sheet?"

"Shall I inspect it, your Majesty?" asks Ximena. She poses the question calmly enough, but from my view, I can see her hands shaking behind her back.

Rage steps forward. "Or you may possess me," offers the archdemon. "If anyone hides there, I can kill them."

"No," counters Colossus. "I'll explore with my own hands."

Step-crawling back to the center of the room, Colossus slips on the rest of the armor until only the helm remains. Colossus lifts that final piece above his head and grins.

"Let's see what you built for me, Luce." Colossus pulls down the helm, which falls in place on his head with a soft click.

And the magic goes to work.

The room becomes washed in shades of red as Colossus' armor glows with power. My heart sinks at the sight. Colossus was always the worst of the worst, his sole limitation that fact that he could only possess others.

That's done now.

"Ah," sighs Colossus. "The armor has already begun to function. I feel my solidity." He turns toward the crystal clock.

Myla lets out another—*longer*—string of silent cuss words.

Within moments, Colossus stands before the covered clock once more. My mind reels. There must be something we can do.

I glance over to Myla. If anyone can some up with a stunning scheme on a moment's notice, it's my wife. She presses her palms against her eyes. That's her *emergency planning pose.*

Colossus reaches forward. Little by little, he pulls off

the tarp. The clock is revealed in all its perfection. Thousands of apex crystals intertwine and gleam. It's gorgeous, powerful and deadly.

"Let's see now." Colossus runs his many long fingers over the magical clock. "How best to consume this power?"

I scan Merlin and Nimue. If anything, there's less blue mist around them, not more. Then I inspect the dragon queen. Ximena shivers. She isn't running away, but she isn't looking ready to fight, either.

Myla and I lock gazes. My wife mouths a single word, and I couldn't agree more.

Damn.

MYLA

*C*olossus wants to take in the crystal clock's power?

Oh, Hell.

Focusing on Lincoln, I pull out my baculum and flip it between my fingers. The question is there: *Should we spark these up now?*

My guy inspects Merlin and Nimue, who still silently chant. I can almost see the thought bubble over his head saying, *there's still a chance these mages will channel the explosion's power into the* Opus Magica.

Returning his attention to me, Lincoln mouths one word. *Boom.*

I get the meaning here. We have one shot to take down Colossus, and that's when the crystal clock does its thing … while Merlin and Nimue do theirs. Long story short, we simply must wait for the *big bang*. Which sucks. Standing around is not my favorite activity. I glare at the clock with all my held-in frustration.

Explode already!

Colossus grips the clock with such force, a handful of the gemstones snap. A low hum sounds from the device. An electric sense of power fills the air. My skin prickles over into gooseflesh. The clock gleams with golden light. Soon, every corner of the lab is awash with yellow beams.

Then it happens.

Golden cords of power erupt from the device to wrap about Colossus's arms, mummy-style. The clock still shines bright, but now waves of golden power flow from the device into Colossus. With every passing second, the clock grows dimmer. Meanwhile, Colossus's very body begins to glow. Thin beams of golden light peep out between the seams in his armor. No question about it.

Colossus is soaking in power.

I strain my hearing, trying to catch the telltale *tick-tick-ding* that means the crystal clock will explode.

Nothing.

Freaking clock.

Instead of exploding like a good magical device, the clock just sends more and more power into Colossus. Now there's definitely enough energy for the archdemon king to do something nasty. I step a little closer to Lincoln because in situations like this one, he's my *thrax binky*.

"Reveal to me all the magic in this room!" cries Colossus.

Frowning, I process this turn of events. *Okay, this isn't so bad.* Colossus wants to see what else in the laboratory could be useful for him. Logical. And it buys me some time to think of a next step here.

Trouble is, I got nothing.

Long tendrils of golden power rise up from Colossus' arms. The bright cords twist around the room. The thin lines encase the many objects shelved in the lab. Soon a handful of stuff—vials, books, and boxes—now glow with golden light. It's like a blinking yellow alarm that says, *take me home, Colossus!*

All of a sudden, the golden lines speed in my direction. Every nerve ending in my body freezes. I'm no mage. Still, maybe my invisibility spell could be attracting this junk?

Golden cords wrap around my wrists. All thought empties from my mind. *Damn.* I was so focused on Colossus doing his inventory thing, I didn't consider that his spell would detect me. And if it goes after yours truly, the magic will certainly find Merlin and Nimue.

Shit burger.

Sure enough, the golden magic soaks into my skin and vanishes. The spell is over. Did I dodge something here?

One second passes.

Two.

And—POOF—I am now visible. Same thing happens with Merlin and Nimue. Not sure where Fluff got off too. Hopefully the little guy is safe.

For his part, Colossus is not pleased. Ignoring the other mages, the archdemon king glares in my direction.

"I thought you were dead!" he roars.

I make jazz hands. "Fooled ya."

"Now I shall kill you myself." Colossus clasps the crystal clock even more tightly. "Once these apex crystals give me all their power, I can devise new and more bloody ways to slowly end your life."

And I don't doubt it.

Lincoln and I share a look that can only be described as: *oh no.* It's not a question any more of waiting for the big bang. Once Colossus sucks in all the power of the crystal clock, it's game over.

Igniting my baculum as a longsword, I leverage my demonic energy and run straight out. Beside me, Lincoln does the same. My guy's eyes flare blue. Angelic energy. Even Ximena races along at our side.

Across the room, the archdemons notice this turn of events and launch into action. Moving as a single unit, they race off in our direction. Lincoln and I are fast, but these creeps? Lightning velocity.

My brain goes into battle mode. Fast calculations run through my mind. Based on our current speeds, there's no way Lincoln and I will reach Colossus in time. And Ximena's in the same situation, too. While this laboratory may be large, it isn't big enough that she can shift into dragon form.

Strange how your thoughts focus when your world is about to be torn apart. My mind turns to Maxon, Cissy, Xavier and Camilla, picturing all of them smiling in slow motion. If we fail, my friends and family will be gone forever. No more fading angels. No more anything. It's something I never seriously considered before. Despair presses in around me, tight as a vise. Still, I push myself to run faster.

It's no use, though. Colossus remains too far away. Only inches separate us and the other archdemons. Rage has his sword gripped high, pointed in a way that is definitely meant to separate my head from the rest of me.

At some point, we all lose.

This is my moment.

I'm not the only one in trouble, either. Skyn and Bone have their skeletal hands on Lincoln, choking him to death. The remaining archdemons restrain Ximena. Shock, rage and fear battle it out in my nervous system.

Rage's sword comes down. I leap out of the way, but not before the blade nicks my throat. Blood trickles down my neck.

One more swipe from Rage and I'm done.

All of a sudden, a white blob of fur speeds through my peripheral vision.

Unholy Hell. It's Fluff and damn, that little dude is fast.

Extending his tiny claws out, Fluff grabs the helm from Colossus' head. In one whip-fast movement, Fluff tears off the helm and flies straight toward the ceiling. The moment his armor is incomplete, Colossus loses his grip on the clock.

Golden cords die out.

Apex crystals cease to glow.

Ha. No more power for you, Kill Boy.

Colossus points to Fluff. "My helm!" he cries.

Instantly, the archdemons stop trying to destroy us. That's the *cup-half-full* take on this situation.

The *we're screwed side* is how the archdemons now chase after poor Fluff. Skyn, Bone, Null, and Rage all scale up the shelves. Lester shimmies up the armor chain. Plain and Vain transform their silvery cloaks into bat-like wings.

Yipes.

There's no time to worry about the snow imp, though. A new sound echoes through the laboratory.

Tick-tick-ding!

At last. Sheesh.

The crystal clock shatters. Merlin and Nimue cast a sphere of blue power around the device, forcing it to stay in some semblance of its original shape. *A containment orb.* Thanks to the spell, all the matchstick-sized crystals now hover only a few inches apart from their original positions. The explosive power of the clock is mostly held in check, but for how long?

My neck and shoulders tighten in frustration. So far, the containment orb is only preventing an explosion, not channeling any power into the *Opus Magica*. Plus, some energy still leaks free, causing the entire lab to tremble. Shelves buckle. Walls snap. Chunks of ceiling wobble in place.

"My helm!" cries Colossus again.

The archdemons close in on Fluff. Even though the helm is twice his size, the snow imp holds onto it like a champ.

This really isn't going well.

There must be a way to fix things.

An image appears in my mind: the circle I drew on the forest floor. Back then, I called Merlin and Nimue *my knights*. Ever since we entered the lab, I've been waiting for the two mages to do their part.

Maybe their part can't be done alone.

Pulling on my own demonic strength, I race toward Merlin and Nimue. Lincoln and Ximena speed along at my side. How did there end up being so many tables in here? My legs get banged up trying to rush over them all.

At last, we reach Merlin and Nimue. The mages still stand with their fingers laced together. Now I hold Nimue's free hand in my own.

"We just used our inner magic to run here more quickly," I call. "Now ask it to help contain and channel the crystal clock's energy."

Merlin sets the new *Opus Magica* on the ground nearby. We all hold hands, create a circle, and focus our inner powers.

Everything changes.

A magical circuit forms. Lines of blue energy careen around us. The azure magic loops about the crystal clock, pulling it back together into its original shape. The golden energy is more firmly contained within. Will that mean it's easier to take out?

All the while, Fluff zooms through the lab, leading the archdemons on the chase of all chases. How long can the little guy hold out?

Our magical circuit grows stronger. The blue lines create a funnel that stretches from the crystal clock to the *Opus Magica*. Waves of golden energy move from the apex crystals into the magical book. The two cover seals glow with power.

It's happening.

And then, the flow of golden power slows.

My eyes widen as I realize the truth. *Colossus took too much energy from the crystal clock.* There isn't enough left to fully charge the *Opus Magica*.

Rage heats my veins. How can this be the end? My jagged reflection stares back at me from the mosaic of golden stones.

She winks. This isn't something I'm doing.

At this point, I'm ready to scream. What is it with this mystery chick? Giving girlfriend advice? Scaring the crap out of me in lakes? And now, at my worst moment, winking away like she's got some super awesome secret to share? Meanwhile, the flow of golden power grows even weaker.

My reflection rests her hands on her shoulders. Again, this isn't anything I'm doing. Behind her back, a white haze appears. Then, there are wings. Lovely angel wings whose feathers are tipped in gold.

I gasp.

And at last, I understand.

Since I was a kid, I knew about my inner wrath demon. It took meeting Lincoln for me to discover my lust power. But my inner angel? I'd never searched for her. If anything, I've been actively avoiding any thought of her at all.

Yet she exists.

And the way Colossus' spell highlighted yours truly as one of the magical things in the room? My inner angel must be jam packed with spell casting energy.

Instantly, I see the reason for her wink. I can pump extra magic into this entire scene.

So that's what I do.

I've never cast a spell before, but I know how my inner demons work. I imagine something and they make it happen. Right now, the five of us stand in a circle. Power loops around us in great cords. I ask my inner angel to pump more energy into the circuit. It flares bright blue. Fresh waves of power flow into the *Opus Magica*.

Each page takes on a golden hue. The white and red seals atop shine so brightly, my eyes water at the sight.

That's when the archdemons fall.

It begins with Null. Tendrils of gold power reach out from the white seal, grasp the rusted knight and drag him down. The cords yank Null toward the magical portal that is the pale disc. Light flares out from the white seal, and then Null is gone.

I could cheer with joy. One archdemon is back in prison, seven more to go.

The process repeats as one by one, more archdemons are pulled back into the white seal. Rage, Plain, Vain, Lester, Skyn and Bone... all get dragged away.

Only one remains.

Far above us, the archdemon king clings to the rock wall, his claw-like hands digging in to hold him in place... and out of the red seal. All the while, more gold cords wind around his torso and legs. The tendrils grow thicker as they pull Colossus toward the *Opus Magica*.

Boom!

The stone wall that Colossus holds crumbles into rubble. The archdemon king loses his grasp. The colored cords pull taught. Colossus tumbles toward the red seal. Light flares when the archdemon king reaches the *Opus Magica*. After that, darkness.

What was once a laboratory is now a hollowed out cavern filled with broken glass, rubble and shadows.

Every inch of my body goes on alert. Did it work?

On the *Opus Magica*, the red seal flares to life. The disc shines with the symbol of a ram's head. I do a happy dance.

"We did it!" I cry. "We got Colossus!"

Merlin and Nimue hug. Ximena cheers. Lincoln stares at a small pile of rubble nearby. I know my guy and what it means when his eyes narrow in this particular way. He's in *hunter mode*.

Sure enough, the very spot Lincoln examines does something unexpected. It moves. Everyone stops cheering as out from the rubble comes none other than Captain Fluffbottom, the snow imp who saved the universe. Fluff immediately takes to the air and zooms in my direction. Soon, he's sitting on my shoulder while my tail pats his little head.

"Win, win," says Fluff.

Lincoln beams. "That we did, thanks to you."

Fluff taps his chest. "Knight, knight."

"Absolutely," I chuckle. "You're one of the knights of my roundtable."

My eyes widen as I remember. "The armies! They're still outside!"

With all the excitement of fighting Colossus, I'd forgotten that an evil human mega-army awaited us around the mountain. We all race through the exit hallway, stopping when we reach the outdoors.

Lincoln sighs. "It's all good. They're gone."

Sure enough, everything is back to being mountain peaks, snow and heavy clouds. No armies in sight. Xinema's dragon horde has already packed up and flown home.

Odd. I thought Ximena would have asked her dragons to stay. Yet she already sent them off. As a result, her people could think she died in the lab blast. *Something to ask her about later.*

Merlin grips the new *Opus Magica* tightly against his chest. "Now we have other things to worry about, such as how to hide this book."

Nimue rolls her eyes. "Can you celebrate for two seconds?"

Merlin frowns. "No."

"Not one huzzah?" asks Nimue.

"Huzz. Zah." Merlin looks to me with a gaze that clearly says, *help?*

I raise my hand, palm forward. "Merlin raises a good point. And I happen to know someone who's an ace at putting Lucifer's crap in storage where it won't bug anyone."

Lincoln gives me the side eye. "Are you thinking what I'm thinking?" he asks.

"Yup," I reply. "Let's raise my not-a-father from Avalon."

MYLA

*a*n hour later, we're back at Camelot. Nimue and Merlin have recovered the Staff of Avalon. Ximena stands nearby in her human form. Fluff zips overhead. Now Nimue waits by the forest's edge, her arms raised. The Staff of Avalon is gripped in Nimue's fist. Merlin still holds the new *Opus Magica* against this chest.

True fact: There's a certain kind of joy I usually feel when defeating an enemy. I want to do a happy dance, punch my fist in the air, or at least let out a good *mwah hah hah*. After sending the archdemons back, though? I just feel numb.

Maybe that's because I now know there's an angelic entity who's been floating around inside me for *who knows how long*.

On second thought, it's definitely that.

After all, having an inner angel makes sense, considering how I already have an inner *lust and wrath demon combo*. I'm just starting to get really crowded, that's all.

Across the courtyard, Nimue and Merlin whisper their incantations. The golden stones in the Staff of Avalon shine with a yellow light to rival the sun. Lincoln moves closer to my side. We haven't spoken much since the laboratory battle. Even while flying on Dragon-Ximena's back on the way here, we've been more cuddly than chatty.

Perhaps I'm not the only one who's feeling a little overwhelmed.

Lincoln sets his palm on the base of my back. "So what happened during the spell to recharge the *Opus Magica*?"

"You mean when I pumped extra power into the magical circuit we'd created?"

"Yes, that." A sly look enters my guy's mismatched eyes. He so knows I'm avoiding telling him something.

And he's right.

When it comes to my inner angel, there's actually a lot I haven't shared with Lincoln. Mostly because I've been actively avoiding the truth myself. If I told my husband, then the mysterious-me would be a real issue.

"I only ask the best questions," quips Lincoln.

My gaze flicks over to Merlin and Nimue. They're still pretty tired after the whole laboratory adventure, so it's taking them a while to actually get this spell going.

"It's a long story, so I'll just give you the punch line."

"Whatever you like."

"Know how I have inner wrath and lust demons?"

"My favorites."

"Turns out, I have an inner angel, too. And she's a mega-powerful sorceress."

Lincoln's face does that thing where his emotions turn completely unreadable. "Wow."

"I know. Shocker."

"What has she said since the laboratory?"

"Nothing. I haven't asked for her and she hasn't shown up. I'm trying to actively ignore the whole deal." I sigh. "But maybe I should give it a try." Closing my eyes, I call out to my inner angel.

Hey, uh, you. Hi.

Not my best greeting, but this is a super-weird situation. I wait for a reply.

Nothing.

Nothing.

And nothing.

At this point, the ground begins to rumble. An electric charge of magic fills the air. The earth splits. Trees snap. The silver castle of Avalon rises once more.

Some part of me knows that I should focus now. After all, we're about to go inside a freaking castle and awaken my Not-Dad. But the most I can do is go through the motions. I might as well be sleepwalking as we enter Avalon and watch Nimue awaken all the archangels.

The reason is simple. Before, when I was ignoring my inner angel, I didn't care that she wasn't chatty. But now that I called out to her? It's getting on my nerves how she won't reply. I mean, if I think about how Lincoln is hot, then my inner lust power is right there. Should I focus on kicking a horde of Rodentia demons, my inner wrath entity will fire up in my soul.

But my inner angel? She's a no show.

Now sure how I know this, but I'm positive she's still rattling around inside me somewhere. She's just holding out. *What's up with that?*

Lots of time passes while I sulk on this issue. Soon all the other archangels have woken up and flown off. Avalon is back underground. Not-Dad stayed behind for some reason; now he's striding over in my direction.

"I'll give you two a minute," says Lincoln. He kisses my cheek before stepping away.

Not-Dad pauses before me. "Greetings."

I give him a mostly-serious salute. "Hello, General."

"About the Staff of Avalon... You were right."

I grin. *How I love being told that.* "Let it be a lesson to you."

Not-Dad chuckles. "I will." He gestures to the Band of Epochs on my thumb. "You'll be leaving us soon."

"Yeah, I came back in time to stop Colossus from starting the demonpocalypse. That's all done, so I need to head back and hope my reality is fixed again."

"Were there magical visions that drove this journey of yours?" asks Not-Dad.

"Oh, yeah. From both a wrath coven and an oracle angel."

"Then as long as you followed the path of those prophecies, your future is safe." He shakes his head. "By the way, it would be nice to think I'd have a daughter some day, but that's not me. Some souls aren't built for love."

I rock on my heels and press my lips together. It's really tempting to prove I'm his daughter, but I don't want to monkey with the future. If my father knew he'd have a kid, that could change things. I like my reality just the way it is, thank you very much. Besides, I am such a charismatic figure, I bet Not-Dad will already spend centuries wondering who I really am.

"Have a good life, Mika." Not-Dad spreads his wings and takes to the skies.

My mouth hangs open in surprise. *Mika?* Then again, maybe Not-Dad will fly off and forget me in all of five seconds.

Lincoln steps to my side. "Did he just call you Mika?"

"That he did."

Nimue, Merlin, and Ximena step over. Fluff hovers in the air above them. A sinking feeling moves through my insides. I'd gotten really attached to these guys. Now we need to go home.

"What will you do now?" I ask.

"We're not sure," says Nimue. "Maybe rebuild the Pendragon Academy."

Lincoln looks to Ximena. "How about you?"

She scans the skies. "In your history, I'm still locked up. I should like it to stay that way... officially. None of my dragons saw the end of what happened in the laboratory. For all they know, I'm all locked up again." She grins.

"There's a certain freedom to leaving your crown behind and living a simple life. I doubt that makes sense."

"Oh, it makes tons of sense," says Lincoln.

I look to my little group. An image appears. All of us holding hands as we fought none other than Colossus and his archdemons. Words begin to tumble from my mouth, seemingly without any instruction from my brain.

"If you guys are around in another eight hundred years or so, be sure to look me up. I have this problem with fading angels. I bet if we worked on it, we could come up with something cool. After all, we brought down Colossus after an hour's worth of planning." My voice gets a little wobbly as I say the next bit. "You've become my own knights of the round table." I look to each familiar face: Merlin, Nimue, Fluff and Ximena. "I need you."

"We mages live a long time," says Merlin. "But eight hundred years is a stretch."

Nimue sniffles. "We like you, too."

"Love, love," chirps Fluff.

Ximena pretends she needs to clear her throat. It's a trick I use myself to hide when you're tearing up. "You two better go. I have a lot of meaningless meandering to do."

"We'll depart," says Lincoln.

"And thanks," I add.

Lincoln and I pull out our respective last bands, speak the incantation, and snap our rings in two. Purple mist surrounds us as the time travel spell kicks into action.

We're going home.

LINCOLN

*T*he spell ends as quickly as it began. Myla and I soon find ourselves back in Soul Tower One. The place isn't done up like a disco anymore. Even better, the cloud carriers hover overhead. Joy lightens my heart. I pull Myla into my arms and twirl her about.

"We did it!" I cry.

She laughs, and I simply adore that sound. "Go us."

I set my wife down and wave to the control room. "Ho, there!"

A figure steps to the window while the intercom springs to life. "Yes, your Majesty?"

"Do you happen to know if my son is at home?" I ask.

"He is at your Purgatory residence. The Consort to the President is watching him." The sound of paper rustling echoes through the speaker. "In fact, the general contacted us not long ago. He asked you to pick up more maple syrup on your way home."

My gaze locks with Myla's. She's beaming, same as I am. Maxon is safe. Xavier and Camilla are back. Our world has returned. It's everything we'd hoped for.

"We better get moving," I call to the control room. "Thank you for the information."

The voice crackles over the loudspeaker once more. "But your guests are almost here."

Sure enough, the front doors to the soul tower swing open. In walks a group figures, their outlines highlighted by the setting sun behind them. I blink hard, not believing who I'm seeing.

Nimue.

Merlin.

Ximena.

Fluff.

Myla and I race over to them. It's the most natural movement in the world for us to fall into a circle once again.

"What are you doing here?" asks Myla.

"I decided to take a little nap in Avalon," answers Nimue.

Merlin raises his hand. "Same thing."

"Same, same," adds Fluff.

Ximena shrugs. "So I woke them up at the right time. It's not hard to do when your have the Staff of Avalon. And now we're here." She sets her fist on her hip. "You still need some help with those fading angels or what?"

"Yes, I do." Myla's eyes narrow while she steeples her

fingers under her chin. I know that look on my wife. Some kind of scheme just popped into her mind.

Can't wait to see it in action.

EPILOGUE

LINCOLN

ONE WEEK LATER

O ne week later, we're back in Ghost Tower One. Myla paces the concrete floor. I know how nervous she is about today's dry run of the new system for the fading angels. In my opinion, she has nothing to be concerned about.

Myla rakes her fingers through her hair. "This is risky."

Which it isn't.

"No," I counter. "It's brilliant."

Because it is.

The tower is a bustle of activity. Against the far wall, Myla's knights wait by an enchanted mirror on the wall. And by her knights, I mean Merlin, Nimue, Fluff and Ximena. All wear lab coats, even Fluff. For the past week, they've all been locked up in this tower while testing out different spells. Since there are spirits so close by, they can easily ask for souls to volunteer to try out different incantations.

It's a rather small tower, so everyone overheard what Myla just said.

"This probably won't work," agrees Merlin.

"Stop being a worrywart," says Nimue.

"Worry, worry," squeaks Fluff.

"Dragons never fret." That's Ximena. She goes by Lady X now and is a master of taking measurements. Like always, she grasps a clipboard in her hands. Officially, she's a quasi-demon these days and loving it.

Nearby, Maxon plays with his truck collection. He's having a grand time using the concrete floor for races.

I glance toward the front doors. Any minute now, Camilla, Xavier and Walker will enter for the official test of our new system, Camelot One.

At last, the doors swing open. Xavier, Camilla and Walker enter the tower. They're all in human suits, which fits their roles today as the ruling team of Purgatory. I'm in a human suit as well, while Myla opted for her new Scala robes.

After all our hellos and greetings, Myla steps before the mirror to speak. The thing is about give feet tall, oval and with a gilded frame.

"Tell us about your invention," prompts Camilla. In this moment, Myla's mother is every inch the President of Purgatory.

Myla nibbles on her thumbnail. "We don't know if it

will work, just so you know. We haven't had much time for tests."

Being so close to Myla means that sometimes, I have a mainline to her anxiety. Right now, I sense her nervous energy like its my own. She wants so badly for this to go perfectly; that's my wish as well.

Xavier flashes one of his most angelic smiles. "No expectations from our side," he says smoothly. Still, there's a curious twinkle in his eyes. No doubt, Xavier is planning something special for after the test. It's even more suspicious considering how he's been in touch with Octavia. Mother loves nothing more than to plan a party.

Myla inhales a deep breath. Her gaze locks with mine. I shoot her a thumbs=up. Myla grins, straightens and addresses the group.

"We all know how human lives have various *cruxes*. These are key decision points which decide their future and afterlife." She gestures to Merlin. "Can you show the example?"

Merlin touches the mirror. Blue mist rolls over the reflective surface. When the colored haze fades, the mirror displays Drusus sitting on a straw mattress, gripping his lute. A trio of guardian angels stand behind him. Although we can't hear what's being said, there's no question what's happening.

Myla gestures to the mirror. "This human is about to do something terrible. Namely, he's about to sing a song filled with untruths. In some ways, the damage of this song has already been done in terms of history. But for Drusus, this particular concert marks his *crux* of no return. To convince him otherwise, a guardian angel already left a what we call a *serendipity* nearby. In this case, it's song lyrics from another composer."

I think back to the serendipity we saw with Drusus' extended son, Charles. In that case, it was when the guardian angel changed the image on Charles' cell phone. It altered from an email to a picture of Charles' family.

In the mirror, Drusus picks up his serendipity—that parchment—from a nearby table. The bard scans the sheet and pauses.

"As you can see, this *serendipity* has got Drusus thinking," continues Myla. "He's considering singing something else... or skipping the performance altogether."

"This happened long ago," says Camilla. "What became of this man?"

"Drusus doesn't heed the warning. After he died, he was sent to Heaven and became a fading angel. Yet the situation gave us an idea. What if the guardian angel had tried a different song? Perhaps another serendipity could have worked. In the past, guardian angels could only try one thing during a mortal's life. Now, with the Mirror of Avalon, we can give a soul an unlimited number of chances."

My chest swells with pride. In this moment, Myla exudes a heady mixture of confidence and excitement. No other Great Scala has ever attempted to fix the problem of the fading angels. But there's never been anyone like my Myla.

After closing her eyes, Myla raises her arms. I've seen her do this a hundred times before, and it never gets old.

She's calling her igni.

Hundreds of tiny lightning bolts of power appear nearby. Myla lowers her arms and the igni swirl about in a column that reminds me of a school of fish. When the igni disappear, the barest outline of a figure stands before us.

It's Drusus.

And he's almost completely vanished.

Myla turns to him. "Are you sure about this? It will seem like you're back in your mortal life. And it will be hard."

"I want to try," says Drusus. "Did you get my lyrics? Not the ones from the guardian angel, but those I wrote."

"Yes," explains Nimue. "They're already loaded into the illusion."

"Then it's time for me to go," intones Drusus.

Merlin raises his hand. Cords of blue power wind from the mirror and curl through the air. The magical tendrils wrap around Drusus, outlining his body in blue lines. A long pause follows as the spell hangs in space.

Then it moves.

The blue cords pull on Drusus, dragging him into the mirror.

The test has begun.

Inside the mirror a new image appears. It's the same small room we saw before. Drusus sits on his cot while holding his lute. To him, he's alive again. There is no memory of his afterlife, only the present moment. Drusus notices the parchment on a side table and reads it.

And now, after days of practice and planning, both Drusus and Avalon One reach a crossroads. Will Drusus crumple up these lyrics, like he did the other set? Or will he change his life… and all of Purgatory?

Myla nibbles her thumbnail and watches the scene unfold. Maxon makes happy *vroom* noises with his red truck. Seconds pass.

Drusus takes the new lyrics, folds them up carefully, and sets them in his pocket.

Back at Ghost Tower One, a palpable sense of excitement fills the air.

Inside the mirror, the door to Drusus' chamber slams open. None other than King Arthur stands framed on the threshold.

"You're late," says Arthur. "Take your lute and come with me, man."

Drusus rises. "Yes, your Majesty."

"What do you plan to play tonight?"

Drusus slips the sheet out from his pocket. "This."

Arthur unfolds the paper. "The Song of My soul. What's this?"

"A new tune. I *will* play it tonight."

Arthur reads the lyrics aloud.

> *"Let us sing and raise our flagon*
> *Celebrate the man who saved the day*
> *His name was the Pendragon*

His deeds are great and ..."

"Have you gone daft?" asks Arthur.

"No, I've never felt more sane."

Arthur scans Drusus' face. "You know, I think you really mean this."

"I do."

"Then, you're a dead man now. No one will ever hear this filth… And your life is over."

Drusus lifts his chin. "I know."

Merlin touches the mirror. Blue haze rolls over the vision of Drusus, obscuring it. That same colored mist rises from the mirror's surface until a cloud of azure magic settles in the center of the ghost tower. That haze solidifies into a particular form.

It's Drusus the angel.

And he's solid.

I don't remember moving, but somehow Myla and I are in each other's arms, sharing a deep hug.

Drusus steps about in a wobbly circle. "Where am I?"

"Don't worry," says Nimue. "It will take a few seconds for the spell to wear off."

Sure enough, Drusus' eyes widen. "I remember now." He pats his chest. "I'm solid. It worked! Do you think I can return to Earth again and try to help Charles?"

Xavier nods. "I may be able to pull a string or two."

Merlin, Nimue, Ximena, and Fluff all surround Drusus, firing off a long list of questions. This is all part of the test. I kiss the top of Myla's head and then whisper in her ear. "Told you it was brilliant. We should have made that a bet."

Myla chuckles. "Too bad we didn't. I'm still up one win."

She's talking about our bet back at the Arena contest. "I look forward to you claiming your prize."

Camilla approaches us. Myla rushes forward to meet her mother. "What do you think?"

"This is a major breakthrough," declares Camilla. "We've always sorted souls and purged out evil ones before they could get to Heaven. Now we can be purging in terms of cleansing the spirit as well. I love this!"

Walker steps up. "I may have some ideas on how to expand this design. We could build some soul towers that are more mirror towers, if that makes sense."

Xavier joins the group as well. Within seconds, Xavier, Camilla and Walker are in deep into conversations about mirror towers and soul priorities.

Walker waves me over. "Lincoln, do you think we can spare some alchemists? We may be able to use them for more tests."

I hold up my pointer finger. "One second." Scanning the tower, I find Myla looking into the mirror. She's alone. I sidle up beside her. "Is everything all right?"

Myla nods. "She's here."

No question who *she* is. *At last.* All week, Myla has been calling out to her inner angel with no reply.

They're finally speaking again.

MYLA

 y gaze stays locked on the image of myself in the mirror. Only it's not me. This version has angel wings that are tipped with gold. She speaks in my mind.

"You did well."

I reply back in my thoughts. *"I've been calling for you."*

"I'm not one to be summoned or controlled. I am your angelic nature." In the mirror, my inner angel holds up her hand; an orb of blue magic materializes on her palm. *"I had planned to stay silent forever. Yet your desire to help the fading angels brought me forth."*

Let the record show that I've thought about my inner angel a ton over the last week. I'm not missing my chance to get some answers.

"You were the one who sent the visions to the wrath coven. You set up Verus with visions, too. You then enchanted the Band of Epochs to bippity-boppity-boo onto my thumb, and then later,

to fall off as well. You even cast the spell that protected me and Lincoln from the demonpocalypse."

I'd add Remy to the list of things my angelic self magic-ed into motion, but I did snooping last week. Remy got herself into trouble, all on her lonesome.

In the mirror, the image of my inner angel nods. *"Yes. You were willing to do what you could for the fading angels. So I stepped in as well."*

This leads to what I consider to be my big magilla ques-tion. *"I'm in front of mirrors many times a day. You could have appeared to me and given me a heads-up."*

"You could have called for me as well."

I don't really have a great comeback on that one. I always knew my inner demons. But my inner angel? I have to admit, I was never looking for her.

"Will we be friends?" I ask.

"You'll never see me again."

"Ouch. That's rough." My inner angel is kind-of a bitch.

"I'm already in everything you do. The core of your being. Besides, my magic must be conserved so it may pass to your child, the one who'll save the very fabric of the after-realms."

"You mean Maxon?" Because I think of that kid as more El Destructo than a fixer.

"No, I speak of your future daughter, Portia."

The mirror mists over in blue magic. An electric charge of power moves through my body. More magic. When the mirror clears, my inner angel is gone… and my mind is a blank. Closing my eyes, I try to summon the last thing my angelic side said. She spoke a name. Petunia? Penelope? Polly?

Nope, that's not it.

That said, other things about my inner angel stay perfectly clear in my mind. Like how she says I'll never see her again.

She may believe that, but I doubt it. As my inner angel already discovered, I can be very persuasive.

MYLA

J'd feel bummed out that my inner angel is gone, but that's when Dad strolls up. He wears the same shit-eating grin that I see daily on my son.

"Guess what?" For a badass archangel, my father's opening lines can be a little corny. Still, it's beyond awesome to have my real father back and remembering who I am.

"What?"

"I set up a celebration for the success of Avalon One! Or rather, I had the idea and Octavia did the setting up. It's in the Arena."

I blink hard. "The Arena?"

"Yes, Octavia felt there was bad mojo there after the contest, so she wanted to—as she put it—*take back the memories*."

"I love this idea, but…" I wince. "Didn't you wonder if Avalon One might fail?"

"Not for a second." Dad winks. Even if he's lying his butt off, I appreciate the effort. "Now get changed and let's celebrate!"

So that's exactly what we do.

An hour later, we're all in the Arena. Octavia has decorated everything with different colored spotlights. The beams rove across the darkened Arena. As they cross, it creates an otherworldy vibe.

Honestly, I never thought the Arena could look majestic. But Octavia pulled it off.

There are tons of thrax here. You'd think after being their queen, I'd recognize at least half the faces Octavia invited to a party. Not yet.

Mom, Dad and Walker arrive. The Ghoul Reconciliation Convention ended up being, as Mom calls it, a solid first step. My mother is thrilled to be watching Maxon tonight; she missed him while being so busy with the conference.

My new knights have taken over the dance floor. You wouldn't think that Merlin and Nimue had recently lived in the middle ages, considering how they have their pick of dance partners. Even Ximena is chatting up an angel. *That could be interesting*. And Fluff is zooming around and having the time of his life.

Speaking of angels, Drusus made a quick appearance. He's now a *guardian angel in training* with none other than Verus as his sponsor.

And yes, my father does work that quickly.

By the way, Verus corners me to say that if I don't avoid

salty foods, I might start an event chain that ends with an extra-horrible monsoon on Earth. I'm starting to wonder if Verus is an oracle... or if she just wants me to stop eating junk food. I give her what I consider to be a non-binding *maybe* and then slip off to scour the crowd for signs of my bestie.

At last, Cissy and Zeke arrive. I'm thrilled to grab my bestie and hide in the shadows. We spend a full hour updating each other on everything that happened. While my knights and I were on crunch-time with Avalon One, I hadn't had a chance to really tell Cissy much of anything. Now, she's totally loving all details, especially the King Arthur gossip.

It's almost midnight when the wrath coven arrives. I'm bracing for another yucky conversation—the one I had with Verus turned out to be a tad scarring—but the ladies are super-sweet. They tell me how much they liked getting secret visions from my hidden inner angel. They're even working on a regular-sized quilt for me that includes images of all my new knights. And I got a firm confirmation there would be no blood and guts involved.

Oh, and Connor is here, too. He hangs for an hour and then slips off to do... whatever stuff Lincoln's father does these days. I swear, it's like he walks around with his own little raincloud over his head.

My parents beg off early. Mom says she's tired, but I think the real reason is that she wants to put Maxon to sleep. Fine with me. Mom is awesome with my son. A little heavier on the rules than Octavia, and I think that's good for my little man.

It's close to midnight when Lincoln pulls me onto the dance floor. The place is hopping since Octavia found a great DJ. I'm super excited to show off my new little black dress with a flare skirt. It's great for twirling. Lincoln looks sharp as always in his black suit.

A slow song starts and Lincoln pulls me against him. "I wish we could sneak off."

I can't help but grin. Usually, we attend formal balls in Antrum. Lincoln is an expert at knowing every secret passageway in his palaces. Even though Octavia holds court by the exit, we're always able to sneak off early.

Our bodies sway to slow tune. I love the feel of his firm muscles against me. "As a matter of fact, I know a sneaky place."

Lincoln leans in to nip my ear. "Really?"

"It's where I used to get ready for matches."

"Oh, Myla." Lincoln stops dancing. "This is going to be a problem."

"Bad problem?"

"Good problem."

Lacing my fingers with Lincoln's, I guide my guy off the Arena floor. The moving spotlights make it easy to slip off unnoticed into a nearby archway. Then it's a matter of navigating through the back corridors until we reach a small stone room. There's not much to speak of here, outside of some hooks on the walls and a few large wooden trunks.

I step into the center of the space and twirl. "Here it is. Changing room central."

Lincoln slips off his jacket and sets it onto a nearby trunk. "Did you come here after we met?"

There's a certain predatory gleam in my guy's eyes that I'm enjoying very much indeed. "Oh, sure," I reply. "I had lots of matches after we first met."

My gaze lands on a particular trunk. Memories appear. My face turns eleven shades of red.

Lincoln notices the trunk in question as well as my blush. He steps up to the trunk and damn, my fantasies were all correct. The lid comes to just the right height at his waistline.

Lincoln runs his fingers over the lid. "And what is there about this particular piece of furniture, may I ask?"

"No point telling you that I don't know what you're talking about, huh?"

"None."

"Well, I might have thought about you, the trunk and, um, things."

Lincoln steps closer. "Things?"

"I'd put on my dragonscale suit and wonder what would happen if you came into the dressing room or something."

That predatory look returns to Lincoln's mismatched eyes. It makes me feel all woozy inside. Not a bad thing.

"I love this story. So you'd be... what?"

I gesture toward the trunk. "Sitting here."

Lincoln scoops me up and sets me right atop the trunk. "Like this?"

"Uh-huh."

A knowing grin rounds his mouth. "So I could stand before you like this." He rests his hands on my knees. His skin is all warm and rough at once. Little by little, Lincoln slowly guides my legs apart and presses my skirt up to my hips. Then he steps between my knees.

"Almost like that," I say breathlessly.

At last, Lincoln presses himself against me. At this angle, his hardness hits all the right places. "Do you mean this?" he asks.

Fire sparks inside my core. "Exactly."

"I can see the appeal." Lincoln slowly trails his hands over my body. Wherever he touches me, there's an electric zing of desire. Leaning in, he stops when his mouth hovers a breath above mine. "You know what I want."

"I do." I lick along the seam of his lips. "And I'm calling in my prize."

Our mouths meet in a rough kiss. Somehow, my underwear ends up torn off and then—yes—Lincoln is inside me. We make love. I adore the feeling that we're joined.

One person.

One bliss.

Afterward, I decide that it's good to have my own knights of the round table.

But far better to share body and soul with King Lincoln.

This is almost *the end of The Brutal Time.*
What follows next is a bonus story called,
'Barbie Doll Death Match'

BONUS STORY - BARBIE DOLL DEATH MATCH

Introduction From the Author, Christina Bauer

Dear reader,

This tale takes place *before* the events of Angelbound book one. In it, Myla gets a lesson in battle tactics from a magical cat because, of course, she does.

I hope you enjoy the story of *Barbie Doll Death Match*!

Sincerely,

CB

BARBIE DOLL DEATH MATCH

*N*ot gonna lie.

It's not easy being eight years old and teaching yourself to be a warrior … especially when your training ground is the backyard. But that's where Miss Kits comes in. She's a magical cat with black fur and multiple tails as well as the ability to talk. And right now, she's about to give me some actual battle training.

I do a double-take. "What did you say?"

"I'm about to enchant your toys into their first-ever Barbie Doll Death Match," replies Miss Kits.

"Ooo! Which one do I fight first?"

"None. They are fighting each other."

My heart sinks. I bought into this whole 'death match concept' because I pictured life-size opponents.

Huh. Maybe I misunderstood things.

"So." I smack my lips. "We're not training *me*? This is a fight between *my Barbies*."

Technically, they are my mother's dolls because she bought them and plays with them when she thinks I'm not looking. But I digress.

"That's what I promised to do, isn't it?" asks Miss Kits.

I get that. And Miss Kits is a magical cat and all, but I can't help but push it a little.

"Can't we have a part deux where I do fight them?"

"No." Miss Kits does that thing where she blank-stares at you in a way that blocks off any additional chatter on the subject. Total cat superpower.

Miss Kits stalks around the tea table, her multiple tails swaying with each step.

Did I mention that Miss Kits is a magical cat with no less than eight badass tails? She is.

Back to my ME.

Miss Kits scans the toy table carefully. "You've prepared for my demonstration."

"I've been doing extra pushups."

"I refer to the dolls, Myla. You've dressed each one in a unique way."

"Oh, I want to see different fighting styles, so I changed their outfits." I tap the head of the closest doll. "First, there's Boxing Barbie. I stuck blobs of chewed Bubble Yum on her hands to stand for boxing gloves."

"Clever."

"Second is Pokey Chick. I dressed her in a black napkin to stand for ninja robes." I tap Pokey Chick's hands. "These paperclips stand for nun chucks."

"I see." Miss Kits nods slowly. "You wish to learn about boxing technique and projectiles in battle."

"That's right." I move onto the next doll. "Third, there's Archer Barbie. The sewing pins taped to her back stand for arrows. I also made a bow from a long needle and thread."

"And fourth?"

Frowning, I focus on the last doll. "Honestly, I ran out of ideas. She's just wearing a bathing suit, so I have her black ribbon tied around her waist to stand for a quasi tail. I call her Quasi Barbie—that's the name from her box."

Miss Kits prowls around the small table. With each step, her tails keep moving, each in their own way. She stops and sits back on her haunches.

"Perfect."

My pulse speeds. *Sure, A doll-based battle demo isn't ideal, but it's something! Can't wait.*

"And you'll cast the spell now?" My voice is a little needy, and I don't care.

"Yes, each doll will use *your* natural skills, but have her own personality. Except one. You can consider Quasi Barbie to be the only warrior. Essentially, she's a true mini you."

"Did you say the dolls will have my natural skills?"

"I did."

I wince. "Are you sure that's a good idea? I don't know much."

"I'll also give each a basic level of knowledge in the different techniques you specified. Think of them as having completed Archer, Boxer, Nun Chuck, and Myla 101."

"Wait, Myla 101? What does that mean?"

Miss Kits licks her front paw. "You'll see."

There's no point pushing Miss Kits when she isn't ready to share. "All right. Bring it on."

"Stand back."

Miss Kits snaps her claws. That's the way she starts some spells. I don't know how she does it, considering how felines lack both fingers and opposable thumbs, but it's Miss Kits. Anything is possible.

A planet appears on my lawn. It's five feet high and hovering just above the grass, only it's formed entirely of golden light. This is her way of casting spells.

With a flash of brightness, the planet collapses into a baseball-sized sphere before exploding outward in a shower of sparkles. The spell rolls across the yard in concentric waves that remind me of dropping a stone in a still pond, only the effect is with light instead of water.

When the brightness dies down, my dolls still sit at their pink table. All four are the same size as before. What changes is how the toys now move around as if alive.

A chill of awe moves across my skin. All four Barbies are just as I pictured them: Boxer wears gloves, Archer carries her bow, and Pokey totes a sack of nun chucks. As for Quasi, her dragonscale tail sways behind her.

Taking in a deep breath, I soak in this scene. A weight of anxiety falls off my shoulders. Battle training is finally happening.

Boxer leaps up from her seat at the table. She shakes out her arms while hopping from foot to foot. Turning her body at an angle, she throws punches into thin air. My brows lift with interest. I never thought about it before, but standing at an angle must make Boxer a smaller target.

Meanwhile, Archer checks out her needle arrows. Pokey inspects her sack of nun chucks. Quasi plays rock-paper-scissors with her tail. The other Barbies whisper among themselves and shoot sly glances at Quasi.

"Quasi is such a loser," whispers Pokey.

It's true that Quasi is acting a little immature, but it doesn't give the others the right to be rude. Looks like I have me some Mean Girl Death Match Barbies.

Miss Kits sits back on her haunches. "Attention, Barbies!"

All my dolls pause to look at Miss Kits.

"You are about to participate in a free-for-all battle," continues Miss Kits. "There are no rules. Use your talents. The last Barbie standing is the winner. Understood?"

"Yes," cry all the Barbies at once.

"In that case," adds Miss Kits. "Get ready to rumble in three... two... one!"

Archer and Pokey take off across the lawn at a run. Surprisingly, they race *away* from the other dolls. Archer hides behind an old boot. Pokey lurks around the watering can. Soon enough, I see what their plan is. Both are using long-range weapons. Archer and Pokey need cover.

For her part, Boxer doesn't run at all. Instead, she keeps warming up with more shadow punching. Although we don't really have shadows in Purgatory (that would require sunshine), I get what she's trying to do here.

Then, there's Quasi. *The true mini-me.* She minces around. Dances. Sings the tune, *Little Surfer Girl*, at the top of her lungs. Slap-fights with her tail. Does a cartwheel. A ball of dread settles into my stomach.

Quasi is so dead.

Meanwhile, Pokey and Archer keep lurking behind stuff. Every so often, they pop their heads up and chuck something at each other. Direct hits don't happen. Matter of fact, nothing gets even close. Maybe they failed Archer and Pokey 101.

Boxer finishes her warm-up and makes a beeline for her Quasi counterpart. Seems like Boxer could have gone into battle right away, but what do I know?

Boxer and Quasi size each other up as they go around in circles.

"Gonna dance some more?" asks Boxer.

"Always." Quasi shimmies.

Boxer pulls back her arm and tries to connect a hit. Quasi jumps in the air, does a somersault, and lands behind her opponent. Quasi's tail then bonks Boxer on the back of the neck. *Snap!* Boxer crumples forward, unconscious.

Yay, Quasi!

"Now, why did Boxer lose?" asks Miss Kits.

I purse my lips and consider. "When Boxer was warming up, she angled her body to make a smaller target. But Boxer didn't do anything like that when she went after Quasi."

"And that means?"

"Boxer didn't take Quasi seriously."

"Absolutely. And before, what was Quasi doing?"

"She was dancing around and being a goofball." I gasp. "Wait. Do you think she was doing that on purpose so Boxer wouldn't bring her best?"

Miss Kits nods. "That's exactly what Quasi was doing."

Quasi sneaks up on Archer. All the while, Archer doesn't notice a thing—she's too focused on trying to land a hit on Pokey. Quasi uses her tail to drag the tea table behind her.

Archer stays focused on Pokey.

Quasi gets closer. She's twelve inches away.

Six inches.

Two.

Quasi uses her tail to swoop the table in a great arc that aims for Archer's head. *Blam.* Archer gets walloped on the noggin and falls over unconscious.

Two down, one to go.

Finally, Pokey realizes the risk. She starts chucking stuff directly at Quasi. Her aim isn't any better, though.

"Screw you, ditz!" says Pokey. "Just try to come for me!"

"You got it!" Quasi runs in a zig-zag pattern toward the rusty watering can where Pokey hides. Although Pokey starts chucking stuff at Quasi, not one projectile hits its target.

Quasi is within an inch of Pokey's hiding spot. Did I mention that Pokey's aim is crap? It is. Which is why Pokey makes the logical choice. Raising her hands, she comes out from her cover. "I surrender."

Quasi stops. "Happy to accept."

But Pokey doesn't surrender. Instead, she pulls out a long knife and slices the blade toward Quasi.

"Watch out!" I cry.

As the blade closes in, Quasi ducks while her tail swipes across Pokey's neck. A second later, Pokey doesn't have a head.

"Oops," says Quasi. "I thought that was glued on a little better."

Pokey's decapitated noggin looks up from the lawn. "Just jam it back on later."

"Enough!" cries Miss Kits. "Stay in place until ordered to move." My cat rounds on me. "Before we finalize the match, I have a question for you. What's the lesson of that final battle?"

"Don't lie and pull knives on people."

"This is a free-for-all battle. No rules. Would telling the truth have helped Pokey?"

"I guess not." I tap my chin. "Maybe the lesson is not to underestimate your opponent. Pokey could have pretended she was injured and then stealth attacked or something. Just chucking a knife was way too obvious."

Quasi nods toward's Pokey's severed head. "The girl has a point. I saw that strike coming a whole inch away."

"My bad," says Pokey's head.

"And now," cries Miss Kits. "I shall officially declare the winner of the Barbie Doll Death Match. It's Quasi Barbie!"

I cup my hand by my mouth. "Woo!"

Quasi dances around as Miss Kits snaps her claws once more. Another imploding planet-o-magic appears. When the brightness vanishes, my Barbies are back to being regular toys.

Pokey still doesn't have her head, though. I'll have to fix that later.

Miss Kits turns to me. "We've established the other dolls didn't take Quasi seriously. Did you notice anything else?"

I think through the battle, step by step. "Boxer, Pokey, and Archer just weren't that good at their fighting styles. Pokey dropped her nun chucks. Archer kept shooting arrows into the lawn. Boxer was okay, but nothing special. Quasi owned that fight."

"Precisely. It's easy to admire fighting styles that seem glamorous, like sparkling projectiles. But mark my words. There are battle styles that you find interesting … and then, there are ones where you *excel*. All these dolls were magically given your natural skill set."

I tap my chin and consider this. "So I'm better off acting like Quasi?"

"I've seen you with your homemade punching bags. You don't use boxing moves. You jump, kick, and somersault. In my view, your skills are with close-range, hand-to-hand combat in an acrobatic style. It's good to know these other skills, but they aren't closely aligned to your strengths."

I glance around the yard and think this though. *Miss Kits has a point.*

"Do you think I could get an actual instructor to help me with hand-to-hand combat? Maybe you could enchant a doll into life-size. Not Pokey, since her head doesn't stay on all that well. But you get the idea."

Miss Kits stares at my house, I can almost picture the thought bubble over her head, saying: *Can I confront Myla's mother twice in one one day?*

"Later," says Miss Kits eventually. "We'll get to it, but your mother needs time. I'm shocked that I got her to agree to this much."

"Me, too."

Miss Kits sighs. "I'm so glad we're making progress. *He* gets closer to you every day."

I blink hard. Once more, Miss Kits just said something important, but I can't quite remember her words. I tilt my head. "What did you say?"

Squinting, I try to recall everything anyway. Miss Kits said something about a guy, maybe? Whatever the realization is, the thought is gone.

That said, there is one thing I *do* know. Miss Kits is helping me out again.

I turn to her. "Thank you."

"You are most welcome." Miss Kits straightens the golden bow at her neck and saunters off through the dead hedges.

For a long moment, I watch the spot where I last saw Miss Kits. My heart warms.

I'm so lucky she's my friend.

The End (For Reals)

The story continues with ARMAGEDDON, Angelbound Origins 7 and QUASI REDUX, Angelbound Origins 8.

ALSO BY CHRISTINA BAUER

ARMAGEDDON

ANGELBOUND ORIGINS BOOK 7

The story continues in ARMAGEDDON, Book 7!

QUASI REDUX

ANGELBOUND ORIGINS BOOK 8

More Myla-Lincoln fun in QUASI REDUX, Book 8!

LINCOLN

Enjoy Lincoln's perspective with the Angelbound LINCOLN series!

OFFSPRING

Meet the next generation in MAXON, Book 1 of
Angelbound Offspring!

FAIRY TALES OF THE MAGICORUM

A modern fairy tale that *USA Today* calls a 'must-read!' Check out WOLVES AND ROSES!

DIMENSION DRIFT

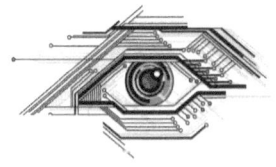

A kick-ass heroine + a swoon-worthy prince + an all-girl heist = the DIMENSION DRIFT series!

BEHOLDER

Medieval mages … Slow-burn love … And heart-pounding action! Check out the BEHOLDER series!

PIXIELAND DIARIES

PIXIELAND DIARIES tells the story of sassy pixie Calla and 'her' elf prince, Dare.

APPENDIX

IF YOU ENJOYED THIS BOOK...

...Please consider leaving a review, even if it's just a line or two. Every bit truly helps, especially for those of us who don't *write by the numbers,* if you know what I mean.

Plus I have it on good authority that every time you review an indie author, somewhere an angel gets a mocha latte. For reals.

And angels need their caffeine, too.

COLLECTED WORKS

Angelbound Origins

About a quasi (part demon and part human) girl who loves kicking butt in Purgatory's Arena

1. Angelbound
2. Scala
3. Acca
4. Thrax
5. The Dark Lands
6. The Brutal Time
7. Armageddon
8. Quasi Redux
9. Clockwork Igni
10. Lady Reaper
11. Reaper Wars
12. Angry Gods

Angelbound Lincoln

The Angelbound experience as told by Prince Lincoln

1. Duty Bound
2. Lincoln
3. Trickster
4. Baculum
5. Angelfire

Angelbound Offspring

The next generation takes on Heaven, Hell, and everything in between

1. Maxon
2. Portia
3. Zinnia
4. Rhodes
5. Kaps
6. Mack
7. Huntress

Angelbound Xavier

1. Archenemy
2. Archnemesis
3. Archangel

Fairy Tales of the Magicorum

Modern fairy tales with sass, action, and romance

1. Wolves and Roses
2. Moonlight and Midtown

3. Shifters and Glyphs

4. Slippers and Thieves

5. Bandits and Ball Gowns

6. Fire and Cinder

7. Fairies and Frosting

8. Towers and Tithes

9. Mirrors and Mysteries

10. Rapunzels and Powers

Dimension Drift

Dystopian adventures with science, snark, and hot aliens

1. Scythe

2. Umbra

3. Alien Minds

4. ECHO Academy

* This is a finished series.

Pixieland Diaries

About sassy pixie Calla and her love-crush-nemesis, the elf prince Dare

1. Pixieland Diaries

2. Calla

3. Dare

* This is a finished series.

Beholder

Where a medieval farm girl discovers necromancy and true love

1. Cursed
2. Concealed
3. Cherished
4. Crowned
5. Cradled
This is a finished series.

ACKNOWLEDGMENTS

If you're reading my freaking acknowledgements, chances are, I should thank you for something. So, for the record: you are awesome, dear reader.

That said, huge and heartfelt thanks must go out to my husband and son for their rock-solid support. Being an author means a lot of early mornings, late nights, long weekends, and never-ending patience. You two are the best guys in the universe, period.

After that, I must thank the extensive network of reviewers, friends and colleagues who helped me build my writing chops in general. Gracias.

Finally, deep affection goes out to my late, much loved, and dearly missed Aunt Sandy and Uncle Henry. You saw the writer in me, always. Thank you, first and last.

ABOUT CHRISTINA BAUER

Christina Bauer thinks that fantasy books are like bacon: they just make life better. All of which is why she writes romance novels that feature demons, dragons, wizards, witches, elves, elementals, and a bunch of random stuff that she brainstorms while riding the Boston T. Oh, and she includes lots of humor and kick-ass chicks, too.

Christina lives in Newton, MA with her husband, son, and semi-insane golden retriever, Ruby.

Stalk Christina on Social Media

Blog:
http://monsterhousebooks.com/blog/category/christina

Facebook:
https://www.facebook.com/authorBauer/

Instagram:
https://www.instagram.com/christina_cb_bauer/

Twitter:
@CB_Bauer

VLOG:
https://tinyurl.com/Vlogbauer

Web site:
www.bauersbooks.com

COMPLIMENTARY BOOK

Get a FREE novella when you sign up for Christina's
newsletter: https://tinyurl.com/bauersbooks

BEVERLY HILLS VAMPIRE

A NOVELLA BY
CHRISTINA BAUER

AUTHOR NOTE

*D*ear Reader,
     Welcome to the end of the book! If you're here, I figure you may want some additional background on THE BRUTAL TIME, so here goes!

In this novel, I wanted to explore a new inner journey for Myla. Specifically, she's always been a solo player—except for a handful of family and friends—and I thought it'd be cool to have her learn how to *play well with others.* That's when I leveraged the extensive library of storytelling that explores this aspect of the heroine's journey.

Just kidding.

I looked around, but I really couldn't find dick out there on this particular topic. Not that it doesn't exist; this might just be my limited searching skills. Anyway, what I did find was a lot of magical powers that showed up without a lot of work. Not helpful.

Let me explain.

One big magilla problem for being a teenage girl (in my opinion anyway) is that one second, you're a kid. The next, you're a sexual being and getting all sorts of attention for your hormones hopping. You don't do anything to achieve this status. It just happens.

All of which is why a lot of stories about teenage girls deal with powers that simply appear. Again, that's totally valid ... but so is the idea that, at some point, working your ass off will take place as well.

Case in point: in the original *Angelbound*, Myla has inner wrath powers, but that in itself isn't enough for her to win. Myla must know each demon type and how to take them down ... which in turn takes lots of research, visiting the arena, keeping notebooks, and thinking through the approach in the heat of battle. This is different from, say, being born with immunity to mind reading or something. Yes, that power may open doors for you, but it wasn't anything you worked to achieve. Again, not an invalid story type as much as one that does't float my particular boat.

That said, I did find some YA fantasy books that described what it was like to be a queen or whatever. The ones I got my hands on mostly described two things: 1) planning outfits and-or parties and 2) barging into a room and yelling at people. I spent thirty years in corporate America working for tech companies like Microsoft and Cisco. In my experience, any major focus on outfits, parties, and scream-fests was 1) pretty rare and 2) a career limiting move in the long run. So none of those approaches inspired me.

When I finally ran across the idea of King Arthur, I was thrilled. There's research showing King Arthur is an Anglican version of Celtic pagan legends. For a long list of reasons, I think Celtic tales retain more of the heroine's journey than other types of storytelling, so it fit with the Myla model. The rest of the book fell out from there.

If I've down my job right, none of that will be super-apparent. THE BRUTAL TIME should just be a kick-ass story that's both satisfying and unique. I certainly hope that's the case for you, and that this note gives you more background on the thinking behind the page.

See you at the next book!

Best,

Christina Bauer

www.ingramcontent.com/pod-product-compliance
Lightning Source LLC
Chambersburg PA
CBHW020508260626
47156CB00006B/1913